"Cole, this isn't a good idea...." Bree murmured, closing her eyes against the seductive feel of his hands on her shoulders.

"I don't know." His breath warmed the nape of her neck. "I think it's a great idea."

She took a deep breath and moved away before she could give in to the hunger coursing through her veins.

Just then, the faintest of sounds reached her ears. She didn't react in any way, but Cole still whispered, "What is it?"

The tiny hairs on the back of her neck had started to rise. She didn't want to think about what that meant.

"It looks like your private little hideaway isn't all that private after all," she said under her breath. "There's somebody out there."

Somebody who could have a gun trained on them at this very moment...

Dear Reader,

Valentine's Day is here, a time for sweet indulgences. RITA Award-winning author Merline Lovelace is happy to oblige as she revisits her popular CODE NAME: DANGER miniseries. In *Hot as Ice*, a frozen Cold War-era pilot is thawed out by beautiful scientist Diana Remington, who soon finds herself taking her work home with her.

ROMANCING THE CROWN continues with *The Princess and the Mercenary*, by RITA Award winner Marilyn Pappano. Mercenary Tyler Ramsey reluctantly agrees to guard Princess Anna Sebastiani as she searches for her missing brother, but who will protect Princess Anna's heart from Tyler? In Linda Randall Wisdom's *Small-Town Secrets*, a young widow—and detective—tries to solve a string of murders with the help of a handsome reporter. The long-awaited LONE STAR COUNTRY CLUB series gets its start with Marie Ferrarella's *Once a Father*. A bomb has ripped apart the Club, and only a young boy rescued from the wreckage knows the identity of the bombers. The child's savior, firefighter Adam Collins, and his doctor, Tracy Walker, have taken the child into protective custody—where they will fight danger from outside and attraction from within. RaeAnne Thayne begins her OUTLAW HARTES series with *The Valentine Two-Step*. Watch as two matchmaking little girls turn their schemes on their unsuspecting single parents. And in Nancy Morse's *Panther on the Prowl*, a temporarily blinded woman seeks shelter—and finds much more—in the arms of a mysterious stranger.

Enjoy them all, and come back next month, because the excitement never ends in Silhouette Intimate Moments.

Yours,

Leslie. J. Wainger
Executive Senior Editor

Please address questions and book requests to:
Silhouette Reader Service
U.S.: 3010 Walden Ave., P.O. Box 1325, Buffalo, NY 14269
Canadian: P.O. Box 609, Fort Erie, Ont. L2A 5X3

Small-Town Secrets

LINDA RANDALL WISDOM

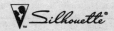

INTIMATE MOMENTS™

Published by Silhouette Books

America's Publisher of Contemporary Romance

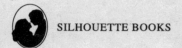

SILHOUETTE BOOKS

ISBN 0-373-27201-4

SMALL-TOWN SECRETS

Visit Silhouette at www.eHarlequin.com

Printed in U.S.A.

LINDA RANDALL WISDOM

first sold to Silhouette Books on her wedding anniversary in 1979 and hasn't stopped since! She loves looking for the unusual when she comes up with an idea, and only hopes her readers enjoy reading her stories as much as she enjoys writing them.

A native Californian, she is married and has two dogs, five parrots and a tortoise, so life is never boring—or quiet—in the Wisdom household. When she isn't writing, she enjoys going to the movies, reading, making jewelry and fabric painting.

Prologue

"We are the Wildcats, mighty, mighty Wildcats!" The cheers sent a rumble throughout the bleachers and beyond. Trumpets sounded the charge.

"It's been a hell of a game," Scott Fitzpatrick remarked, keeping his arm tight around his wife's waist. He nuzzled her neck. "Hey, sexy, wanna relive your teen years and go behind the bleachers and make out?"

Bree laughed throatily. She pushed him away, but the smile on her lips promised there would be no pushing away later that night. "And get caught like we did the last time? Remember how mortified Sara was when she heard about it? She went on and on, saying how dare we old folks do such things in public? Besides, you don't want to miss seeing your son make the winning touchdown, do you?"

"Hell, no." Fitz chuckled, keeping his hand tucked into the back pocket of her jeans.

Bree gave him a bump with her hip as they walked past the concession stand. To look at him in his faded jeans and sweatshirt, no one would guess he was a highly respected FBI Special Agent in Charge. With her working as a homicide detective for the Los Angeles County Sheriff's Department, it was said they were the rare pair who made it work in more ways than one.

Bree liked to tease him they were probably the rare instance of local law enforcement and the feds working together extremely well.

After eight years of marriage, the man still made her heart thump the way it had the first time she met him. He complained his hair was graying at a faster rate than he'd like, but she always reminded him that the fire in the furnace burned brightly no matter how much snow was on the roof.

With his son and daughter from a previous marriage, and their own shared son, they made a close-knit family that blended well.

Bree was celebrating the wrap-up of a tough case and was eager to watch her stepson help win the league championship. She'd turned to say something to Fitz when she noticed his gaze focused toward a dark corner. The curse that dropped from his lips would have cost him a five dollar bill in the family Cuss Jar.

"What?"

"Looks like a drug buy going down," he murmured.

Bree kept a smile on her lips, but her expression had turned all-cop.

"Anyone we know?"

"That kid I said looks like a moron? The one who was hanging around Sara."

"You've called every boy who's even talked to her a moron." Bree slid her gaze sideways, now seeing what he did. There was no doubt the boy was handing over a few plastic bags of pills to another boy, who gave him several bills. Damn, not one security officer around.

"Wanna be my backup?" he asked.

"Since this is more my jurisdiction than yours, it's more like you'd be mine." She thought of her weapon, nestled comfortably in the small of her back. Since she'd come directly from the station, she refused to leave her weapon in her SUV, even with it locked. "Nobody's taken anything over state lines, bud."

"He's mine." Fitz moved forward. "Sorry, guys, you're

busted. FBI,'' he called out, just as he reached them. "Just stand easy and it will be painless for everyone.''

Bree saw the dark flash of metal before Fitz did. She instantly reached for her weapon.

"Gun!" she shouted, swinging her weapon up. "L.A. Sheriff! Put it down! Put it down now!'' she screamed, infusing her voice with authority.

The boy swung around, saw her, and panic filled his face. He looked at Fitz and shot. Bree fired her gun just as the boy shot at her.

She felt the fire enter her chest the same moment she saw Fitz drop to his knees. The stunned look on his face told her he hadn't fully realized what had just happened.

But she knew. There was too much blood flowing out of him. The bullet must have nicked an artery, because with every heartbeat, more blood gushed. She tried to get to him, but her body failed her. All she could reach was the tip of his finger.

As the world turned dark around her, she heard the screams and the roar of the crowd.

"Touchdown!"

Chapter 1

There was too much blood for one person. It covered her hands and clothing. No one could lose this much blood and survive. She looked down at the man lying lifeless in her arms.

"Fitz!" She sat upright in bed, positive her screams echoed off the walls.

There was no pounding on her door. No demands to know if she was all right. At least the scream remained in her head. This time.

Bree's fingers trembled as she pushed a damp lock of hair away from her face.

She'd thought the dream had finally left her. It was bad enough, dreaming of Fitz's death, but having each episode detail it differently only made it worse. In reality she hadn't held his dying body in her arms. His blood hadn't covered her hands. When she fell after being shot, only her fingertips had been able to touch him before she lost consciousness.

The dream was her punishment for not being able to save him. From the first time she'd had it, she saw it that way.

Fitz dying in her arms. Fitz never having a chance to say a

word to her nor Bree given the chance to say anything to him. No goodbye. No "I love you."

She pulled her pillow around, holding it tight against her chest as she rocked back and forth. She ignored the voices that screamed inside her head. After all this time, it was getting easier to overlook them.

"Dammit, Fitz, you weren't supposed to die that night," she whispered, feeling the anger build up as it had so many other nights. Anger that didn't exactly override the pain but merely accompanied it. "You were supposed to be here when David graduated from high school. I need you to help keep the boys away from Sara and just watch…" she blinked rapidly to keep the tears from falling "…just watch Cody grow up."

She knew she had to be up in three hours, but didn't bother trying to fall back to sleep. Past experience taught her it would only mean a return to her dream. Instead, she lay back with the pillow nestled in her arms. It was a poor substitute.

"I knew we shouldn't have moved here. I couldn't sleep all night because of all the horrible noises I heard," Sara Fitzpatrick announced in the dramatic tone only a fifteen-year-old girl could adopt. "Either we have ghosts in this house or there's rats in the wall."

"Rats?" six-year-old Cody asked, wide-eyed with horror. He swiveled to face his mother. "Big rats like in that movie?"

Bree shot her stepdaughter a silent warning. "According to the inspector who went through the house for me before we moved in, there are no rats in this house," she said. "You have to remember this is an old house. Old houses make noises."

"Right," David muttered, as he spooned raspberry jam onto a slice of toast. "The Addams family would love this wreck."

"Enough," Bree said firmly, noting her youngest son's distress. She cut the omelette she'd made in two and slid half on another plate, placing it in front of Sara.

Sara recoiled as if the plate held a nest of vipers.

"That is loaded with cholesterol and fat!" She pushed the offending plate toward David. He shrugged and picked up his fork.

If time hadn't been running against her, Bree would have confronted her daughter on her eating habits. Or lack of. She knew she would have to have a long, heartfelt talk with Sara that evening. But now she had to get them all out of the house and off to school. She also couldn't afford to be late her first day on the job.

She still resented her superior for giving her the choice of either taking a desk job or finding a position in a smaller town. Bree knew the lieutenant had her best interests in mind. He'd told her that enough times. She'd fought it as long as she could, just as she fought the tension that took over anytime she approached the scene of a violent crime.

She felt she would have worked through it if it hadn't been for that last crime scene. She'd walked into a living room that would have been warm and homey if it hadn't been for the blood staining the walls and furniture. A man brutally murdered by a former business associate and a wife sitting in the kitchen, silent from the shock of coming home to find her husband dead.

The memories had flooded Bree's mind so swiftly she'd almost shut down functioning. Lieutenant Carlson took one look at her when she returned to the station and knew what had happened. Twenty-four hours later, she was called into his office and given a choice: take a desk job, or better yet, take a post where she wouldn't have so much pressure.

Bree hated him for forcing her to make the decision. He knew she wouldn't like being chained to a desk. He knew her so well that he had already called in favors and found her a detective's position in Warm Springs, a small inland town northeast of San Diego. His reason for choosing the community was the low crime rate in the area. San Diego was an hour's drive away for times when the family wanted more sophisticated entertainment, he told her. And Bree should expect him and his wife down there in a few years when he retired.

She resented Lieutenant Carlson for pretty much accepting the position on her behalf.

And the kids resented her for going along with it.

From the day they moved out of their home in Woodland

Hills, they'd made sure she knew they weren't happy with her decision.

Bree bolted down her breakfast and set the plate in the dishwasher. "You don't think you'll have any problem finding the high school?" she asked David. "Or the grade school when you go to pick up Cody?"

Instead of the good humor he usually displayed, his expression was almost sullen. "Oh yeah, I'll have a tough time finding two schools that are all of two blocks apart in a town that's, what? Three blocks total?" he muttered, taking his own dishes over to the dishwasher. He may have been angry with his stepmother for the move, but he was responsible enough to not ignore his chores.

Bree took whatever small favors she could get. She looked at her stepson and saw her husband in the handsome features that she knew would one day be stamped with his sire's character. All these months, they'd dealt with anger over Fitz's death. Then they'd moved from a city they'd lived in all their lives. Abandoned friends, familiar places. She told herself the old cliché about time healing all wounds. She was learning about patience.

Although David never said a word, she knew he had to be hurt and angry that he left behind his football team during his all-important year. And he registered at his present school too late to try out for football. He'd muttered he'd try out for the baseball team and she hoped he would.

She handed Cody's backpack to him, verified that all three children had lunch money, and herded Cody into her Expedition, with Jinx, her K-9, hopping into the back seat. The German shepherd sat down with his tongue lolling happily in anticipation of the ride.

"If I stayed in my old school I would have Mrs. Allen for my teacher," Cody said with a sigh. "She lets her class do really neat things. And her class has a hamster and two guinea pigs."

Bree hurt because she knew Cody hurt. She was aware this move was the hardest on her youngest, who was just beginning first grade. She'd hoped that moving here a couple weeks before the beginning of the school year would help. Instead she'd battled with three kids who constantly complained that their new house wasn't like their old house and there was no one to hang out with. Since his older brother and sister weren't interested in doing anything he wanted to do, Cody was on his own most of the time, and suffered the most.

Bree wasn't worried about Sara and David getting along in school. The two siblings never had a problem making friends. They'd complain about the area, but in time she knew they'd easily fit into a group. It was Cody, quiet and shy, who had difficulty in new situations. Even more so since his father's death.

"I understand that your teacher here, Miss Lancaster, is very nice," she said. "I also heard that her class does a lot of neat things. They take a lot of field trips. Maybe she has a hamster in her room, too."

"Not like Harry Hamster," he whispered, his lower lip trembling.

He still didn't look convinced things were great by the time Bree stopped the vehicle in front of the sprawling building that housed classrooms for kindergarten through the sixth grade.

"Do you remember where your classroom is? Would you like me to walk in with you?" she asked.

He looked out the window at the kids milling about. When he turned back to her, his small face was set in a determined look she wryly recalled seeing on her own at times. His rusty-colored hair had been combed before they left the house, but it was already unruly. She tamped down the urge to smooth it back with her hand.

"I'm not a little kid, Mom," he replied with little-boy dignity. "I go to room 108."

She didn't dare sniff, much less cry, the way she had on Cody's first day in kindergarten. It would mortify him.

"Don't forget that David will pick you up after school," Bree reminded him.

"Don't talk to strangers. If anyone tries to talk to me, run to a teacher and tell 'em," he recited. "Or yell really loud. And stand by the front door of the school until I see David."

Bree swallowed the lump in her throat. And swallowed the need to hug him tightly and kiss him. Which he would only rebuff for fear that his classmates would see her display of affection.

She settled on a basic mom statement. "Be good."

For all of Cody's bravado, he was still exceedingly slow in opening the door and climbing out of the SUV. As he stepped onto the sidewalk, he paused long enough to turn and offer a brave smile and wave.

Bree waited until Cody was safely inside the building. Then it was her turn, and she headed for the Warm Springs Sheriff's Department.

"Hope you're ready, fella," she told her K-9 partner as she parked in the department's parking lot. She paused long enough to loop his chain collar around his neck, complete with a deputy's shield attached to it.

Since detectives weren't required to wear a uniform, she had chosen coffee-colored linen pants and a matching vest, paired with a cream-colored, short-sleeved blouse. Her detective's shield was clipped to her waistband, and her weapon, settled in a holster against the small of her back, was hidden by the three-quarter-length-sleeve, coffee-colored linen jacket. For easy care, she kept her bright auburn hair layered in short waves, tucked behind her ears. Jinx walked regally at her side.

"Good morning, Detective Fitzpatrick." The office receptionist greeted her with a small smile. The nameplate pinned on her chest revealed her name to be Irene. Like the deputies in the station, she wore a navy polo shirt and khaki pants. "I'll let Sheriff Holloway know you're here." She eyed Jinx warily, as if she wasn't sure Bree's four-footed partner was safe. "We've never had a dog here before."

"Jinx is a full-fledged sheriff's deputy," Bree reminded her.

"Detective Fitzpatrick?"

Bree turned and faced her superior. He, too, was dressed in a navy polo shirt, and his khaki pants had a razor-sharp crease. His dark brown boots were so highly polished she imagined he could use the surface as a mirror. She'd say Roy Holloway was a man who valued his image. She'd even say he was good-looking, with his broad smile, his blue eyes holding a touch of humor. She doubted he was a pushover, though. He looked like he had what it took to keep his people in line. He held out his hand.

"Sheriff Holloway." She smiled as she put her hand in his. "I'm sorry we weren't able to meet the last time I was here. I understand you and your family were on vacation then."

"Relaxing at my favorite fishing hole," he admitted. His eyes dropped to the dog sitting by her side, and again he grinned. "I'm not used to seeing a deputy with four legs."

She grinned back. "He would have been perfect if I could have trained him to drive."

Roy chuckled. "Come on back to my office and we'll talk." He jerked his head toward the rear of the building.

Bree murmured a command to Jinx, who moved smoothly alongside her. As they walked toward the sheriff's office, she noticed that the men seated at desks were watching her with undisguised interest.

"Have a chair," Roy invited, as he settled behind his desk.

Bree took the one opposite, with Jinx sitting sedately on his haunches beside her.

"I'm going to be up front with you," her boss said crisply, all-business now. "I didn't think we needed another detective. This county is growing, but I wasn't thinking of adding anyone to the force just yet."

"Token female detective?" she said lightly.

"Probably. They've gotten on the politically correct bandwagon with a vengeance lately," he admitted. "I'll be honest with you, Fitzpatrick—I'm not one for surprises. I like to know what's going on in my department. I like to do my own hiring."

"I had no idea," Bree said honestly.

"You've got some heavy hitters in your corner, however." He glanced at the file folder lying open on his desk. "A kennel has been set up near the parking lot for the dog." He fixed her with a piercing stare. "It's your job to keep it clean."

"Of course," she said without hesitation.

Lieutenant Carlson had said she would be better off in a small town, where she wouldn't be up against the kinds of violent cases she'd handled in L.A. He hadn't said anything about her new boss not being entirely happy with her arrival there. Still, he was friendlier than most would be in this situation.

"Since you've already got the training, I'll just throw you into the shark pool," he told her. "Fine by you?"

"The only way to do it," she replied.

Roy nodded. "But let me tell you. You screw up and I come down hard. I don't care if you do have a dog that can eat me for breakfast." He warily eyed the German shepherd. "Literally."

"Jinx hasn't bitten an officer in, oh, at least a month," she said, matching his tone.

He chuckled. "How'd a deputy K-9 end up with a name like Jinx?"

"He comes from a distinguished line of police dogs," she replied. "His sire is Ace, as in Ace of Spades. His dam is Allie, as in Poker Alice. The litter Jinx was in was born on Friday the thirteenth. Each puppy received a similar name. The breeder's twisted logic."

"And he left L.A. when you did."

"It happens a lot. When you work with a dog as your partner, you develop as close a relationship as you do with a human partner. In many ways, closer."

Roy's eyes tracked her every feature. "Then you'll understand that we're a close unit here, Detective. We've all worked together a long time."

"And new people have to prove their worth before they can hope to be accepted," she stated, finishing his thought. "I understand that. I believe in pulling my weight."

"Good." He stood up. "I'll show you your desk."

Bree didn't say a word when she was led to a battered desk stuck in a corner. Roy rattled off names as he passed each desk. She nodded and offered each deputy a brief smile. She wasn't surprised to receive speculative looks in return.

It was a good thing she hadn't expected an open-armed welcome.

Jinx lay down next to her desk and rested his chin on his paws. She idly scratched the top of his head.

"It's only the first day, boy," she murmured.

* * *

"Tell me, oh powerful one, do you plan to do anything useful today or just sit there and look cute?"

Tipped back in his chair, his feet propped up on the desk, Cole Becker looked up at his assistant. This was his favorite position when he needed to proofread the advertisements for that week.

When his uncle died, leaving him the newspaper, Cole took it over. He became not only the owner of the *Warm Springs Bulletin,* but reporter and staff photographer. He wore many hats in the office.

"I am doing something useful." He gestured to the sheaf of papers he held in one hand. "I'm making sure Whitman's name is spelled correctly. I don't think he'd be so amiable if it happened again."

Mamie Eichorn chuckled. "I don't know. Substituting an *S* for the *W* told everyone what the mean old coot is really like."

"Maybe so, but that mean old coot pays his bills on time," Cole reminded her.

"And each time acts as if we're bleeding him dry." She rolled her eyes.

"I hear there's a new cop in town," he commented. "A story about her would make a good human interest piece. Nothing better than a mom with kids. And there's even a dog. Makes you feel all warm and fuzzy inside, doesn't it?"

"I heard the dog is her partner," Mamie noted.

"Even better on the human interest angle." Cole picked up a sheet of paper from his desk. He believed in doing his homework ahead of time. By talking to a couple of contacts in L.A., he'd been able to pick up a lot of information about the former Los Angeles Sheriff's Detective, Bree Fitzpatrick. He'd even had a photograph faxed to him—of the widow standing tall at her husband's funeral. Cole had heard an impressive listing of the woman's accomplishments.

Unlike the proper widow, Cole was a complete contradiction. He looked like one of those guys who didn't move a muscle unless it was absolutely necessary. Only those who knew him well understood that his body and mind could move swift as lightning when he needed to.

"I called over to the station, but the new detective is in with Roy." He spoke in a low rumble that slid like warm lotion over a woman's skin. "Think you could find out the new detective's home telephone number for me?"

Even Mamie, who'd been happily married for the past fifty-six years, wasn't immune to Cole's lethal charm.

"The woman hasn't even settled in and you're already calling her up for a date? She has children, Cole. I thought you drew the line at women with families."

He agreed. "I do. Too much trouble. This is business, Mamie."

"Like I'll believe that," she retorted. "You're not getting any younger, Cole. Finding someone with a ready-made family is a good way for you to go. Saves a lot of time."

"You make it sound like my sperm's in some retirement home. Herb Dickinson became a father last year, and he's in his late seventies," Cole pointed out in his defense.

Mamie shook her head. "Herb needs new glasses. That baby looks more like their pool man than he looks like Herb, even if the kid's as bald as his alleged daddy."

"There you go." He grinned. "Herb doesn't care who the baby looks like. He's just happy everyone's calling him a stud."

"Some stud," she snorted with disdain. "Herb has an artificial hip, a glass eye and high blood pressure."

"And a twenty-eight-year-old wife. I'd say the man did something right."

Mamie blithely ignored him as she continued. "If you don't do something about your social life, you'll be worse off than him."

"That's why I go out of town."

Mamie shook her head. "So what's next on your agenda?"

Cole flashed her a warm smile. "I guess I'll just have to call over to the sheriff's station again. See about setting up an interview with our new sheriff's detective."

His assistant shot him a knowing look. "And you say it's business only."

Cole played it cool. "You got it."

Mamie started to leave the room, then paused. She stared at him for several moments. "What's really going on, Cole?"

He gave her a bland look. "Working on next week's edition."

She shook her head again. "I don't know what's going on in that mind of yours, but I have a feeling it might not be good."

Cole flashed a smile that had warmed many a woman's heart. "Just doin' my job."

This time she wasn't fooled.

Bree hated first days. Cody's first day of first grade. Sara's first day as a high school sophomore. David's first day as a high school senior. Her own first day with the Warm Springs Sheriff's Department.

While Sheriff Roy Holloway was helpful, her peers weren't. They didn't make it difficult for her, but they didn't make it easy, either.

She arrived home to find Cody almost in tears. He looked at her and declared he hated school.

"We only have a dumb parakeet," he muttered, with a slight whine to his voice.

"I've heard of some smart parakeets," she offered.

"Not this one." His eyes plaintively beseeched her. "I want to go back to my old school, Mom."

"Sweetie, it's only your first day," she murmured. "You have to give it time."

He shook his head.

Bree looked at her stepson and stepdaughter. They didn't look all that happy, either.

"Don't tell me you only have parakeets in your class, too," she said lightly. Her joke fell flat.

David was tight-lipped about his day. Sara announced she was going to her room.

"And how was your day, Bree?" she asked herself as she checked the casserole she'd popped in the oven as soon as she got home. "Just fine. Thank you for asking. The sheriff is an okay guy, but I can't say much for everyone else. The deputies treat me as if I carry the dreaded plague, and the dispatcher informed me she's allergic to dogs.'' Bree pulled out makings for a salad and began tearing a head of lettuce into pieces. ''Now I learn that Cody's convinced everyone hates him. David hates his school and Sara is positive she won't make any new friends. How do I know that's how they're feeling, when they haven't said a word to me? Easy. I'm a detective. I read minds.'' Her movements were almost violent as she tossed a variety of vegetables into the bowl.

When the phone rang, she snagged it before the first ring faded away.

She glanced at her caller ID and noticed it listed *Warm Springs Bulletin* as the caller.

''Fitzpatrick.''

''Detective Fitzpatrick? I'm Cole Becker with the *Warm Springs Bulletin.*'' A man's lazy drawl drifted across her mind the way a soft comforter covered her body. ''Welcome to our fair town.''

Bree felt a tingle begin deep inside her body and move upward. She wasn't sure if it was warm in the kitchen or just her. She feared it was all her.

''Thank you,'' she said warily.

''I was wondering if there was any possibility we could get together?''

''Why?'' she asked.

''I'd like to interview you for the newspaper. See how you feel being Warm Springs's first female detective. What prompted you to move to Warm Springs. Human interest stuff,'' he explained.

Stuff? He didn't sound like any reporter she'd ever come across.

''I'm sorry, Mr. Becker.'' She didn't sound the least bit apologetic. ''But right now, I'm in the midst of fixing dinner.''

''How about we talk over breakfast tomorrow?''

''I like to have breakfast with my kids.''

''Lunch? They'll be in school then, right?''

She gave him points for figuring that one out.

''This isn't a good time, Mr. Becker. I'm still settling in.'' She wasn't about to tell him she hated interviews. People usually spelled her name wrong or made her sound as if she was an avenging angel with PMS. "No free time at all."

"I'm sure you are busy, Detective. But wouldn't you want the people to know about the woman behind the badge? Show them that while you're wearing that badge and carrying a gun, you're still a mom and a human being?"

"Not my style," she retorted.

"Then why don't we talk about something that is your style," he suggested. "Something I think you'd like to know."

Bree felt a familiar tingle at the base of her neck. She'd never ignored the warning signal before, and a few times it had even saved her life.

How could something happen in this small town when she was barely unpacked? She could feel her jaw tightening. She didn't know what was going on, but felt this was more than a request for an interview.

"Tomorrow. Lunch. One o'clock," she rattled. "I'll leave the choice of restaurant up to you. I haven't learned which ones are better than others."

"Then I'll make it easy for you. Two doors down from you is The Eatery. I'll see you there at one." He hung up.

Bree stared at her phone before she set it back in the cradle. "It's not as if you're marrying the man, Bree. Just think of it as a free meal," she murmured as she turned to the oven when the timer dinged. "Dinner!" she called out.

Instead of the clatter of three sets of feet that normally followed her announcement, three quiet souls marched into the kitchen. They started to take their seats, then instantly rose up in response to their mom's telling stare.

Sara headed for the refrigerator and pulled out the bottles of salad dressing. Cody filled glasses with iced tea and milk, while David carried the casserole dish over to the table.

Bree pasted on a bright smile as she sat down. "So, tell me about your day," she urged in her best June Cleaver voice.

They all looked at her as if she'd lost her mind.

"So Cole Becker's going to interview you today?" Roy grinned at Bree's look of astonishment. "No secrecy in this town, Fitzpatrick. Someone asked about you when I stopped for coffee. You'll have to get used to everyone knowing your business."

"I should have cleared it with you first," she said uneasily, silently damning Cole Becker to hell. "He said it's purely a human interest type story about the new arrival in town."

"Don't worry about it, Fitzpatrick," the sheriff replied. "Becker's like one of those bloodhounds who refuses to give up. Believe me, if you hadn't agreed to the interview, he would have found another way. He's one persistent son of a bitch," he said without rancor.

"You don't need to worry about my saying anything I shouldn't. I've dealt with the press in the past without any dire consequences," she assured him. Her stomach was already roiling at the thought of sharing a meal with a man who sounded like the devil incarnate. "I can tell him I can't make it."

Roy shook his head. "I can tell you haven't dealt with this man. Don't worry about it. Take advantage of him picking up the tab. Sit there and smile at the guy. Tell him you came out here so your kids would grow up breathing clean air."

Bree grimaced. "I really prefer not talking about my children to the media," she told him. "I think you can realize why."

Her superior looked at her and nodded in understanding. As police officers, they were fully aware of just how vulnerable kids today were.

"Bree, you're living in a small town now. Everyone knew everything there was to know about you within ten minutes of you moving in. I'll be the first to tell you your kids are safer here than they would have been in L.A. I'm not saying we haven't seen problems with drugs, but we've been pretty successful in keeping the gangs out, and any kid caught with drugs finds out just how stupid he or she is. Cole's looking for human interest fluff for his readers. Give him what he wants and he'll go away. Trust me," he told her in a soothing voice.

"If it was my choice I'd rather have a root canal without anesthesia," she muttered, rising to her feet.

Roy laughed out loud. "Yeah, but you don't get a free meal out of a root canal."

"Then maybe you should do the interview," she murmured, leaving the office.

Bree's first alert that something was wrong was the way Jinx stood by her desk. His entire body vibrated with the need for action.

"So what did they do, huh, boy?" she whispered, sitting at her desk. She didn't have to look around to notice everyone's attention was centered on her, even if no one looked in her direction. "Let's find out, shall we?"

She didn't miss the sound of Frank Robert's malicious chuckle from the other side of the room.

She swiftly reviewed past misdeeds thought up by co-workers. The flour bomb left in a desk drawer. Her picture pasted on top of a *Playboy* centerfold. Fake vomit placed under her desk chair. She affectionately called the perpetrators her own juvenile delinquents. And she did her own damage when the occasion arose.

She found what she was looking for in the second drawer. As soon as she opened it, a triangular head slid upward and a narrow, forked tongue flicked out to test the air. Bree leaned back a bit as a long, sinuous column swept toward her, seeking the heat of her body.

"Well, aren't you a cutie," she cooed, picking up the snake, which immediately wrapped itself around her arm. "And what did they arrest you for?" She glanced at Jinx, who whined in displeasure at having such a creature invade his partner's private space. She had no doubt every eye was on her. "A rosy boa, isn't he?" she said to no one in particular. She stroked the reptile's head. "My oldest son has one."

Keith, one of the deputies, rose to his feet. He looked a little uneasy as he approached her. "So that's where he got to," he chuckled, but the sound came out forced. "Mabel's my son's snake," he explained, walking over with his hand outstretched, ready to take the boa from her.

"Mabel," Bree murmured as she studied the reptile, which seemed content to remain wrapped around her arm. "Interesting name. Ours is named David Boa." She grinned.

This time Keith's chuckle was more natural as he understood

the twist on words. As he turned, he caught sight of Frank's dark expression. He turned away immediately.

"Keith, do you have some place for Mabel or should I just put her back in my desk?" Bree asked. "She seemed to have made herself at home there."

His face reddened even more. "Ah, I've got a box in my locker."

"She can stay here until you get back." She set the snake back in the drawer.

Bree noticed some of the men looked wary, but a few still appeared hostile. She sensed this was just the beginning of pranks meant to test a new colleague.

But Bree wasn't easily intimidated.

Since it was getting close to the time for her lunch meeting, she walked Jinx outside to the small fenced enclosure fixed up for him. She made sure he had plenty of water before she closed the gate after him.

"Can you believe those guys thought they could scare me with a measly snake?" she asked her canine partner. "As if that would do it. I have teenagers, for God's sake!"

She went back inside and stopped in the ladies' room long enough to freshen her lipstick and cologne. She knew her outfit was professional looking, with a touch of femininity—a square of lace peeking out of the pocket on her navy houndstooth vest, topping navy linen pants. She made sure her pager was switched on, then grabbed her purse and left.

Now to see if the man looked as good as he sounded.

The man looked even better than he sounded.

Bree might not have met Cole Becker before, but when she stepped inside the restaurant, she had no problem targeting her quarry.

He sat in the last booth, his back against the wall. Long jean-clad legs were stretched out in front of him. Neatly shorn black hair flecked with silver framed a blatantly male face, whose signs of wear and tear only accented his rough good looks. A faded gray, cotton button-down shirt matched the equally faded jeans.

He looked like a man who had all the time in the world. As if nothing mattered except what he was going to order for lunch.

Bree knew better. There was something in that deceptively lazy gaze wandering over her that said this man probably knew everything about her down to her bra size. Just from that look.

An energetic Beatles tune boomed out of a jukebox near the front door. The first thing that hit the people who entered the restaurant was the black and hot-pink decor. Hot-pink vinyl bench seats framed black tables of the booths, and pink and black vinyl alternated on stools at the counter. Most of them were occupied, Bree noted. Chatter momentarily halted as the occupants paused and identified the newcomer.

Her gaze returned to the man sitting in the booth at the rear of the room.

Oh my God. No man should look this good.

She resolutely kept her jaw up off the floor as she walked toward him. This man didn't need to worry that the lines by his eyes and mouth had been stamped there by time and the sun. They only intensified his good looks. He watched her with an expression that also betrayed a hint of amusement, as if he was aware of her thoughts.

He has to be used to lots of feminine appreciation.

Storm-gray eyes that matched his shirt tracked her movements. He rose to his feet in one fluid motion and held out his hand.

He had to be a good six feet two inches to her five feet eight. She wasn't used to men towering over her, and it had been a long time since a man looked at her the way Cole Becker was. As if she was today's blue plate special.

"Detective Fitzpatrick, I'm Cole Becker." He spoke in that kind of supremely masculine voice that wouldn't sound out of place in a woman's bedroom.

Where did that thought come from? She firmly shook it off before it gathered too much momentum.

"Please, have a seat." He gestured toward the bench across from his, then looked past her. "Did you leave your partner back at the station?"

She mentally gave him points for knowing about Jinx. But then, as Roy had told her, there's no privacy in a small town.

"His table manners can't always be trusted," she replied, sliding across the hot-pink vinyl seat.

"Too bad. I was hoping to meet him." Cole sat down. "I can guarantee everything they serve here is fantastic," he added, nodding toward the menu. "And it's on me."

Bree arched an eyebrow. "Some might see that as bribing a police officer."

"I don't think Holloway would consider a $5.95 hamburger a bribe," Cole murmured with amusement. "But if you order the steak sandwich, favors will be asked for."

"Hey there, hon." A waitress stopped by the table. Her gaze was filled with unabashed curiosity as she stared down at Bree.

"Annie, this is the town's new detective, Bree Fitzpatrick," Cole introduced. "Detective, this is Annie, the love of my life who keeps me well fed."

Annie shot him her "get out of here" look.

"Nice to meet you, hon," she said warmly. "What can I get you to drink?"

Bree smiled back. "Iced tea, please."

She nodded and started to walk away.

"Hey, Annie, I don't get asked?" Cole said with mock hurt.

She laughed. "Oh, hon, the day you don't drink black coffee is the day the sky will turn plaid." She wiggled ample hips encased in denim. "I'll get your drinks now. That'll give the detective time to figure out what she wants to eat." She pointed her finger at Cole. "You, I already know."

"Eat here often, do you?" Bree asked, entertained by the waitress's lively chatter.

"Only two times a day, seven days a week," he admitted. "But we're here to talk about you. I understand you have three kids. Two from your husband's first marriage, the third yours and your husband's."

The light in Bree's eyes dimmed a bit. As if obeying a command from within, she pasted on her professional expression.

"I consider all three mine," she replied, pausing long enough to murmur her thanks as the waitress deposited her drink in front of her. "But I really prefer we not discuss my children. I like to keep my work and personal life separate."

The lines fanning out from his eyes crinkled as he grinned. "You've never lived in a small town before, have you? The favorite entertainment around here is learning everything you can about your neighbor. Once the residents know all the little details, they consider you one of their own. It's already common knowledge you bought Mrs. McGyver's place. As for your job, the city council liked your credentials, which I have to say were impressive, and your hire was almost immediate. Detectives with your credentials don't usually come to a place like Warm Springs," he told her. "Of course, it doesn't hurt when you've got some city politicians on your side."

Bree's gaze could have cut through him like a hot knife through butter. He didn't look the least bit cowed. If anything, he smiled more.

She looked up when Annie returned to take her order. Bree quickly examined the menu and asked for a bacon, lettuce and tomato sandwich.

"I'll have my usual," Cole said.

Annie gave an unladylike snort. "Like I didn't already know." She moved away.

"One day I'll order something different," he called after her.

"Sure, and tomorrow Harrison Ford is going to show up and take me away from all this grandeur," the waitress snickered.

Bree smothered her chuckle. "Stand in line."

Cole looked at Bree and decided she was one fine-looking woman, even if she did carry a gun and could probably pin him up against a wall with a minimum of effort.

He'd never thought of freckles as sexy until he noticed them lightly dusted across her nose. They went with the red hair tucked behind her ears and wisped across her forehead. Her tailored clothing stated she was no-nonsense. Probably had to give that impression because of her occupation. But the citron studs in her ears, gold filigreed chain around her neck and the hint of perfume proclaimed her femininity to anyone who cared to look for it. His gaze flicked downward. She wore no wedding ring, so she must have laid her husband to rest even in her heart.

Cole was positive she'd deck him if he told her she was cute.

Besides, she was not his type. Law enforcement officials he'd met in the past were pretty regimented in their thinking. And the woman had three kids.

No, not his type. Even if just looking at her made his day.

This meeting was purely business, however. He'd dangled a little mystery in front of the lady to get her here. After all, who was more qualified to solve a murder than a homicide detective?

He wondered if he could trust her.

"How about if I start off with some humor," he suggested. "What was one of the funniest things to happen to you on the job?"

Bree thought for a moment. "The first year I worked patrol, we were called to a carjacking scene. We were only a block away and arrived in time to see the suspect take off. We wasted no time in going after him. We apprehended the suspect and told him we were bringing him back for an ID. The minute we pulled him out of the car to face the woman, he said, 'Yep, that's the lady I robbed.' He was dead serious when he said it, too. My partner and I couldn't stop laughing. Good thing we'd Mirandized him the minute we grabbed him. There was no way his confession could be thrown out. That good enough for you?"

Cole chuckled. "Definitely. You gotta love an easy confession like that."

"It did make it a lot easier for us," she admitted.

"I would think Warm Springs would seem pretty quiet after the fast pace in L.A.," he commented, looking up to smile at Annie as she set their plates in front of them. As always, his hamburger was grilled to perfection, the sauteed mushrooms on top of the meat finishing the work of art. The onion rings were golden brown and crispy. "Marry me, Annie," he begged.

"The day I say yes is the day you'll hotfoot it out of town," she hooted.

"That's what you eat every day?" Bree asked curiously, as she sprinkled salt on her French fries.

He shook his head. "Only on Wednesdays. I believe in a varied diet. So tell me, how long did you work for the Los Angeles County Sheriff's Department?"

"I was with the department for twelve years, the last three in homicide."

"I guess Warm Springs seems pretty tame after all the excitement you had in L.A.," he commented.

Her smile rivaled that of a shark moving in for the kill. "Sometimes what looks tame on the surface isn't. I've heard that can happen in small towns."

Damn, he should have known better than to underestimate the lady. It was as if she knew exactly what he was leading up to. But would she accuse him of chasing shadows that weren't there?

She pushed her plate to one side so she could rest her arms on the tabletop. She fixed him with a steely gaze that had prompted more than one suspect to confess all. "Cut to the chase, Becker. Why are we sitting here having this conversation? No BS, either."

"I'm just making conversation," he drawled, falling back into the good-ole-boy routine that had lulled more than one subject he'd interviewed in the past. And gotten him some good quotes in the process. "I like to write up an accurate article. There's nothing worse than a sheriff's detective ticked off because I spelled her name wrong."

Her verbal rejoinder to his glib reply was succinct and to the point.

Cole's grin was slow to appear, but earth-shattering to the senses. "Damn, woman, I like your style. Something tells me you're going to give this town the kind of shake-up it needs." He leaned back, resting one arm across the back of the bench seat. He cocked his head to the side, watching her with piercing eyes that seemed to probe past any defenses she might erect.

Her return smile would have scared off a great white shark. "Lordy, Becker. Compliments like that will only go to my head," she purred.

Cole looked stunned, but quickly recovered. He opened his mouth as if he wanted to say something, but waited until after Annie paused by the table to see if they needed anything.

"During your time in homicide, did you ever have a funny feeling about a case? Something that just didn't feel right?" Cole asked when they were alone again. "A feeling that what was in front of you wasn't what it should be? That while everyone else said it was fine, you knew deep down it wasn't?"

Good. The lady looked intrigued.

"That's not unusual for any good cop," she said with a hint of caution in her voice. "When you've been on the job long enough, you learn to follow your instincts."

"Even if it means stirring up trouble?" he pressed. "What if there's an excellent chance that there's someone from your own department involved in something illegal?"

She returned his gaze with an equally bold one of her own. "Then you do what you have to do. Just because somebody wears a shield doesn't mean they're exempt. Your job is to arrest the bad guys," she said candidly.

"No matter who it is?"

"No matter who it is," she repeated.

Cole shrugged. "The mind-set of a police officer is interesting. You not only have hard and fast rules to follow, but you need to follow your instincts, too."

He noticed she absently placed her hand against the back of her neck, as if something bothered her.

"So what are you not telling me, Becker? What conspiracy do you believe has cropped up in Warm Springs?" Her emerald eyes glittered. "I'm sorry, I haven't read your newspaper long enough to know what your views are—if you think aliens are landing in the desert or a wild coyote boy is living out there."

Cole didn't miss the mocking implication.

"Why don't you eat your lunch first. Then we'll talk."

"I hope this doesn't mean I don't get dessert," she murmured, as she picked up her sandwich.

Cole finished his hamburger in record time. With every bite he kept an eye on his companion, as she, too, ate with relish.

Bree Fitzpatrick wasn't what he'd expected. It wasn't as if he hadn't met more than his share of female detectives, some of them downright gorgeous. But there was something about her that fascinated him.

When he'd learned the city council had hired a new detective, he'd been curious about what kind of officer they'd chosen. He hadn't expected Detective Fitzpatrick to be a widowed mother of three, two of them teenagers. He thought he'd meet a hard-nosed cop who'd worked toward her twenty years on the force and looked every one of those years. A woman no one in his right mind would want to cross. He would hazard a guess that no one in his right mind would cross this woman, and for all Cole knew she was a hard-nosed cop. But there was more to her than that. He'd say Bree Fitzpatrick was made up of more than grit.

He also hoped she had good instincts.

"Dessert?" Annie asked cheerfully.

Bree looked past him so she could read the brightly marked board on a wall.

"Pink lemonade pie?"

Annie nodded. "You'll love it."

"I'll take your word for it."

"Coconut pie for me, my love," Cole said.

Annie rolled her eyes. "As if you'd ever have anything different." She moved away.

"It sounds as if you've dug yourself into a rut," Bree commented. "Maybe you should shake things up a bit yourself by ordering something different next time."

"Maybe I will."

Bree looked at the chalkboard set next to the dessert board. She read the brightly colored words and laughed. *Customers using cell phones in here will be treated with the same courtesy as anyone lighting up a cigarette.*

Next to the board were two hooks. A squirt gun hung from the first and a waterfilled, clear plastic bucket hung from the second. A cell phone rested in the watery depths.

"The cell phone belongs to a businessman who'd stopped for lunch and didn't believe the sign," Cole said, noticing her interest. "He threatened to sue until he discovered he wouldn't have a chance of winning, since the sign is up where everyone can see it."

"I'll remember to keep mine turned off," she murmured, as the waitress dropped off their desserts.

Bree quickly discovered that pink lemonade pie was some-

thing very close to heaven even if there wasn't one hint of chocolate in it. She finished the rich pie in no time and knew she'd
be back for more.

Cole waited until she ate her last bite before he spoke. "Tell
me something, Bree. Have you ever thought an accident or suicide could have been a homicide? Did you go even further and
try to prove it?"

She looked intrigued by his question. "Any reason for asking?"

"Curiosity."

Bree silently regarded him. He kept his expression blank.

"There have been times when something hasn't seemed what
it is," she said finally.

"What if you were the only one who saw it? How do you
handle that kind of situation? Do you go along with what's already been determined, or try to make things right?"

Her expression tightened. "What's important about any case
is that it's closed properly. I do whatever it takes. So why don't
you tell me exactly why you're asking me this?"

Now it was Cole's turn to regard her. "Some people get lost
in the cracks."

"Only if the investigator hasn't done his or her job," she
retorted. "You've got sixty seconds to tell me exactly why
you're asking me these questions before I get up and walk out."

Cole waited fifty-nine of those seconds before he leaned down
and reached into his battered briefcase, which lay at his booted
feet. He pulled out several sheets of paper and pushed them
across the table.

"I'm trusting you with something I wouldn't like to have get
out, Detective," he said quietly.

Bree picked them up and began reading. She noted the neatly
aligned columns that listed names, dates and cause of death.

"Not very informative for an obituary," she commented.

"These aren't obits. These are not accidents or deaths by natural causes, either," he said quietly, tapping the papers with his
forefinger. "These are all murders."

Chapter 2

Bree scanned the contents, then looked back up at Cole.

"What makes you think foul play?" she asked. She leaned slightly forward. "What you have listed here are traffic accidents, accidents in the home and death by natural causes. Considering the average age of people in this county, it's expected."

"Then can you give a good reason why the death toll has risen twenty-four percent in the past two years?" he challenged her.

He noticed she again placed her hand against the back of her neck, as if something bothered her. Maybe the same something that bothered him when he realized the death toll was just a little too high?

Bree shrugged her shoulders. "It still goes with the population growth. More senior citizens are moving here because of the temperate climate, affordable housing and low crime. When the median age is high, you have to expect more deaths."

Cole shook his head. "The percentage still shouldn't have risen that much."

"Are you thinking you'll discover some heinous plot directed toward the elderly?'' she asked. "That you'll write your way to a Pulitzer Prize?''

"There's more involved here than some damn prize,'' he said without heat, but there was no mistaking the intensity in his voice. "Someone has gone to a lot of trouble to cause these deaths. And usually everything boils down to money.''

She glanced down at the papers again. "Do you know if any of these people had extraordinary amounts of insurance?''

Cole shook his head. "We're not talking millions.''

Bree gazed off into the distance. "I'll look into it.'' She held her hand up to indicate he should remain silent. "There's probably not anything to this, but I will do some checking,'' she announced, sliding out of the booth. "Thanks for lunch, Becker. Hope you got enough for your article.'' She sounded as if she couldn't care less.

"I'm not going to apologize, Fitzpatrick. I wanted a professional opinion,'' he told her. Then he added, "You free sometime for dinner?''

Bree laughed softly and shook her head. "In your dreams, Becker.'' She walked away.

"Shot you down but good, big fella,'' Annie said, as she collected the plates.

Cole shook his head as he watched Bree walk past the front window. "Naw, she's just playing hard to get.''

Bree couldn't stop thinking about Cole Becker's real reason for seeing her.

It wasn't the first time someone had sought her detecting skills for an alleged crime, and it wouldn't be the last.

He's a good-looking man, a little voice whispered in her ear.

"I had a good-looking man,'' she muttered to herself. "I don't need another one.''

Fitz wouldn't want you to be alone.

"Like I'm ever alone. Jinx sleeps in my room and he snores worse than Fitz ever did.'' She waited for the faint ache that happened each time she invoked her husband's name to settle deep within her body. "Oh, Fitz.'' His name came out on a soft sigh. "Damn you for leaving me.''

The ache was still there. Not as strong as it had been in the past. But instead of Fitz's face swimming in front of her, Cole Becker's rugged features appeared.

She hastened back to the office and walked around to the rear, where Jinx's kennel was set up. The German shepherd was ecstatic to be let out.

"Heel," Bree ordered. The dog obediently fell into step by her left side as she entered the building. She stopped at the call board that indicated which deputies and detectives were on duty, and marked herself in.

"Fitzpatrick! You want to come in here, please?" Roy appeared in his office doorway. Assured he'd gotten her attention, he turned around and disappeared back into the room.

"Boss man yells, we jump," Irene murmured as she walked past Bree.

"I haven't been here long enough to have done anything wrong," Bree mumbled, thinking of a past superior who believed the louder the voice, the faster the response from his people. It generally proved to be true. She parked Jinx at her desk and walked back to Roy's office.

By the time she stepped inside, he was already seated behind his desk.

"I have to report to the courthouse in an hour regarding a case," he announced, looking up at her. "Seems it got moved up at the last minute. Probably something to do with that idiot of a defense attorney," he grumbled. "The thing is, I'd promised to give a safety lecture at the senior center this afternoon."

That area in the back of Bree's neck was now tingling like crazy. The chance to meet some of the town's senior citizens was too good a chance to pass up. "Okay," she said, easily guessing the direction he was taking.

"Glad to hear you're volunteering for the job." He grinned.

"I did?" She pretended surprise. Why did a boss always try to make it sound as if you were volunteering for the last possible job you'd want, when in actuality you were being volunteered? With no way to get out of it.

"Sure, you did." He tossed a sheet of paper across the desk. "Speaking to the group will give you a chance to get to know some of the county residents. And for them to get to know you in a more relaxed atmosphere than you showing up at their door because you're investigating a crime. The talk is the usual—street smarts and not letting yourself look like a victim. You've probably given your share in the past.''

She picked up the paper and read. The block letters announced a safety lecture to be given by Sheriff Roy Holloway at two o'clock in the sunroom at the Warm Springs Senior Center. All were encouraged to attend this informative talk on how not to be a victim in today's tumultuous times.

"Aren't these usually handled by the deputies?'' she asked.

He eyed her sharply. "You don't think you can give a simple talk on street smarts, Fitzpatrick?''

"I have given talks like this,'' she admitted.

"Good, because I have an idea the good people at the center will enjoy the talk more coming from you than from me.''

Bree silently cursed her big mouth.

"Actually, I like the idea of everyone doing their part,'' she said, hoping she didn't sound as if she was trying to flatter her boss. "I'd hoped a smaller town meant a chance to get out more and meet with the people.''

He nodded in agreement. "Be there at quarter of two and ask for Joshua Patterson. I'm sure you'll do fine.''

Hearing the dismissal in his voice, Bree left the office and walked over to her desk.

"Community relations are very important,'' she instructed herself, as she stared at the too clean surface. No pink message slips were waiting for her. She told herself it was a good thing, since the only people who would have tried to get hold of her were from the kids' schools. "The public gets to know the officers who protect them. Nobody can say I'm not being thrown into the fray.''

"Sheriff Holloway said to give these out at your talk.'' Irene set a small cardboard box down in front of Bree. "We just got them in. They're magnets they can stick on the refrigerator. They have the phone numbers for the sheriff's department and fire department, plus blank spaces where they can write in their doctor's and pharmacy's numbers,'' she explained.

"Sounds like a good idea," Bree said approvingly, looking at the white squares with red lettering. "Is this senior citizens center pretty active?"

"They have something going on all the time," the receptionist replied. "Dances, bingo, day trips to San Diego for plays and concerts. You name it."

"Definitely a better social life than mine," Bree told Jinx, who lay under her desk.

The moment Bree and Jinx entered the Warm Springs Senior Center, they were approached by the administrator.

"We're grateful you were willing to step in at the last second and take the sheriff's place, Detective Fitzpatrick," Josh Patterson said after he'd introduced himself. He clasped Bree's hand in a warm grip.

While the man's weathered features indicated he had to be in his mid- to late seventies, his demeanor was that of a man a good twenty years younger. His silver hair and mustache gave him a dashing look that reminded her of Douglas Fairbanks Jr. Bree wouldn't be surprised if he'd been told more than once about the strong resemblance.

"Thank you. Hopefully, this will be a good chance for me to meet some of the county residents, and in turn, they can begin to get to know me," she replied with a warm smile, finding it easy to fall under the spell of his courtly charm.

He looked down. "And I see you brought your partner with you. Excellent." He beamed. "That box looks heavy. Let me help you with it," he offered.

"Oh my, the man is doing it again. I swear he can't be trusted to keep his hands off any female."

Josh turned his head at the sound of the woman's voice. His mouth broadened in a smile and his eyes softened with an expression Bree remembered well and ached for again.

"Detective, this is my wife, Renee." He made the introductions. "Renee, this is Detective Fitzpatrick. She's taking over for Roy today."

"And I must say it's a definite improvement." Renee smiled

at Bree and held out her hand. "Roy is a dear man, but there are times when he can be a real tight-ass," she confided.

Bree smiled back. Just as Josh was movie star handsome, Renee equaled him in looks. Her hair was as silver as her husband's and brushed back in thick short waves. Fashionable glasses were perched on her small nose. Her dusty-blue silk pants and a print polo-style top coordinated with her husband's navy slacks and navy-and-white-striped shirt.

"You have to excuse Josh. He likes to believe he's still a stud," Renee confided, tucking Bree's arm in hers as they walked across the center's spacious lobby to a side room. "The dear man can't understand that he's in his declining years."

Bree chuckled. "I can't imagine the man is even close to his declining years."

The older woman leaned closer to say in a low voice, "He's not. I just don't want him to know that. Makes him too self-confident."

People milled around the end of the room where a long table held a coffee urn and cups. Several turned and looked curiously at her and the dog walking next to her.

"It's nice to know they've finally gotten smart and hired another woman over there," Renee told Bree as she guided her toward the front of the room, where a podium and several chairs were set up. "Oh, I know the department has a female deputy, but they need more women in there. Roy Holloway can't help being your typical male chauvinist. He was brought up to believe women belong in the home and so on. His wife is Suzie Homemaker with a capital *H*. As for his children...well, there's no reason I should give you all the gory details at once." Her brown eyes twinkled with amusement.

Bree was amazed at her frank speech. "So far, he's been fine with me," she confessed.

Renee chuckled. "That's because he knows a good thing when he sees it." She squeezed Bree's hand. "Please don't let my words scare you off. Something tells me you can handle the man."

"I'll do my best," she promised, keeping in the lighthearted spirit.

"I think you will." The woman looked around and gestured for people to be seated. "Would you like a glass of water or some coffee?"

"No, thank you." Bree set the box of magnets on the floor by the podium.

"Will everyone be seated now?" Renee called out. She waited until the group did her bidding. "As you all know, Sheriff Holloway was going to speak to us today on personal safety. Unfortunately, he isn't able to be with us, but he has sent his newest detective, Bree Fitzpatrick. Detective Fitzpatrick worked for the Los Angeles County Sheriff's Department and is now with the Warm Springs Sheriff's Department. Please give her a warm welcome."

Bree looked around the room, noting the audience's age bracket ran from late fifties to late eighties. She'd lost count of the number of talks she'd given to various groups over the years, so this was nothing new to her.

So why did she feel this talk could be the most important one she'd delivered to date?

"Thank you, Renee," she said warmly. "Good afternoon, everyone. My name is Detective Bree Fitzpatrick. Before coming to Warm Springs, I was a homicide detective with the Los Angeles County Sheriff's Department for twelve years, the last three in homicide. I am also a K-9 officer, which means my partner is a dog. Which I'm sure more than one officer has said about their human partners," she said, to expected laughter. "Jinx here comes from a long line of K-9s. Right now, his three brothers are working for the Los Angeles Police Department and Sheriff's Department. He is considered a bona fide member of the sheriff's department. He even has his own specially fitted Kevlar vest. If anyone dares to shoot or, God forbid, kill him, the investigation and conviction would be treated the same as firing on any human police officer."

"But he's a dog," a woman said, almost apologetically.

"A dog with very special training," Bree replied. She went on to explain what his training entailed. "And now to the reason for my being here." She looked from one face to another. "I wish I could say that there are places and communities where you don't have to worry about crime. But, sad to say, those days are over. It's lovely that the crime rate is low in this county, but everyone still needs to be cautious. To use your common sense and street smarts so you won't become a victim. At night, park in a well-lit area, as close to your building as possible. When you leave a building and head for your car, make sure you already have your keys in your hand. Be aware of everything going on around you. Keep your head up, walk with a confident stride. Before you get in your car, take a few seconds to glance at the back seat to make sure no one is hiding there. The minute you're inside your car, lock the doors.''

''What if you feel someone is following you?'' a woman asked.

''Marian, we'll have a question and answer period after the talk,'' Renee chided.

''She did bring up a good point,'' Bree said. ''If you feel you are being followed, never go home. Drive directly to the police station or someplace that's well lit and busy. If you have a cell phone, call the authorities and explain your situation. Once you reach the police station, and if you're afraid to get out of your car, honk your horn repeatedly. Believe me, someone will come out to investigate.''

Bree felt herself relax as she gave a talk she knew she could give in her sleep.

Then the rear door opened and someone slipped inside, making his way toward one of the chairs in the back row.

Bree felt herself start to falter as she locked gazes with Cole Becker. He smiled and tipped his head in a silent greeting as he sat back in the chair. He pulled a notebook out of his briefcase and settled his ankle on the opposite knee. She purposely ignored him and continued speaking.

It wasn't easy pretending he wasn't there. Not when he was staring unflinchingly at her.

What is he doing here? He's not old enough to be a member of this center, unless he's better preserved than I thought. And if that's the case, I want to know his secret.

One way or another, she was determined to finish her talk without stumbling over any words.

What was it about Cole Becker that affected her this way?

If it wouldn't ruin her future with the sheriff's department, she'd just shoot the man and get it over with.

She mentally heaved a sigh of relief when she finished her speech and waited for questions. She nodded at one woman sitting in the second row.

"But what about when someone tries to rob you?" the tiny, gray-haired lady asked in a trembling voice. "I know you're not supposed to fight them, but I can't just allow them to take my money, either."

"Better to lose the money than lose your life. However, what we've seen is that many thieves preying on the elderly are actually cowards. They tend to choose people they don't think will fight back," Bree explained. "If you feel you have a chance, then show them you aren't that easy. Especially if they're not carrying a weapon. Things you can do are stomp down on their foot really hard, plant your knee between their legs, and if possible, poke at their eyes. And yell as loud as you can. Some people feel yelling 'Fire!' gets more action than yelling for the police. Do whatever you think will get you assistance."

"That's why we need to carry guns of our own," one man grumbled. A low rumble moved through the audience. "That way the bastards will know who's really in charge."

"Not at all a good idea," Bree said firmly. "I've had to work on too many crime scenes where the victim's own gun was used on him or her."

"Then what should people do, Detective Fitzpatrick?" Cole called out from the back of the room. "What do they need to do to protect themselves?"

"Carry a personal alarm. The kind where you pull a cord and it emits a screeching sound. That will attract attention. Take a course to learn how to properly use pepper spray," she recommended. "Take a self-defense course that will not only teach you how to defend yourself, but will give you a little confidence to boot."

"What about a large dog?" someone else asked.

"They're a good deterrent and make for good company," she agreed.

"I can see our time is up." Joshua stood up and moved over to stand next to Bree. "I'd like to thank Detective Fitzpatrick for coming here and giving us some good ideas on how to protect ourselves." He started clapping and the others joined in.

What Bree noticed most was the tall man now standing in the back of the room.

"I've brought some magnets for you to put on your refrigerator or by the phone," she said, holding one up. "Please, help yourselves."

Bree stood by the podium as many of the seniors made their way to the front. She smiled and spoke to each person Joshua and Renee introduced her to.

"Thank you for explaining who we need to beware of," one frail silver-haired woman said, laying her trembling hand on Bree's arm. She lowered her voice. "Sometimes I feel very frightened."

Bree had only to look into her eyes to see that she wasn't speaking lightly. Fear spoke a stark message in her gaze. Bree didn't hesitate. She plucked the magnet out of the woman's hand, dug a pen out of her pocket and quickly wrote on two of the empty lines.

"This is my cell phone number and this is my home number," she said quietly. "If you need to, call me directly, all right?" She tucked the magnet back into the woman's hand and curled her fingers over it. "I am very serious. You call me anytime, day or night."

The woman offered a tremulous smile, then turned away to walk slowly to the door. Bree watched her thoughtfully.

"Estelle Timmerman," Renee murmured in Bree's ear. "Poor dear. She used to be such an incredible woman. She was in the Women's Army Corps during World War II. She faced each day with a smile. She and her husband did everything together. After his death, she seemed to change overnight. Became timid. Quiet. I've tried countless times to find out what's wrong, but she tells me it's nothing. I've been able to persuade her to go on some of our day trips, but it hasn't been easy. I worry about her."

"Sometimes what someone sees as something very wrong,

we would see as nothing," Bree murmured back, making a mental note to check on the woman.

She was meeting the last of the group when her senses picked up Cole Becker's presence. She turned and offered him a brief smile that wasn't the least bit friendly.

"I found your talk informative, Detective," he drawled. "I think our senior citizens will feel safer after knowing their options. I know I do."

"Something tells me that most criminals would run the other way if they ran into you," she said.

He nodded sagely. "True. Power of the press and all that."

Bree suddenly realized that everyone else seemed to have disappeared, leaving her and Cole alone. He appeared to have realized it, too.

"Lunch tomorrow?"

"I'm busy."

"Dinner tomorrow night?"

"Busy," she said glibly.

"March 7, 2004?" Cole asked without missing a beat. He reached for the box of magnets, but she beat him to it.

She smiled. "Dentist in the morning. Seeing my psychic in the afternoon, and I'll be washing my hair that evening." She headed for the door. "Have a nice day, Mr. Becker."

As Bree entered the reception area, Renee approached her.

"Don't tell the sheriff, but I believe I got the better deal, too. I didn't have to familiarize myself with mountains of paperwork," she confessed with a big grin.

"Next time you must show us what your dog can do," the older woman requested.

"He's a working police dog. He doesn't do tricks," Bree warned.

Renee chuckled. "Don't worry. We don't expect him to shake hands or sit up. Perhaps you could show us how he catches a suspect."

"Now that he can do," she assured her.

"Come back anytime," Renee invited.

"I'm not exactly in the right age group."

Her eyes twinkled with laughter. "Don't worry, we'll give

you a special dispensation." She laid her hand on Bree's arm. "Perhaps you'd be free for lunch one day. I'd like the chance to get to know you better."

"I'd enjoy that," she said sincerely.

Renee's smile was sly. "Poor Cole must not have said the right words." She turned away when one of the women called her name. "Thank you again, dear," she said to Bree as she took her leave.

Bree walked out to the truck with the box nestled in her arms.

She disarmed the vehicle alarm and set the box on the floor of the back seat. She expected to see Cole Becker in the area and found herself feeling strangely disappointed that she didn't.

"I am *not* going back there!" Sara's strident voice could be heard as Bree pulled the Expedition into the garage.

She could hear every word even with the vehicle's windows closed.

Jinx whined and pawed at the back of the seat.

"I hear them, too," Bree said with a deep sigh.

"What are you complaining for? I was the one who got the dork of the year award," David yelled back.

"When're we gonna eat? I'm really hungry!" Cody wailed.

Bree shut off the ignition and pulled the key free. Her fingers hovered over the garage door opener button.

"Maybe we should go out for a hamburger," she mused. Before she could give in to her first thought, she pushed the button. As she climbed out of the SUV, she listened to the whir of the garage door sliding downward.

When Bree opened the back door, the first thing she noticed was the sudden silence that dropped over the room. Then the spicy scent of garlic and oregano tickled her nose.

"Spaghetti?" she asked, walking through the room. "It smells good. Thanks for starting dinner, Sara."

The girl shrugged her shoulders.

"Mom?" Cody was right on her heels as Bree headed for her bedroom.

"Give me a minute." She pulled her lock box off the closet shelf and deposited her weapon inside. "What is it, honey?"

"I got to feed the parakeet today," he told her.

Bree dropped onto the bed beside him and wrapped her arms around him.

"So it's not so bad, after all?" she asked.

He gave a fleeting grin and shook his head. Before he could say anything, shouting erupted from the kitchen.

"I don't give a—!" David yelled at his sister.

"Cuss jar," Cody whispered, burrowing closer to his mother. "That's a dollar word."

Bree urged him onto his feet and together they walked back to the kitchen. She found brother and sister facing off in what she knew was only the beginning.

"Did you pay your dollar?" she asked her stepson.

David muttered something under his breath as he reached into his pocket, then pulled the cork top off a large earthenware jar with Cuss Jar engraved on the front.

"Add another dollar to it," Bree instructed.

"He's being a sh—!" Sara's complaint was cut off by Bree's upheld hand.

"Dollar from you, too. Want to go for two?"

"But I didn't say it!"

"No, but you were ready to." Bree pulled open a cabinet door and withdrew a bag of dog kibble. She filled the large plastic dish set by the refrigerator. Jinx wasted no time heading for his bowl. "Dare I ask if anything good happened today?"

Sara swiped her hand across her eyes. "They're all lame at school," she complained.

"You're the one who's lame," David muttered.

When the kitchen timer dinged, Bree felt as if she was listening to the gong announcing the next round in a championship fight.

"David, drain the spaghetti and pour the sauce over it, please," she directed. "Sara, you want to get the garlic bread out of the oven?"

Bree watched her stepson set the bowl on the table as they all sat down.

"It looks good," she said cheerfully.

Her rule regarding no battles at the table held true. The children's conversation was chillingly polite.

After dinner, Bree loaded the dishwasher while the three children disappeared into their rooms to do their homework.

She enjoyed the peace and quiet in the kitchen as she rinsed off dishes and placed them in the machine. For the next half hour, her only companion was Jinx, who lay sprawled on the floor.

"If I could get you to do the dishes, you'd be the perfect partner," she informed the dog.

She should have known her quiet time wouldn't last long.

"Mom!" Sara yelled. "Where's my pink lace top? I want to wear it tomorrow."

"Mommy!" Cody joined the chorus.

Bree threw up her hands. She looked down at the dog, who looked back at her with a quizzical expression on his face.

"Who are these children and why do they call me Mom?"

Chapter 3

Cole should have been working on next week's column. He knew what he was going to write. Had already drafted it in his head. It would be easy enough to type the words into his laptop computer. He'd done it many times before.

Trouble was, he didn't want to write his reflections on the new school year compared to his memories of school. Not when something in town had been brewing for quite a few years now. All he had to do was find some hard facts to back up what he'd only been able to suppose so far.

He was hoping Bree Fitzpatrick would be able to help him in that matter. A reminder of another story that needed to be written.

He stared at the bulky file folders and the contents he'd been accumulating for the past year. They were stacked haphazardly around the easy chair in his living room.

With all the research he'd done so far, why hadn't he been able to find some hard proof that he could take to the authorities? Considering the stories he'd investigated and written in the past, this one should be a piece of cake. It had started late one night when he'd been feeling stuck on what to write about. He'd pulled out some of his uncle's files, looking for ideas for his column. A sticky note attached to a file folder had caught his attention. *Too many are dying.*

Cole knew his uncle wouldn't have written such a cryptic note unless there was something behind it. Sometimes, he feared that note had something to do with his death. So he'd done some digging of his own. And discovered, indeed, too many people were dying.

Even with the large senior citizen population in the county, the numbers were still too high for his peace of mind. He did what digging he could, but he still couldn't find enough solid evidence to indicate foul play.

Cole's gut told him a lot of these deaths weren't accidents or from natural causes. Now he just had to find the connection.

He'd mentioned his suspicions to Roy once. The sheriff had listened and, when he was finished, explained that he could understand his concerns, but that Cole had to look at it from the sheriff's point of view. What he was talking about sounded a hell of a lot like some sort of conspiracy theory. If Cole came up with some evidence Roy could follow up on, then he'd be happy to do whatever was necessary to investigate.

Cole figured Roy had mouthed all the right words and hoped he would move on to something else.

Cole did. After all, he had a newspaper to put out.

But it didn't stop him from gathering information every chance he got. "Casual" talks with victims' friends gave him insight into their lives that he couldn't have gotten any other way. He'd drunk gallons of coffee and eaten pounds of homemade coffee cake while discovering bits and pieces about various residents that he kept filed away. Pieces of information that didn't always make sense.

Sure, it was possible for someone suffering from inoperable cancer to succumb to a heart attack. No reason why someone diagnosed with impending blindness as a complication due to diabetes wouldn't die from slipping in the shower. Some of the deaths Cole could have believed were suicide, but there was just something about them that didn't add up in his mind.

Maybe he was looking for a story that wasn't there. Seeing things that didn't exist.

Except for Uncle Charlie's notes.

Uncle Charlie who hadn't had one fanciful bone in his body.

Cole leaned back in the easy chair that faced his big-screen television set. He had CNN on now, but the sound was muted. An open pizza box had two pieces of mushroom pizza remaining. A can of beer sat on the table by his elbow. For now, he was content to think about Bree.

Ordinarily, he kept his distance from a woman with children. Trying so hard to get her to go out with him wasn't his usual *modus operandi*.

He didn't consider himself good relationship material. A failed marriage had taught him all he needed to know—he wasn't good in the long run. After his ex-wife told him his work came before anything else and she was tired of not meaning anything to him, he'd decided she was right.

Except things weren't the same after she left. He felt as if he'd failed. Going after any and all stories, no matter how dangerous, was his way of coping.

Amazing how a bomb almost turning him into confetti had got him to make a few changes in his lifestyle. He took life a little easier now. But one rule was still hard and fast with him: any woman he dated knew from the get-go he wasn't the commitment type.

Marriage and family weren't meant for him. But that didn't stop him from enjoying an evening, and maybe even all night, with a woman.

It wasn't the thrill of the hunt Cole thought about when it came to Bree. He'd outgrown that behavior years ago. No, what he felt was a tug toward the lady. All he wanted was the chance to follow through on his interest.

But first he had to convince her he wasn't such a bad guy.

"Did you look through the files I sent you?"

Cole's husky drawl filtering through the telephone line was surprisingly devastating to a woman who believed she was immune to the man.

Bree thought of the manila envelope delivered to her home. There was no note inside, but there didn't need to be. She knew the identity of the person who'd sent her copies of accident reports and a few doctors' statements. Clipped to the first page of each report was a lined sheet of paper filled with neatly printed comments.

No way he could have fallen in the shower. He preferred baths.

Medical report more fiction than fact.

Any reason why only Holloway signed off on most of these accidents?

Heatstroke theory doesn't wash.

"Tell me something, Becker. Why me?" she asked now.

"You look like a lady who likes a challenge."

Bree picked up her pen and began doodling on the pad in front of her. Anyone looking at her would think she was taking notes.

"Did anyone ever tell you you're as irritating as poison ivy?" she asked.

His chuckle was like a warm breeze in her ear. "That's a new one. Trust me, I've been called worse. Come on, Bree, help me out here."

"Again, why me?"

"Because you're new to the area. You don't have any pre-conceived ideas about any of these people or their deaths. Because you worked homicide and were good at it. And because you don't believe anyone should die unnecessarily." The humor had leached out of his voice as he spoke quietly, but with a note of determination.

"You have no proof," Bree stated.

"There's proof out there. And I plan to be around when it shows up." He was silent for a moment. "I feel that proof is there on your end."

"Why?" she asked.

"Think about it. Whenever there's a cover-up it usually goes back to the cops."

She straightened up so quickly, Jinx raised his head to watch her.

"Don't go there, Becker," she warned.

He couldn't miss the ice in her voice. "All right, big mistake. Let me apologize by taking you out to dinner."

Bree laughed in spite of herself. *The man never quits.* "I would think you'd have dates running out of your ears. If I were you, I'd think twice about trying for a woman who has three children, two of them in high school."

"Ordinarily, I'd be running the other way," he said candidly. "I guess there's just something special about you."

"No, there isn't." She matched his candor with some of her own. "You're not used to being turned down. Good-looking guy like you."

"You're weakening, Detective. You just admitted you think I'm good-looking."

"Tell him I'll call him back," Roy could be heard saying to someone.

Bree looked up just as he stopped at her desk.

"Please, ma'am, don't apologize for calling," she said in her calm official voice, as if she'd been occupied with a business call. "If you think your handyman has been seen on *America's Most Wanted,* you should call us right away. We'll certainly check on it. Thank you for calling."

"Coward!" She heard Cole's accusation as she laid the receiver in the cradle.

Roy dropped a file folder on her desk.

"It's one of those cases that should be simple, but isn't," he told her. "A uniform was out there early this morning to take the initial report, but the complainant is still up in arms. She wants action. This is a situation that's been escalating for some time now. I'm hoping that sending you out there will diffuse it. I'll warn you, Mattie Williams isn't too easy to deal with and, personally, these calls are more crank than legit. But I'm not going to have anyone say we didn't follow up on a call just because we don't take it seriously. The day could come when it would be serious."

"Yes, sir. I'll get right over there." She picked up the file and opened it. She realized the man was still standing by her desk. She looked up. "Is there anything else, Sheriff?"

"The Pattersons said you gave a good talk," he said.

"I'm glad they were pleased," she replied, warmed to know her first public appearance was well received.

"It was a good beginning for you. You might want to attend the city council meetings, too," he suggested. "I like my people getting involved in the community."

"I'll do that."

He nodded and moved away. The moment his office door closed after him, Bree noticed everyone else's eyes shift back to their desks.

She picked the case folder up again and began reading. Once finished, she kept it in her hand and stood up. The moment she rose to her feet, Jinx got to his. The dog immediately moved to her left side.

"I think I'd rather have a human for a partner than a dog," Frank Roberts said. "At least then I'd know my backup was carrying a weapon."

"Oh really?" Bree's expression was bland as she kept her gaze centered on him. There was no inflection in her voice, nor did she glance at the German shepherd. "Jinx. Detain."

The dog moved so swiftly, the man didn't have a chance of blinking, much less moving, before the German shepherd cut off any hope of retreat. He gently, but firmly, held the man's trouser leg in his mouth.

"Hey!" Frank snarled, but he was no match for the dog keeping him in check. "Tell him to let go." Frank started to jerk backward, but Jinx's low growl changed his mind.

Bree knew he'd be furious, but she wanted to make a point. "Jinx. Keep close."

Frank froze when Jinx's jaws now landed a bit too close to the crotch of his slacks.

"If you'd had a weapon in your hand, he would have immediately disarmed you," Bree explained. "And you know the nice thing about having a K-9? He doesn't spill coffee on the seat, he doesn't complain about his wife and he doesn't nag me about my driving. If the situation came up, he would also take a bullet for his partner. Something you can't always count on with a human partner."

Frank's eyes blazed with temper, but he quickly masked it when he realized the dog picked up on his reaction.

"Who do I apologize to? You or the dog?" he asked, keeping his voice low and even.

"Jinx is the one you disparaged."

He took a deep breath. "Jinx, I'm sorry if I saw you more as a dog than as an officer," he muttered.

"Jinx, stand down," Bree said softly.

Jinx released his grip on the man's pant leg, took two steps back and settled back on his haunches.

"Say hello, Jinx," Bree instructed.

The dog lifted his paw. Frank looked as if the last thing he wanted to do was shake the dog's paw, but too many people were watching. He circled his fingers around the paw and shook it.

Bree stepped forward. "I'm not trying to embarrass you, Frank," she said in a low voice, meant for his ears only. "But I want to make the people in here understand that Jinx isn't just a dog who happens to have a shield attached to his collar. He's been trained as a deputy's partner, which frees up someone to work elsewhere. He was one of the first to work in a trial program to work with detectives also."

Frank's jaw worked as he thought about her words. "Just as long as he doesn't have fleas," he said grudgingly, drawing on anything to preserve his dignity before he returned to his desk.

"You should worry more about me than him on that count." She offered him a smile.

He didn't return her smile. She didn't take it personally. She sensed he was of the mind-set that didn't believe women belonged in law enforcement. Nothing new to her.

He looked around at their audience, officers that pretended not to be interested. "I see one dog collar or chew bone on this desk and there'll be hell to pay." He gave a growl worthy of Jinx.

"Our cue to leave. Jinx. Heel."

Bree walked out to her SUV and opened the rear door for Jinx to climb up inside. "Domestic dispute," she murmured with a sigh, switching on the engine. "My favorite kind of case."

She didn't have any trouble finding the location of the dispute. The first thing she noticed was Cole Becker standing on the sidewalk. He was busy studying what looked like a major war zone. She hazarded a guess that the day before, the green lawn had been lush and flowers bordering the front porch had added a colorful accent to the neatly painted house. Today it looked as if a deranged gardener had been let loose on the lawn. Flowers were torn up and thrown every which way. Chunks of sod were tossed up onto the porch and ground into the steps. And some kind of strange design was burned into the lawn.

Bree winced as she studied the destruction in front of her.

Then she sneaked a peek at Cole, who stood nearby. It was a sin a man could look so good in a pair of jeans.

Keeping her eyes off his illegal rear end, she parked in front of the house and got out. She let Jinx out of the truck and walked up the driveway with him at her side.

The morning breeze sent a hint of lemony aftershave her way. The man smelled as good as he looked.

"What did you do so wrong that you caught the Williams-Baxter feud?" he asked, snapping off a couple of photos.

"Don't tell me, you not only write the stories, you take the photos, too," Bree commented.

"I'm a Renaissance man. I do everything," he admitted.

A woman stepped outside. "Who're you?" she asked in a raspy voice that had an accent more commonly heard in Brooklyn, New York, than Southern California. She wore baggy shorts and a faded blue T-shirt that hung on her bony frame. Chipped red polish adorned her toes and fingernails. A cigarette dipped dangerously from her lower lip. She had the look of a woman who'd lived a hard life and didn't mind if it showed. She cast a suspicious eye in Jinx's direction. "He won't pee on my lawn, will he?"

As if that would hurt it more! Bree thought to herself.

"Mrs. Williams, I'm Detective Fitzpatrick." She moved forward, holding out her hand. The woman took it in a brief shake. "I understand you've had some vandalism."

"Hell, yes, I've had problems. You can't miss them, can you?" Her eyes flashed fire. In between puffs on her cigarette, she mouthed a few colorful phrases detailing what she thought of the vandals. "Teresa and her spawn are the ones who made this mess on my Harry's lawn. He works damn hard to keep it looking beautiful and they've ruined it. I want them arrested."

"Why do you think Teresa is to blame?" Bree's nose twitched at the acrid smoke. She'd quit smoking when she learned she was pregnant with Cody, and every once in a while that craving for nicotine hit her. Thanks to Mrs. Williams, it was rearing its ugly head.

"Teresa is my sneaky sister. How do I know she's behind this? I know because this is something she'd do. Or she'd have her son do it." She squinted in the plume of smoke rising upward.

"Come on, Mattie, tell her the truth why you think it was the Baxters," Cole suggested.

She glared at Cole. "Everyone knows why, Cole. This detective is here to arrest them. Not hear stories."

"Mrs. Williams, I can't arrest someone just on your say-so. I need proof," Bree explained.

The other woman snorted. "It's not as if I know they're out here so I run out with a camera. Besides, that's your job. Proving they did it," she insisted. "You just go on and do your job and put the two of them behind bars! This yard was just fine last night. That means they did it between the time I went to bed after Letterman and sometime before I came out for my newspaper this morning after the morning news." She waved her cigarette for emphasis, sending ash flying everywhere.

"Stand on the sidewalk where you can get a better look at the lawn," Cole advised in a low voice.

Bree did just that. As she stood on the sidewalk and looked at the grass, she realized it was more than some kind of design burned in the lawn, it was words.

"Interesting choice, wouldn't you say?" Cole asked, moving over to stand next to her. "No crop circles for this person."

"Whoever did it can't spell worth a damn," she muttered.

"Considering this could be considered a favorite obscenity, you'd think they'd know how to spell it."

"All you need to do is ask someone to spell this word and see if they use two *k*s instead of a *ck*," he commented. "Too bad that last school bond was voted down. Seems like our schools really need to do something about the students' spelling skills."

"When my Harry gets home and sees what those Baxters did to his lawn, he's going to bust a gut," Mrs. Williams said. "You have to arrest them!"

Bree took a deep breath, then wished she hadn't when she inhaled a hint of smoke. She was going to have to dig through the glove compartment and hope she could find a stick of gum. A mint. Anything that would help the craving. She blinked when something appeared in her range of vision.

Cole held out a square of bubble gum.

"It's the only way I can be around Mattie for more than thirty seconds," he said quietly. "And a hell of a lot safer. If I tried to take that cigarette from her, she'd have me flat on my back before I knew what happened."

Bree pulled off the paper wrapper, popped the pink disk in her mouth and started chewing.

"Mrs. Williams, I'm going to have a talk with Mrs. Baxter," she told the other woman. "But I'd like to ask you a few more questions first." She pulled her notebook and a pen out of her bag.

It didn't take her long to realize that all Mrs. Williams cared about was Bree arresting the entire Baxter family and putting them away for the next hundred years. Cole made no pretense of pretending not to hear. What irked Bree most was the tiny smile that tugged at the corner of his lips, as if he knew something she didn't.

He was walking toward a battered pickup truck when she finished talking to Mrs. Williams.

"Becker," Bree called out, just as he opened the door. She picked up her pace and headed toward him. "Okay, what's the big joke about this feud? And if you tell me the Baxters are aliens from another galaxy...'' She left the threat unspoken, but no less powerful.

"Whoa, Detective, I'm not packing heat." He held up his hands in surrender. "You're not even close with the alien guess. But you have to meet the Baxters to understand where Mattie is coming from. Or not," he muttered. He climbed inside the truck and closed the door after him. The window lowered. "Let me know how your meeting with the Baxters goes."

"You know something," she accused.

"Nothing that can help the case. See ya, Detective, honey." The window rolled upward and the engine rumbled to life.

Bree remained on the sidewalk, watching Cole drive away.

"You're seein' the Baxters today, arn'cha?" Mattie Williams called out to her.

"Yes, ma'am." Bree headed for her vehicle. She had an idea this case wasn't going to get any easier.

Bree knew it for a fact the moment she rolled to a stop in front of the Baxter house, situated a few miles outside of town.

She guessed the two-story dwelling had been built in the 1940s, but the paint job was pure 1960s—hot-pink with orange and purple daisies decorating the shutters bracketing each window, and an equally bright green door. As she walked up the obviously handmade stone walkway, she surreptitiously gave a few sniffs. The only smoke she detected was the tangy aroma of mesquite, not the sweet odor of something illegal.

When she reached the door, she found a multicolored rope hanging there. She gave a yank and listened to melodic chimes echo from inside the house.

"May I help you?"

She turned toward the side of the house. The woman she faced wasn't who she expected after listening to Mattie Williams ranting and raving about the people destroying her life. This woman dressed as if she still lived in the sixties in a pale yellow peasant-style blouse with a drawstring neckline and a brightly colored skirt that swirled around her bare ankles. Her brown hair was liberally streaked with gray and hung straight to her waist.

"Mrs. Baxter?"

Her smile was serene. "I prefer Teresa."

Bree moved forward. "I'm Detective Bree Fitzpatrick." She pulled out her shield and identification.

"Mattie sent you," she said softly. "Please, come on back." She stepped around to the rear of the house. "Would you like some tea?"

"No, thank you." Bree looked at the greenhouses set away from the house. "What do you grow?"

Teresa smiled as if she found her question amusing. "I supply orchids to local florists. Would you care to see them?"

She saw it as a chance to learn about the woman. "Yes, I would."

The first thing Bree noticed as she stepped inside the glass enclosure was the heavy moisture in the air. At first she felt as if she was breathing water.

"Do you feel as if you've suddenly traveled to the tropics?" Teresa asked. "Orchids prefer this type of atmosphere."

For the next hour, Bree was shown varieties of orchids. She expressed her astonishment at the colors arrayed before her.

"What is Mattie saying I've done this time?" Teresa asked, after she led Bree out of the greenhouse.

"She insists you carved designs in her lawn." Bree told her the words adorning the yard.

Teresa chuckled. She gestured for Bree to follow her inside the house. The kitchen was as brightly colored as the exterior, but very much set in the present. The two women sat at the butcher block table set with red-and-black cloth place mats.

"Mattie has blamed us for everything from her water heater going out to her cat having a hairball to her husband's erectile dysfunction," she said serenely as she set a teakettle designed to look like a duck on the stove.

Bree swallowed the laugh that threatened to crawl up her throat. "Any reason why she would think that?" She pulled out her notebook.

"Her reason for me to be in jail is very easy. She believes I stole this property from her."

Bree paused. "Any reason why she would think that?"

"Possibly because I married the man she thought she was in love with." She poured tea into a cup and carried it over to the table. She sat across from Bree. She nodded as if Bree had said something. "It's not a new story. Two sisters attracted to the same man. The man chooses one over the other. The spurned sister plots revenge."

"How long has this been going on?" Bree asked.

She closed her eyes in thought. "It's been a good thirty years."

"Even though she has Harry," Bree said.

"Harry *is* the man in question. We divorced fifteen years ago and he married Mattie. I received the house as a settlement."

"But you've since remarried," Bree said, hoping she could keep this straight.

Teresa nodded. "And divorced again. Harry and I had a son who is now nineteen. Adam helps me with the orchids."

Now Bree felt lost. "If Mattie has the man she's wanted for so long, why would she accuse you? And her husband's son?"

She smiled. "That's Mattie's way. She thinks I still want Harry. But I don't."

Bree shook her head, amazed at the woman's story. And believing it because it was too bizarre not to believe.

Teresa sipped her tea. "I don't want her husband, Detective Fitzpatrick. But Mattie refuses to believe me. So she does whatever she can to try to get me into trouble. This is an ongoing thing," she explained. "And I'm afraid since you're new to the area, you had no idea what you were in for." She got up from the table and headed for the stove. "I think you'll take that tea now."

"Let me get this straight. You married the man your sister was in love with?"

Teresa nodded.

"You had a son. Later, you divorced the man and your sister married him. You married someone else."

"Correct."

"But your sister thinks you want him back, so she's making all these accusations." Bree hoped she was filling in the blanks properly. "For what reason?"

"If I'm in prison, I can't chase after Harry," Teresa said evenly. "I have to say the vandalism of her front yard is a new twist. Before, it's been trash strewn around on the lawn or flowers dug up. What you've described is much too imaginative for Mattie. I hope she hasn't made an enemy.'' She shook her head in sympathy. ''She can sometimes come across as a bit abrasive.''

Bree didn't doubt it.

An hour later, she left Teresa's house feeling as if she had been Alice traveling through the Looking Glass. She didn't doubt Teresa's story. Bree was familiar with liars. In her line of work, it was a given. She also noticed that when someone lied they had a habit of coming up with a complicated story, as if it made them sound more credible. She usually had a pretty easy time finding the truth. However, she didn't doubt Teresa's convoluted tale.

''Mattie wants Teresa in jail. Teresa hopes Mattie will get a life,'' she said out loud as she pulled onto the highway leading back to town. With the windows down, she could inhale the varied scents from produce fields planted on either side of the road. After the rich perfumes of the orchids, they seemed almost fresh. A thought suddenly occurred to her. ''He knew. Dammit, he knew and he let me walk right into it!'' She slowed down and pulled over to the side of the road. She snatched up her cell phone and punched in three numbers for directory assistance. After receiving the number, she disconnected, then punched it in.

''Good afternoon, thank you for calling the *Warm Springs Bulletin*. How may I direct your call?'' a woman said in a cheerful voice.

''Cole Becker, please,'' Bree crisply requested.

''May I say who's calling?''

She unclenched her jaw. ''Tell him it's his worst nightmare.''

Bree ignored the music playing in her ear that was meant to be soothing but only further fueled her anger.

''Becker.'' His voice was like rough velvet in her ears.

''Nice story here. Sister accusing sister. Accuser's husband used to be Mattie's brother-in-law.''

''You can't tell me you haven't investigated cases like that in L.A.,'' he said.

"I worked homicide," she reminded him. "The victim wasn't a mutilated lawn."

"As if Teresa would do anything like that. She's a nice lady, isn't she?" Cole commented. "Hard to believe she and Mattie came from the same family. I can't believe that Harry would marry Mattie after being married to a nice woman like Teresa, but then Harry's not all that bright. His idea of a good time is a can of beer and Monday night football."

Bree ignored Jinx's soft whine and his head bumping against her arm.

"Are you going to show up everywhere I go?" Bree asked.

"Only the interesting places," he drawled.

She gave him her best cop voice. "In this state that can be construed as stalking. Not a nice thing to do, Becker."

"And that's not a nice thing to say, Detective," he told her. "You have a chance to look over the papers I sent you?"

"Not yet. I said I'd look them over and I will. Seems you want to add to the list of bad guys I'm dealing with. You're not a bad guy, are you?"

"Only if you want me to be."

Bree took a deep breath. There was no denying Cole was trying to seduce her over the phone. Not what she wanted. But it sure felt good.

"Down, boy," she said dryly.

"Not what a guy likes to hear."

She ignored his mock mournful tone as she disconnected the call.

Chapter 4

"**Y**ou can look at those papers all you want, but it still won't change a thing," Mamie scolded as she stopped by Cole's office to tell him she was leaving for the day.

He looked up. "Why do you think that?"

She shook her head. "Darlin', I don't know what you think you're going to do with all that material you're gathering, but I can tell you one thing. You won't get the answers you're seeking."

Cole narrowed his eyes. "What do you know about this, Mamie?"

She waved a hand in the air, her heavily laden charm bracelet making a tinkling sound. "Considering you haven't said a word, I've had to try to figure it out on my own. Which means I don't know as much as I'd like to." Suspicion rolled off her like a heavy fog. She speared him with a look that had never failed with her children when they were young; they'd confessed in record time. Sad to say, it never seemed to work with Cole. "What's really going on, Cole? You lock up file drawers that were never locked before. You've encrypted your computer in such a way I don't think even the CIA could break into it. Come to think of it, you're more paranoid than the CIA.'' She stepped inside and took the chair across from him. ''Tell me what's going on.''

He shook his head. ''Nothing's going on, beautiful.''

''You can't pull that on me. I've known you since you were a kid with skinned knees. Something's bothering you.'' She made it a statement of fact.

He leaned back in his chair, the springs squeaking slightly. ''Don't you have a date tonight?'' He lifted his coffee cup to his lips.

''Oliver can wait.'' She airily dismissed his question. ''It's not as if he's going to get lucky tonight. Even if he thinks he will.''

Cole hurriedly set his cup down before he dropped it. He coughed so hard that Mamie jumped up and ran around to thump his back.

''Do not say things like that!'' he wheezed. ''Do you know what pictures that conjures up? Dammit, it's like thinking of my mother and father...oh God!'' He waved her off.

Mamie chuckled, clearly enjoying his discomfort. ''It'd be better if you'd think about you and some nice woman doing the horizontal tango.'' Her smile dimmed a little. ''Hon, don't take on something that could land you in trouble. I don't want to have to break in another boss.'' She kissed him on the cheek and left the office.

''Gee, Mamie, thanks for all that confidence in me,'' he called after her. ''It's comforting to know I'll be missed if anything happens to me.''

''Don't worry, we'd hold a real nice memorial for you,'' she called back. ''Hello, is there something I can help you with?''

''Only if you'd like to hold your boss down for me.''

Cole winced as he heard a familiar feminine voice. The biting tone told him she wasn't there to finally accept his dinner invitation.

''Detective Fitzpatrick, I suppose.'' He could hear his assistant's dry tone and guessed she had a broad smile on her lips.

Damn, she was enjoying this way too much.

''Thank you,'' Bree told the woman.

She appeared in Cole's office doorway ten seconds later.

"Right about now I wouldn't mind finding a way to toss your butt in jail." Bree entered the office and took the chair opposite him without waiting for an invitation.

"Women can't get enough of me." He laced his fingers together and cradled the back of his head in his hands. "What can I do for you, Detective?" He decided to lean back and enjoy the scenery. She wore black pants and a black knit shirt brightened up by a red jacket with the sleeves rolled up. Her detective's shield was clipped to her waistband. Her auburn hair was tucked behind her ears, revealing gold hoops. A real no-nonsense lady. "You still mad at me because I didn't tell you more about Mattie and Teresa?"

"It wouldn't have hurt you to tell me."

He grinned. "Yeah, but you're the cop. It's your job to learn the details."

"Thanks a lot," she said without any sincerity. She looked around. "I'd have thought the owner would warrant nicer digs."

"An office with a view would tempt me into looking outside instead of working."

She picked up a metal monkey that sat on the corner of his desk. She wound it up and set it back on the desk. The monkey's paws, holding cymbals, began clapping together. She did the same with the tin duck next to the monkey, which quacked, and a dog that barked.

"Where's your model train?" she asked.

Cole pointed upward. Bree's gaze lifted to a shelf running along the walls, where a small train remained stationary.

He shrugged. "Everyone's got to have a hobby. Mine is collecting antique toys. You get a chance to look through those papers?"

"Enough to know there has to be more," she replied. "Where's the rest?"

He spun around in his chair and tugged open a file drawer. He pulled out a bulging file folder and dropped it on the desktop.

Bree looked from the folder to Cole. "You have been busy, haven't you?"

"It's amazing what you get when you ask the right questions." He smiled briefly.

She leaned forward and placed her hand on the folder. "Do you trust me with it?"

"This is a copy," he told her.

Bree stood and picked up the folder. "I can't make any promises," she warned.

"I didn't ask for any."

She inclined her head, then walked out of the room.

Cole's desire to stay and work disappeared along with Bree. He wasted no time in locking up his desk and getting out of there.

He was feeling optimistic that he'd be hearing from the lovely detective.

Bree parked in the garage and tapped the garage door opener before getting out of her vehicle.

Even with the back door closed, she could hear sounds of an argument. Jinx gave a low whine and pawed at the door. "Serve them right if I put you in working mode," she muttered, reaching for the doorknob.

The minute she stepped into the kitchen she felt as if she'd entered a war zone. Sara stood at the counter with a knife in one hand and a tomato in the other. Her face matched the vegetable in color. Cody stood on a chair, preparing to pull plates out of the cabinet. A grim-faced David stood next to a girl Bree didn't recognize.

Sara turned, then spun back to her brother. "You are so busted," she told him.

"Bite me," he sneered.

"Enough!" Bree didn't need to raise her voice to gain attention. She turned to David.

He ignored her as he muttered to the girl next to him, "Let's go."

"Let's not," Bree said silkily. "Hi, I'm the crew's mom, Bree Fitzpatrick. And you are?"

"Lacey Danvers," she mumbled, not looking up.

Bree knew she was feeling like the typical mother as she

visually examined the girl and found too much wrong with her. Her skirt was too short, her top too brief and low cut, her pale blond hair too long, flowing halfway down her back. Her makeup was too heavy, and her short nails were painted a deep burgundy that matched her lipstick. Bree could smell the smoky aroma of cigarettes coming from the girl's clothing.

"It's nice to meet you, Lacey." Bree's gaze went over the girl's head and straight to David.

"We were just going," he said defiantly.

"Where exactly are you going?" she asked.

David didn't back down. "Lacey and I are going out."

Bree shook her head. "Not on a school night. Make plans for the weekend, but not tonight."

"Then I guess you wouldn't mind if I drive Lacey home?" he asked sarcastically.

She shot him a telling look, a warning any mother would give a child who was verbally getting out of hand. "Since it is after dark, it would be the appropriate thing for you to do."

Satisfied he'd follow her rules, she left the kitchen.

She winced when she heard muttered voices, then the door slam shut. She silently blessed David for having the good sense not to rev the engine as he left the yard.

"I told him he'd be so in trouble with you for bringing her home when you're not here," Sara announced with her usual air of drama when Bree returned to the kitchen. The girl occupied herself placing croutons on the salad with mathematical precision. "And why would he want to go out with her, anyway? Everyone knows what she is."

"Sara." Bree punctuated her warning with a sideways glance in Cody's direction. She swore her son's ears were pointed toward them.

The girl rolled her eyes. "Everyone knows," she muttered.

"Not everyone. Cody, why don't you go wash your hands for dinner," Bree suggested.

"Aren't we going to wait for David?" he asked, clearly afraid if he left he'd miss something important.

"I'm sure he'll be back soon. Just go wash your hands." Bree waited until she heard the bathroom door open before she turned back to her stepdaughter. "All right, Miss Gossip. What exactly does everyone know about Lacey Danvers?"

Sara lowered her voice. "It's not gossip. It's the truth. She's done it with just about every guy in the senior class. She doesn't care what anyone thinks of her."

Bree was disgusted with herself for even asking. "We don't know that for sure."

"Come on, Mom. David doesn't care what anyone thinks about him. Which ruins any future I can hope to have at that school." Sara carried the salad bowl to the table and set it down. "I might as well drop out now."

"Save it for drama class, Sara." At the sound of a buzzer, Bree grabbed pot holders and pulled a baking dish out of the oven. "I don't want to find out you've been spreading these rumors."

"I told you, Mom, they're not rumors. David doesn't care. This is his senior year. He doesn't have to worry about three more years there," Sara groused. "He doesn't think about others."

"Since I doubt you can know the girl all that well, we will dispense with the subject," Bree ordered. "And we will sit down and have a nice family dinner." She finally took a good look at her stepdaughter's attire. "Please tell me you did not wear that to school."

Sara looked down. Her yellow top stopped a couple inches above the waistband of her navy capri pants. "There's nothing wrong with what I'm wearing," she exclaimed, defending her choice.

"Oh yes, there is something wrong with it. From now on you make sure your midriff is covered when you go to school."

"The school lets us wear midriff tops as long as they're not a sports bra," Sara argued mutinously.

"I don't care what the school allows. *I* don't allow it. If I catch you wearing a top like that to school again, I will choose clothing appropriate for a private school," Bree said in a voice that brooked no nonsense. "I'm certain you know what I mean. Plaid skirts. White blouses with those cute little collars. Knee socks and loafers."

Sara blanched as if her stepmother had just announced she would have to wear burlap to school. "You wouldn't," she gasped.

"Sweetheart, please don't tell me what I will or won't do. I own your life until you turn eighteen, so I will cheerfully interfere in it until that day. And even after that if I can get away with it." Bree dug the serving spoon into the casserole dish. "This looks wonderful, honey." She silently wished her stepdaughter would try a recipe that didn't have the word casserole in it.

Sara managed a tight smile.

"She put broccoli in it," Cody muttered, accepting his share.

"You think anything green will kill you." Sara rolled her eyes.

"Some green stuff can kill you," Cody said seriously.

"But not broccoli," Bree assured him. "That's very good for you."

"I bet you didn't believe your mom when she told you it was good for you," he muttered, stabbing a piece of chicken with his fork.

"Sure, I did," Bree cheerfully lied. "My mom didn't believe in doing anything that was bad for me."

"Sure, anything to keep us in line," David muttered, entering the kitchen. He ignored her silent warning glance and sat down at the table. His usually good-looking features were sullen as he spooned a helping of the casserole onto his plate.

"That was a fast trip," Bree commented. "I hope you didn't merely slow down and push Lacey out of the car."

He didn't look up. "She only lives a couple miles from here."

From experience, Bree knew not to question him further. She was ready to break her long-standing rule when a beeping sound echoed in the room.

"Oh yeah, Mom's totally in the work mode," David drawled sarcastically. "They beep. She jumps."

"Shut up, David," Sara ordered, keeping an eagle eye on her stepmother as Bree got up and walked over to the counter, where she'd left her pager. She checked the display and picked up the phone.

"All right. I'll be there in ten minutes," she said crisply. As Bree hung up, she looked at the trio watching her. "I have to go out."

"What did they do before you arrived?" David stared at her with defiance darkening his eyes.

Bree shook her head. "It's my job, David," she said quietly. "You know I can't tell them I can't go out. You all know the drill." She dropped a kiss on top of Cody's head, rested her hand briefly on Sara's shoulder and paused by David's chair. When he concentrated on his meal as if his life depended on it, she moved on. She retrieved her weapon from its lock box and settled the holster against her back as she headed for the door leading to the garage. "Jinx, time to work." The German shepherd rose from his spot by the door and padded over to her side.

Bree felt the weariness settle in her bones as she drove away from the house. Sensing his partner's unease, Jinx whined and pawed at her shoulder.

"Damn, why can't they understand I'm hurting just as much as they are?" she told the dog. "It hasn't been all that long, so I can't expect things to be the way they were. Don't they think I hate having to leave them alone at night? Going on wasn't easy, but there was nothing else for us to do but go on."

Bree half listened to her police-issue radio as she drove swiftly to what she already knew would be a nasty scene because of the crime that would greet her there.

Once home, Cole had planned on a night of football and beer—the best kind of night he could spend. Instead, he received a phone call, a voice whispering across the line, and he was out of his house within minutes.

He wasn't surprised to find Bree standing on the other side of yellow crime scene tape strung across the driveway of a sprawling ranch-style house. She glanced over her shoulder at the sound of his truck, arched an eyebrow and turned back around. The man she spoke to looked shell-shocked.

Cole stepped out of the truck and started to walk toward her. "Nothing here for you, Becker," Ted Carson, one of the deputies, said in an officious tone. He walked toward him with a bit of a swagger.

"How about something for the citizens of Warm Springs?" Cole countered. "What happened?"

The deputy kept a fierce expression on his face as he hitched up his belt, keeping his hand resting lightly on his holstered weapon. "Shove off, before I run your ass in," he snarled.

Bree looked over her shoulder. "Ted, you're canvassing the neighbors, right?" She made it more a suggestion than a question. She didn't spare Cole a glance.

"I'm helping secure the scene," he explained.

"It's secure," she said firmly. "What we need now is to find out if the neighbors saw or heard anything. You and Roberts start talking to them." She glanced past him at Frank and one of the rookies hovering on the sidelines. "How much canvassing has Larkin done in the past?"

"Randy hasn't been with us all that long. He hasn't had a chance to do any yet," Ted replied.

"Why don't you take him with you. Have him do some of the questioning, too."

Frank Roberts glared at her before he called out to Randy Larkin to follow them, then moved off with Ted.

Cole waited by his truck as Bree finished speaking to the man he knew as Kirk Bennett, an electrical contractor. She looked resigned as she walked toward Cole.

"You're late, Becker," she mocked. "I would have thought you'd be hot on our heels a good three hours ago."

"Even we hotshot reporters have to have some downtime." He looked past her. "What happened?"

"Typical B and E." She used slang for breaking and entering. "Mr. Bennett is now minus a big-screen television set, three VCRs, his computer, scanner, printer, fax machine and a nifty copier."

"Did Kirk tell you his wife left him a week ago?" Cole volunteered the information.

Bree smiled as he figured she did when her son said something incredible. For a moment Cole thought she was going to go so far as to pat him on the head.

"There were clues. Such as the half-empty closets and fast-food containers overflowing the trash cans, yet there wasn't enough dust lying around to consider him a lifelong bachelor. I hate to tell you this, Becker—" she lowered her voice "—I've been doing this for a while. Clues are my business."

Cole grinned as he thrust his hands in his pockets and rocked back and forth on his heels. "Anything concrete I can report?"

She shook her head. "Not at this time."

He reached out and touched her arm. "Bree?"

She froze and just looked at him for a moment. "Good night, Becker." She turned around and walked away.

"Power of the press, Fitzpatrick," Cole called after her.

She waved her hand over her head in dismissal. "Goodbye, Becker."

"You'll look back," he muttered as he stood by his truck, watching her walk away. She didn't look back once. "Lady, you're tougher than I thought."

When Bree finished with the crime scene, she felt ready to crawl into a corner somewhere and sleep. Those two spoonfuls of dinner were nothing more than a dim memory. But reports had to be written and filed.

When she walked into the station, it was quiet, with only the dispatcher and one deputy seated at a desk in the rear. She snagged a cup of coffee and found a stale bagel in a box on the table in the small break room. She sat down at her desk and started filling in her report on the burglary. By the time she finished her eyes burned with fatigue and the caffeine rush from the coffee was long gone.

"Miss."

She looked up into the wizened face of an elderly man. "Can I help you?" Then she noticed the large cart of cleaning supplies next to him.

His smile lit up his face. "I'm sorry to disturb you. I just wanted to empty your wastebasket," he explained.

Bree obliged by moving back. She picked up her wastebasket and handed it to him. He dumped the contents into a large trash bag and set it back down.

"I heard you're a real good detective," he said. "Maybe you can help us."

"Help you?" she questioned, not sure what he meant.

He nodded. He looked around. "Some things aren't what they seem," he whispered.

"What do you mean?" she asked.

"Please, do the right thing for us," he said in a low voice before moving on.

She watched him walk slowly from desk to desk, emptying wastebaskets.

Do the right thing for who?

She returned to reading over the report. Satisfied every *i* was dotted and every *t* crossed, she signed it and put it on Holloway's desk. On the way out, she stopped by the dispatcher's desk. Joe, the dispatcher who worked nights, looked up.

"The janitor? What is his name?" she asked.

"That's Leo," he replied. "A nice old guy. He lost his wife about eighteen months ago. Seemed really lost, so the sheriff offered him the job here, since our previous cleaning service wasn't too reliable. We've never had to worry about Leo. He doesn't disturb working surfaces or tell anyone what he sees here. There's times we worry he'll try to pick up something too heavy for him, so we tend to make sure he doesn't overdo it."

Bree nodded. "Leo." She tapped her nails on the counter surface. "I'll remember that."

She thought about the elderly man's strange words. She'd have to bring it up with Cole. See if he could tell her anything more about the old fellow.

She was thinking about raiding her refrigerator the moment she got home, until she remembered that with two teenagers and one growing boy in the house, she'd be lucky if there was a crumb left. Jinx halting and emitting a low growl was her first warning something wasn't right. She looked across the parking lot and saw Cole standing by her vehicle. Her gaze zeroed in on the two insulated containers he held. She almost snatched one of them out of his hand at the same time he held it out to her. She inhaled the bracing aroma before sipping the hot coffee.

"I'm not here as a member of the press," Cole assured her.

"In fact, I would have brought you a doughnut, too, but I was afraid you'd shoot me for going the cliché route."

"You would have been safe as long as it was one of the custard ones with chocolate frosting on top. All they had left inside was a stale bagel." She took another sip of coffee as she leaned back against her door. "If you try to sneak in a glazed doughnut you will be in serious trouble." She named the item most identified with law enforcement.

"Did Kirk accuse his wife of taking the items?" Cole asked casually.

She shot him a look filled with suspicion. "What makes you ask that?"

"Come on, Fitzpatrick, I already told you she left him. Sure, he'd want to blame her. She stopped by the office to bring her newspaper account up to date. She was pretty steamed at Kirk. Seems he'd been slipping off for nooners with his office manager, and Margaret found out."

"They'll always get caught." Bree looked around. Storefronts were dark, the street deserted. She wasn't used to the quiet, but she knew it was something she could easily grow to like. No smog to cover the stars in the sky. She hadn't wanted to come out here, but she was seeing that it was the right decision. "What do you know about the man who works as a janitor in the sheriff's department?"

"Leo?" She nodded. "A really nice guy."

"That I've already heard. Tell me something I don't know."

Cole tipped his head back, so he could look upward. "Leo and Anna, his wife, moved out here about thirty years ago. His wife had problems with her lungs. Needed drier air. He owned a hardware store on the edge of town, did a good business. He sold it when his arthritis started to flare up. They did some traveling to visit their kids, and Leo got involved at the senior center when they were here. Almost two years ago, Anna died. Leo took it really hard. Understandable, since they'd been together for almost sixty years and they'd been childhood sweethearts. I heard Holloway asked him if he'd be interested in working there."

"He thought I could do something," she mused. "But he didn't say what."

"Maybe he knows something," Cole offered.

"We'll see." She finished her coffee and, with a smile, handed him the cup. She activated her door remote. The click of the locks sounded loud in the quiet night air. She opened the back door and gestured for Jinx to jump in. "Thanks for the coffee."

"My pleasure. Consider it my contribution to our police force." He touched her arm lightly.

He noticed the same fleeting look in her eyes that he'd noticed when he touched her a few hours before. She felt what he felt. Something arced between them that couldn't be ignored for much longer. She stepped back to break the tenuous connection.

"Just as long as you don't expect me to fix your parking tickets," she said in parting.

"This time, she'll look back," he murmured as he watched her drive away. When her vehicle was out of sight, and she hadn't, he added, "Damn. It's a good thing I'm not a betting man."

The house was dark and quiet when Bree let herself in through the back door. Jinx immediately headed for his bowl of kibble.

"Gee, kids, you could have saved some for me," she murmured, after looking in the refrigerator and realizing she'd been right. No leftovers.

She settled for a container of cottage cheese and cut up a peach to go with it.

As she sat at the table eating her meager late-night dinner, she thought back to other nights when she'd come home after overseeing a crime scene.

Those nights she'd usually find a plate of food in the refrigerator and the coffeepot on. Even better to her was Fitz waiting to listen and offer opinions if she asked for them. She knew he hadn't liked her working crime scenes at all hours of the day and night, but he'd never asked her to switch over to a desk job. Never asked that she cut back. From day one, he'd understood how important her work was to her.

She recalled how he'd tease her that he was the one working a desk most of the time, tracking down white-collar crime, while she dealt with murderers. She told him that was fine with her, since she was too impatient with computers, while he considered them a valuable tool.

There had been more than talk about crime. They'd had discussions on David's future. Whether they'd survive Sara's teenage years. Playful arguments whether Cody's stubborn nature was inherited from her or Fitz. Late-night talks that led into the bedroom.

Then the day came when she'd lost her husband. For a time, Bree thought about giving it all up. About finding a cave where there was no crime and she could keep the kids safe. But with time came reason. Fitz wouldn't have wanted her to shut themselves off for fear that what happened to him would happen to one of them, also. She'd returned to work, but it wasn't the same. And her superiors knew it. Because of that, she was now living in a smaller town, where her area of expertise wouldn't be needed as much. Maybe it was a good thing it wasn't.

Thoughts of Fitz led to thoughts of Cole. She thought of him standing out there with a cup of coffee for her. Unwittingly, a smile tipped the corners of her mouth.

"A smile? What'd you do? Arrest a clown?" David asked, stepping into the darkened kitchen. He walked over to the coffeepot and poured himself a cup.

Bree opened her mouth to remind him he had school in the morning and coffee would only keep him awake. Luckily, she shut it before she opened another rift. She hoped his friendlier nature meant he'd gotten over his earlier anger. She wanted nothing more than to return to the loving relationship they'd shared before.

"Breaking and entering," she replied. "If you hear of anyone selling a sixty-inch TV cheap, will you tell me?"

"Oh, right. That will make me Mr. Popular in school," he muttered, spooning sugar into his coffee. "I find out a kid at school suddenly has a big-screen TV and I mention it to my cop mom."

"That's why we call them confidential informants," she said

glibly. "Don't worry, I wouldn't ask anything of you unless someone's life was involved." She spooned up cottage cheese and a slice of peach.

"You trying to lose weight again?"

"Excuse me?" She pretended offense. "Again? I haven't gained an ounce since I lost the extra weight after Cody was born."

His grin sent a little pang to her heart. A grin that was identical to his father's. "Sure, that's why you went nuts trying to lose ten pounds before that dinner when Dad was honored."

"That was a special occasion and I was planning on wearing an extremely expensive gown. You guys never understand." She finished her snack. "Cody go to bed without any argument?"

"After he went out to his tree house to leave his treasure box in it," he replied. "Sara did her usual suffering-soul routine. I told her she should try out for drama. She told me, well, you can imagine what she told me."

Bree sighed. "Yes, I can." She pushed the cottage cheese container to one side and rested her forearms on the table. "David, we can't have the fights. We're all trying to make a new life here. We need to work together. We can't do that with all these battles."

He looked at the table as he spoke. "I don't want the fights, either, Mom. But you have to remember we didn't want to move. All the books say not to make a major change right away. What could be more of a major change than resigning from your job, selling your house and moving more than a hundred miles away from everything we've grown up with?"

"I didn't want to move, either, but I also couldn't stay in my job. You know what was going on. It was getting to where I wasn't functioning efficiently. It came down to no choice but the one I made. In making it, I was thinking of all of us," she told him. "Sara hated going to school every day. She couldn't walk past the stadium without crying. You were angry all the time. Cody was just..." she paused to find the right word to describe her youngest's frame of mind "...sad."

David got up and carried his mug over to the sink. He rinsed it out and put it in the dishwasher.

"Dad's dead, Mom. He died and you almost got killed," he said bluntly. "But you didn't die and we all went on. We're all doing it our own way, and we would have been fine back where we knew everyone."

"I'm sorry, David," she said softly. "Sorry for not talking to the three of you more about this. Maybe we should have kept up with the counseling longer."

He snorted. "Are you kidding? That psychologist didn't understand us. He kept wanting us to show our feelings with drawings."

"Until you drew a very unflattering picture of him."

David grinned. "I thought it looked just like him." He walked over and dropped a kiss on her cheek. "Okay, I'll try not to give you such a hard time. G'night."

"Good night, David," she murmured.

Bree cleaned up her own dishes and set the house alarm.

When she went into her bedroom, Jinx laid down on the carpet just outside her door.

When she finally fell asleep she realized that instead of Fitz's face crossing her mind's eye as it usually did, Cole Becker's crept in instead.

"Dammit, Becker, do you have to be everywhere?" she cursed, punching her pillow into submission as if it was the man himself.

Chapter 5

The bulging folder insisted on calling her name. She had no idea why she kept it. At first, she used the excuse that it wasn't something she could just throw in the trash. Every time she'd seen Cole, she didn't have it with her, so couldn't return it to him. That she could have just slid it into a big envelope and dropped it in the mail hadn't occurred to her.

Instead, it lay on her nightstand along with the mystery novel she'd been reading. So far, she'd been able to ignore the silent call, and pick her book up instead.

It wasn't as easy tonight as it had been the night before. She settled in bed with the covers draped over her drawn-up knees. She picked up her book, dislodging the beige folder, which fell to the floor, spilling out its contents.

"Damn," she muttered, climbing out of bed to gather them up. After she'd put it all back together, she started to toss it back on the nightstand. Except something stopped her. Instead, she tossed the book aside.

"The killer's the brother-in-law, anyway."

Bree sat cross-legged as she pulled out the papers. She fanned them in front of her, glancing at each page, determining what order she would put them in. She grumbled under her breath as she reached for her reading glasses and perched them on her nose.

In the end, she arranged them according to date of death. Then she picked up the one that was the oldest and began reading. Before she finished the first paragraph, she absently reached for a pen she kept in her nightstand drawer. As she read, she underlined sentences, scribbled in the margins and marked anything that stood out.

"How did you get hold of these, Becker?" she murmured, once she finished the third report. "Who did you blackmail?"

When Bree had read all the reports, she sorted them again, this time putting accidental deaths in one pile and deaths by natural causes in another. Then she picked each up and read it again, sorting further.

Two hours later, the papers lay in an orderly manner across the width of her bed.

She saw them as an excellent reason to call Cole, and not just because she wanted to hear the sound of his voice.

"He's not the only man in the world, Bree," she told herself.

You haven't seen anyone better, have you?

"No, but why him? He's irritating as hell."

Irritating, maybe. Cute, a definite yes. Call the man.

"I don't know his number," she said in a righteous tone.

That's what directory assistance is for, smartie.

Bree gave up the argument with herself.

She picked up the phone, and a few moments later had the number she'd requested.

"What?" A sleepy, and grumpy, male voice echoed in her ear.

"Gee, Becker, I've had friendlier greetings from serial killers."

"Fitzpatrick?" He perked up. "Do you realize what time it is?"

She glanced at the clock. "A little after midnight. You have a problem with that?"

"If you don't, I guess I don't, either." The soft rustle of bedclothes sounded across the phone line. It brought intriguing images to her mind. "You going to tell me why you felt the need to call me in the middle of the night?"

"I just finished reading all those lovely reports you gave me."

"And you felt the need to call me at midnight to tell me that?" he grumbled. Then her words acted as an effective wake-up call. "And?"

Bree chuckled. "Gee, Becker, that got your attention, didn't it? I have to say, it's interesting reading." She grabbed the second pillow and placed it behind her, punching it into shape to provide the proper backrest.

"There's something there, isn't there?"

"You definitely know how to dig for information," she told him. "I can understand why you feel there were some inconsistencies."

"There were. Look at Elsie Tremaine. She was never sick a day in her life. Not even a cold." Anger and frustration colored Cole's voice. "She taught a couple exercise classes at the senior center. Then all of a sudden, she falls and breaks her hip. Within three weeks, she's dead from a post-operative infection."

"Cole, when some people grow older, their bones are more fragile," Bree told him. "I've also heard that they're more prone to infection."

"You didn't know Elsie. No germ would dare take her on. It would lose."

"I'm not arguing." She settled the phone in a comfortable position between her chin and shoulder. Once it felt secure, she snagged a bottle of body lotion that smelled like vanilla. She poured a healthy dollop into her palm and began smoothing the rich lotion down her leg. "I'm merely playing devil's advocate." She began rubbing lotion into her other leg. She again heard the rustle of sheets from his end. The question of what he wore to bed entered her mind. She ruthlessly pushed it out before mental images started to take over.

"But you still feel the deaths weren't what they're reported to be?" His voice dropped to a murmur.

Bree rubbed lotion into her arms. The spicy fragrance of vanilla filled her nostrils. "Yes, I do." Automatically her voice lowered to a throaty purr.

Maybe it was the late hour. Or the fact she was in bed. She didn't know the man very well, but right then, she felt as if they were sharing something intimate. She sat up straighter and threw back her shoulders.

"I just wanted you to know I read the reports and I'll see what I can do. I can't make any promises, but I'll do some double-checking." She sought to put distance between them by giving off official vibes. "I think what happened was people tended to look at the deceased as being of an age where it wouldn't be a surprise if they died—for one reason or another."

"But it happens," he pressed.

"Yes, sad to say, it happens. And as I said, I'll see what I can do."

"And I thank you for that. Good night, Fitzpatrick."

She heard the soft click, then listened to the steady hum of a disconnected line.

"Damn him," she muttered, clicking the button and setting the phone back in its cradle. "I was supposed to hang up first."

Jinx lifted his head and uttered a soft whine.

"Not you," she assured the dog, who was lying quietly on his spot in the hallway. "You're one of the very few males I can trust. He's one of the many males who likes to mess up a woman's life."

Jinx plopped back down and closed his eyes.

Bree tossed the extra pillow to one side and slid all the way under the covers. She didn't care that she hadn't picked up the papers or that they were falling to the floor. The late hour had finally caught up with her, and she knew she would be asleep within three minutes.

Then why was it more than an hour before she finally fell asleep?

"Nice article, Detective," a man called out as Bree walked down the sidewalk. He gave her a wink.

"Thank you." She could feel her face turning red.

It wasn't the first time someone had mentioned the article Cole had written about her.

When Bree saw her picture on the front page of the paper and began reading the article, she'd assumed it would be a straight-forward piece on the new cop in town.

What she forgot was that Cole Becker was the author.

While he'd detailed her qualifications as a law enforcement officer, he'd also brought up her single status.

Response at the station ranged from positive to pointed comments as to whether she was there as a detective or sex symbol. She thanked people for the former and ignored the latter.

She hadn't intended to use her lunch hour to run errands, but she wanted some time outside after spending the morning finishing up paperwork. Picking up coffee was at the top of her list of things to do. Irene told her the best place was the Coffee Spot.

She easily found the shop and entered.

"I'm just taking a wild guess here, but I bet you're our token female detective," the woman standing behind an old-fashioned wood counter said in greeting. While the shop displayed the look of another era, the espresso maker, coffee bean grinders and trio of coffeepots kept it firmly planted in the present. The owner looked chic with her tan suede skirt ending several inches above her knees and a russet knit top that could have been painted on her lean torso. Her long nails and lips matched her top.

The rich music of Tchaikovsky seemed appropriate for the surroundings.

Bree paused long enough to breathe in the rich aromas of coffee and baked goods. Her mouth watered even as her brain warned her the treats might taste wonderful but they would only end up on her hips.

"And here I thought it would be easy to stop in and pick up a pound of coffee," she said, examining the glass containers holding a large variety of coffee beans. "I'm in coffee heaven."

"Coffee heaven. I wish I'd thought of that for the name of my store. Honey, no one comes in here for just a pound of coffee." The proprietress walked over to one of the pots, poured some of the dark liquid into a mug and brought it to the counter. Along the way, she placed a rich-looking pastry topped with chocolate curls on a plate. She set both on the counter. "Welcome to Warm Springs. I'm Greta Watson, owner, clerk and cleaning woman for the Coffee Spot."

Bree eyed the pastry filled with rich custard. "I'm not so sure I should accept."

"It's not a bribe," she assured her. "I do this for everyone new to town. I find it's the best way to advertise that I carry the best coffees and pastries you'll ever find."

Bree picked up the pastry and nibbled. The combination of flaky pastry, custard and chocolate seduced her tastebuds. A sip of coffee, a rich French Roast, turned out to be a perfect balance.

"I think I'm in love," she moaned, setting the pastry back on the plate, which had an old-fashioned design in keeping with the store's decor. Bree felt this was a place where one could come in and be soothed by music and chocolate. The coffee was turning into a nice added touch.

"Of course you are," Greta said confidently. "The Coffee Spot is known for its goodies."

Bree finished the pastry in record time and wiped her fingers on a napkin before she did the unthinkable and licked them clean.

"What kind of coffee are you looking for?" Greta asked.

"What I thought about and what I'm seeing here says I'll be getting something entirely different than I'd planned," Bree confessed, reading the labels. "French Vanilla sounds perfect for breakfast. What's Holiday Treat?"

"Cinnamon, a little clove. It's pretty much considered a Christmas coffee," Greta replied. "A lot of my customers like it all year round, so I'm now carrying it all the time. Chocolate coffee for those special days when we can't get enough of it." She lifted a delicately arched brow. "You name it, I either have it or know where I can get it."

Bree chuckled. "Sounds like a drug dealer I once met. Throw in a half pound of the Holiday Treat, too."

"Whole bean or do you need it ground?" She began scooping beans onto a scale.

"Whole bean." Bree began exploring the back of the store, studying coffee cups that ran the gamut from delicate designs that wouldn't look out of place in a formal dining room to the large and functional for serious coffee addicts. "I wonder if they'd mind my working out of here," she murmured.

"I'd never complain." Greta grinned as she poured a cup of coffee and lifted it to her lips. "All those lovely coffee drinkers in town have me using a lot of black ink in my books. So what do you think of our fair community? How are your kids settling in? Most especially what do you think of Cole? Although, knowing how he can be, you'd probably want to take the Fifth."

Bree laughed at Greta's last sentence and prudently ignored it. "Warm Springs seems like a lovely town. The jury's still out as far as the kids are concerned."

Greta nodded knowingly. "Still not enough amusements. Mainly no mall close enough to use as a hangout. Understandable. I heard your oldest son is hot looking, your daughter has cute clothes but an attitude—" her expression silently apologized for the statement "—and your youngest is very polite."

"They weren't happy about the move," Bree explained.

"Considering the large number of senior citizens in the area, we do offer lots of sports activities for the kids. But it must be difficult when they're used to having so much more around them. There are times when I get antsy for some nightlife. That's when I close up the shop for a couple days and drive into San Diego or one of the beach cities for some fun."

"I would think your customers go into major withdrawal when you're gone," Bree commented.

"No, it just makes them buy more when I get back." She secured the bags and smoothed on each a black-and-gold label with graceful script stating the coffee's flavor. "Bless their little caffeine-addicted hearts."

Bree walked up to the counter and pulled out her wallet.

"I'll put you in our coffee club. You receive a free pound for every ten pounds you purchase," Greta explained, punching in keys on her register.

"Sounds like a plan. How did you end up in Warm Springs?" Bree asked.

"I married the former mayor five years ago," she replied. "He already lived out here and I thought it would be a nice place to open a coffee store. Luckily, it's done well from the beginning. Liam passed away two years ago.''

"I'm so sorry," Bree said sincerely.

"He was only fifty when he died," she told her. "Poor man was hospitalized when his flu took a turn for the worse. There were complications." Her smile dimmed a bit. "Liam was a wonderful man."

Bree nodded, understanding that kind of pain.

"I needed something to keep me busy after he was gone," Greta said, smiling as if she read her thoughts. "Liam had owned one of those small companies that larger ones like to buy. He made a tidy fortune and decided to retire. He was very active in charity work before he died."

"But you needed more," Bree guessed.

Greta nodded. "Very much so. They kept me on their mailing lists. And invite me to their lovely formal functions. They probably hope I'll put them in my will," she confessed with a twinkle in her eyes. She leaned forward, resting her arms on the counter. "Stop by here or the Shear Desire if you want the latest gossip," she advised, also naming one of the town's hair salons.

"Maybe I should take notes so I can keep everything straight," Bree said with a poker face.

"Whatever works."

As Bree later left the Coffee Spot, she knew she had met someone who could easily turn into a friend.

While putting her purchases in her vehicle, she straightened up when she noticed the German shepherd's alert posture.

"So that's your partner."

She turned around to find Cole standing on the sidewalk. She blamed the strange feeling in the pit of her stomach on the aftereffects of the chocolate-and-custard pastry she'd consumed.

"Don't you ever work?" she asked.

He looked around him. "I run a newspaper, which means I write about the people in the area. The best way to find out news is to walk around town." He jerked his head in her direction. "Do I get an introduction?"

"As long as you don't try to pet him. Jinx, Cole. Cole, Jinx."

"Jinx?"

"He was born on Friday the thirteenth." Bree leaned against the door. "What's your excuse?"

His smile may have been slow in coming but was no less devastating. "I've got one better. I was born February 29."

"Ah, a leap year baby. Women would love that birthday because they'd only count those years."

"Greta give you one of her killer pastries?" he asked out of the blue, while keeping his eyes firmly focused on her face.

Bree couldn't remember a man so intent on her.

"Yes, why?" she asked warily.

Cole stepped forward until he stood right in front of her. The scent of soap and man filled her nostrils.

"Because you have a chocolate smudge right—" he used his forefinger to touch a corner of her mouth "—here."

Bree's mouth dried up like the Sahara as she watched him put the chocolate dot into his mouth.

"I could have taken care of it with a moistened towelette," she said once she finally regained her voice.

His eyes crinkled with amusement. "Wouldn't have done the job as well as I could," he murmured. "Time to give up and have dinner with me."

This was familiar ground to her. As long as she kept her mind on delivering a firm "no" she would be just fine.

"I am a widow with three children," she answered. "I don't have time to go out."

"Sure, you do," he said, undeterred. "Just because you're a widow and a mother doesn't mean you can't go out with a grown-up every so often. Believe me, that's all it would be."

"How considerate of you to let me know how things would be," she mocked.

He shrugged. "That's me. Considerate to the core. So how about dinner tonight?"

"As the saying goes, Becker, when pigs fly."

He looked upward and past her. His broad grin was her first warning. Her second was watching the slow ascent of his hand, the forefinger pointing upward. Feeling as if she was moving in slow motion, she turned around and tipped her head back.

A biplane flew overhead with a banner flapping behind it.

No matter how many times she told herself what she saw was a mistake, she knew it wasn't.

The banner was bright pink and shaped like a smiling pig. The message You'll Go Hog Wild Over Allie's Country-style Bacon was tacked onto the pig's tail.

"Damn, I should have said not until hell freezes over," she muttered as she turned back around.

Cole looked a little too victorious. "What a world we live in," he murmured. "Did you ever think we'd see a flying pig?"

"If I didn't know better, I'd swear you set me up," Bree said evenly.

"Maybe someone's on my side." He tipped his head to one side, looking too engaging for her peace of mind.

"Tomorrow night, dinner at my house, six-thirty," she said before she could rethink her invitation. "Take it or leave it."

Cole nodded and started to move off. "And maybe while we're washing the dishes, we can discuss my theories."

"Don't push your luck, Becker," she warned him. "You're coming over for dinner only."

"I'm looking forward to it," he said, as he ambled off.

Bree watched him walk away and knew she'd just stepped into a mess of trouble. Her hunch was confirmed when she saw Greta looking out the window with a big smile on her face. She waggled her fingers in a wave.

"You're just loving this, aren't you?" Bree muttered, waving back. "What he doesn't know is dinner at my household isn't all Beaver Cleaver nice."

What she didn't see was another pair of eyes watching her. They weren't amused one bit.

"You're *dating?*"

Bree winced at the strident sound of Sara's voice.

"This is not a date," she said for what she believed was the hundredth time. "Mr. Becker is merely coming over for dinner."

"He's a man and you're a woman," her stepdaughter said stubbornly. "You're both single. That means a date."

"Not with you three chaperoning."

Sara fixed her with a look that informed her she was *not*

pleased with her comeback. "How can you do this?" she hissed, her body quivering with indignation.

Bree took a deep breath and counted to ten. "Sara, you will be polite to Mr. Becker and that is all I'm saying on the subject. Now where is Cody?"

"Out in his precious tree house. Did you know he put a sign on it saying Everyone Keep Out?"

"He needs something he can call his own. Besides, I didn't think you'd want to climb up that tree."

"It's the principle of the thing."

"Why can't you lay off him for more than five minutes?" David demanded of his sister as he entered the kitchen. Before he realized it was a bad idea, he was put to work slicing Italian bread into thick slices and covering them with butter and garlic. "The kid isn't doing anything wrong. He's outside playing and staying out of our hair."

"I'm glad to see the two of you keep an eye on him," Bree said sarcastically, opening the oven door to check on the lasagna. "David, once you finish the bread, please call Cody inside so he can get cleaned up."

David slid open the patio door leading to the backyard. "Cody, get in here for dinner!"

Bree resisted the urge to cover her ears. "Thank you, David. I would have had to use a bullhorn to get the same effect."

"He's coming," he said, not picking up on her sarcasm.

"I won't like him," Sara insisted, blending ingredients for salad dressing.

"Then don't." Bree started to smile, then masked it before it bloomed.

Cole would never know what hit him.

Never date a woman with kids.

That was a rule Cole had adhered to from the time he started meeting single mothers. They had to worry about finding a baby-sitter. A simple sneeze could cancel a date. Kids looked at him as if he was either their next daddy or the devil incarnate. Even worse, there was no privacy at the lady's house when it came to some fun and games.

The Fitzpatrick kids belonged in an entirely new category.

David, the oldest, looked at him as if he knew every one of Cole's secrets. Sara smiled and was polite, but a little aloof. Cody, the youngest, who had his mother's eyes, looked at him curiously, as if Cole was some alien being to figure out.

Jinx looked at him as if he was to be the main course—for the dog.

"Mr. Becker owns and runs the newspaper in town," Bree said as she introduced him to the trio.

"You're the one who wrote the article about our mom," Sara announced with her usual dramatic flourish.

"Drama queen," David muttered under his breath, earning a warning look from his mother.

"Would you like something to drink, Cole?" Bree asked, "We have wine, beer, soda and iced tea."

"Wine sounds fine."

"David, why don't you take Cole onto the patio. Since the weather's so nice, I thought we'd eat outside," she told Cole. "I'll be out in a minute with our drinks."

David led him through the sliding glass door that led to the patio.

The first thing Cole noticed was a neatly trimmed lawn bordered by colorful pansies. The seductive scent of night-blooming jasmine floated toward him from bushes planted around the house. He looked at a large tree standing sentry in a corner of the yard, with a plank-sided tree house built among its large branches. Pieces of wood nailed to the trunk served as a ladder. A yellow T-shirt he guessed to be Cody's hung from the cut-out window. A football lay in one corner of the yard and a swing set was installed near the tree.

The evening breeze moved the wind chimes, filling the air with their light music.

A yard set up for a family, he decided with a feeling that was almost wistful. A family like this one.

He looked over at an umbrella-covered, oblong, glass-topped table already set up for the meal. David gestured toward the chairs.

"That was some story you wrote about Mom," the teenager commented, sitting down across from him.

"People enjoyed it," he said, secretly amused that David had deliberately sat him facing the setting sun. Cole was beginning to think he should have worn his sunglasses out here. Luckily, they wouldn't be needed in another moment.

The young man seemed to think otherwise. "Maybe because you made her sound like a babe."

He nodded. "Like Betty Grable during World War II."

"From what I've heard," David said dryly. "That was a bit before my time."

Cody appeared by Cole's side. "Do you carry a gun like Mom does?" he asked.

"No, Cody, I don't," he replied. "I'm lucky that I never really needed one in my line of work."

"Then it's good you don't have one," the boy said. "Guns are dangerous unless you know how to use them properly."

Cole wanted to smile at the gravity in Cody's voice. That he was quoting his mother, and probably his father, was evident.

"Yes, I've heard that," he said. "Probably why I stay away from them."

"Here you go," Bree announced, carrying out two filled wineglasses. "Cody, you need to go in and wash your hands. David, will you help Sara bring the food out?"

He nodded as he pushed himself out of his chair.

"Are they always this polite?" Cole asked in an undertone as he accepted the glass Bree held out.

"No, usually they settle for tearing a person's heart out with their teeth. If it will alleviate your mind any, Jinx won't follow their commands."

"Relieved? Not at all. You're the one I need to worry about," he said candidly.

"Really?" She affected wide-eyed innocence.

"Damn straight. You're the one who can cause me a boatload of trouble."

"Then there's only one thing to say," she said softly, tapping her glass against his. "Don't tick me off."

He chuckled. "I'll make a point not to."

"Hope you're hungry," Sara announced, setting serving dishes on the table.

The rich aroma of tomato and herbs was Cole's first clue he was in for a treat.

He looked at the first home-cooked meal he'd had in some time. He hoped he wasn't drooling, but the lasagna oozing tomato sauce, meat and cheese looked, and he soon learned, tasted much too good. He vowed not to make a pig of himself even as he took a second slice of garlic bread. Even the red wine tasted delicious.

He had to admit the lady knew how to put on a spread.

He also discovered it wasn't so bad sharing a meal with humans under the age of twenty-one. Cody chattered about his day at school. Sara lamented that there wasn't a mall in the vicinity, and David kept an eye on Cole as if David was the parent and Bree the child.

"This is great," Cole exclaimed after he'd enjoyed his second helping.

"Thank you." Bree smiled warmly.

"May I be excused now?" Sara asked, sounding about as long-suffering as any teenage girl could.

"It's your night for dishes," Bree said. She turned to Cole. "Do you want some coffee?"

"Sounds good to me."

"Why don't you go into the family room and I'll bring it in there." She directed him to the proper room before she went into the kitchen.

Bree turned on the coffeemaker while Sara and David rinsed dishes and loaded them in the dishwasher.

"I'll make sure Cody takes his bath and stuff," the girl said. "I suppose you want to be alone." She speared her stepmother with that knowing look only teenage girls can give.

Bree silently vowed to apologize to her mother for all the hell she'd put her through when she was a teenager. Even if her mom used to swear Bree would find out what it was like when she was the mother of a teenager.

"I didn't think you'd start dating," Sara said, as if it was a distinct impossibility.

"We've been discussing a case," Bree said.

"So that's what they call it nowadays," David said, tongue in cheek.

When Bree returned to the family room, she found Cole standing in front of the bookcases, looking up at the wall. He was studying the photographs they'd dubbed the Fitzpatrick Rogues Gallery.

She knew what he'd see. Collages made up of school photos through the years. David in his football uniform. Sara at ballet recitals, from age eight to the year she turned thirteen and decided she wanted more than dance. Cody in his soccer togs. Pictures of Bree and Fitz. With and without the kids. Some of Fitz's commendations framed and mounted on the wall.

Dressed in jeans, a V-necked, charcoal-colored sweater with his T-shirt showing white against the dark gray, Cole looked comfortable in his surroundings. Damn, she didn't want to think about that.

"A true family unit," he said, without turning around.

"Yes, we're an oddity because we're so normal." She set down the tray, which held two mugs and a carafe. She poured coffee into the cups and walked over, handing one to him.

He sipped the hot liquid and nodded his approval. "What happened to his first wife?"

Bree glanced up at a photograph of a very young David and Sara with their mother and father. "She died in an auto accident ten years ago. I was the investigating officer."

"And he was pleased with your detecting skills?"

She shook her head. "We didn't see each other for about another year, and then we ran into each other at the courthouse. The trials we were giving testimony at were in adjoining courtrooms. He asked if I'd like to have coffee with him afterward, and as they say, the rest is history." As always, she waited for that sting she felt whenever she mentioned Fitz. The dart of pain was so faint she almost didn't know it was there.

She made the mistake, an error in her mind, of looking up at Cole.

He'd obviously shaved before he came because, being so close, she could see a faint nick along his jawline. He had dark eyes framed by thick lashes any woman would envy. Eyes that seemed to hold a sense of amusement as they studied her in return.

His eyes match his sweater, she thought illogically, snared by the intensity in his gaze.

"It takes a special woman to be willing to raise someone else's kids," he said in a low voice.

"Actually, they're pretty low maintenance," she admitted. "As long as you feed them three times a day, they're happy."

"It still couldn't have been easy with your kind of work."

"We managed back then and manage now." She walked over to the couch and sank onto it, silently cursing herself for not taking one of the chairs when he sat next to her.

"Always good to hear. So are you finally ready to figure out why those deaths happened?" he asked suddenly.

Chapter 6

Thrown by the quick change of subject, she set down her mug, using the time to come up with a reply.

"What bothers me is not finding any hint that these were nothing more than accidental or natural deaths," she said, forcing herself into an official mode. "We both know if there had been, someone from the sheriff's department would have followed up. Cops don't like people getting killed for any reason."

Cole's eyes darkened. "You'd think so, wouldn't you? There're too many people dead. People whose time hadn't come. I'll concede that not all of them are homicides, but I can't believe all are natural, either."

"Fine, let's say there's something hinky going on here." Bree turned to face him, tucking one leg under her. She rested her elbow on the back of the couch, using her hand to emphasize her point. "For some incredibly crazy reason, someone has decided to kill people who happen to be over the age of sixty-five. Why? Are they all part of the Witness Security Program? Did they all have connections to some major crime underworld?"

"Hinky?"

"It means something very wrong." She spat out the words.

"Mom."

Bree looked over her shoulder. "Yes, Sara."

The girl's lip curled slightly upward. "Cody's ready for bed."

"I'll be right there." When Sara didn't move, she added, "Thank you, Sara."

Sara heaved a deep sigh and left with her head held high and her nose in the air.

"She's looking for an Academy Award," Bree murmured, rising to her feet. "I'll be back as soon as I tuck in my son."

"Would you bring your copies of the reports?"

"Yes."

When Bree walked into Cody's room, she found her son under the covers, propping up his favorite Dr. Seuss book on his tummy.

"So we're going to read about Horton tonight?" Bree asked.

"Uh-huh." He nodded, sliding over to give his mother room to perch on the side of his bed.

She took the book from him and began reading. The cadence of the story suited her mood tonight. But it didn't keep her mind from wandering out to the family room and wondering what Cole was doing.

Looking at more family photographs? Inspecting their video and DVD collection?

When she finished the book, she closed it and put it aside. She adjusted the covers across Cody's chest and leaned down to rub her nose against his and kiss him on the forehead.

"May the angels come down and be with you through the night. And may they sing sweet songs to you while you sleep. And may you have happy dreams." She whispered the words she had said every night since his birth.

"I would sleep really good if we had a kitty," he whispered back. "He could sleep with me."

"We have David Boa," she said by way of reminder.

Cody wrinkled his nose. "You can't play with him. All he wants to do is sleep on David's neck or eat mice. I could play with a kitty."

Bree would have preferred not thinking about the mice. One

of her ironclad rules was that David feed the snake himself and not expect anyone else to do it.

"I'll think about it." She used the time-honored excuse parents use.

His face fell. "Which means no."

"Which means I'll think about it," she said, kissing him again on the forehead. She made sure the door was left open the requisite six inches when she left the room.

She made a stop in her own room to pick up the files. When she entered the family room, she found Cole where she'd left him. He was settled back against the couch with his legs stretched out in front of him.

"You've done an excellent job of ferreting out so much information, but you don't list any suspects," she said, placing the files on the coffee table. She dropped down onto the couch. "You must have come up with some idea who could be behind it."

Cole had rested his head against the back of the couch. He turned it so he could see her. "Personally, I don't think it's one person," he replied.

She nodded in agreement. "Someone within the department, a doctor, maybe even someone else. There's money involved somewhere. There always is," she murmured.

"Money for whom?" he mused. "I haven't seen the surviving spouses come up with large financial benefits."

"Don't you find that interesting?" she commented. "All the people who died were married or lived with a close relative such as a brother or sister. The surviving relative gained insurance benefits—not large amounts, but something that should have allowed them to live quite comfortably. But have you seen that happen?"

Cole thought for a moment, then shook his head. "No, nothing significant." Then it hit him. "Which has to mean payoffs."

Her lips curved. "Exactly."

He couldn't stop grinning. "Damn, we're good. I knew you'd help me figure out some of those missing pieces. Care to tell me who the mastermind is?"

"The butler did it."

Cole groaned at one of the most clichéd pronouncements known to man.

"Okay, I know when to stop." He looked around the room, which held a baseball bat in one corner, a hockey stick in another. A bottle of mint-green nail polish sat on the coffee table.

At least they weren't a tidy family.

He turned back to Bree. "I have to give it to you, Fitzpatrick," he said. "You manage to have it all."

She looked surprised by his change of subject. "If I had it all I'd still be back with the Los Angeles Sheriff's Department doing what I do best."

Cole shifted around until he faced her. He rested his elbow on the back of the couch, his cheek braced against his palm.

"But then you wouldn't have met me," he murmured.

Bree smiled. "And that would have been a bad thing?"

"Sure it would." His free hand reached out. His fingers grazed the side of her jaw. "The cases were the first reason why I contacted you. But after that day, they were secondary."

"Secondary?" She felt a tiny shock in the area where he touched her. Her breath hitched in her throat. "Becker, you're starting to travel in dangerous territory."

His fingers danced along her jawline. "Danger is my middle name."

She wrapped her fingers around his wrist with the intention of pulling his hand away from her face. Instead, they lingered. She sensed the warmth of his skin under her fingertips. The comforting sensation felt way too good.

"This is not a good idea," she whispered.

His hand moved around the curve of her jaw and upward to cup her nape.

"You didn't think going out with me was a good idea," he told her.

"I haven't gone out with you," she reminded him.

"And you told me you'd go out with me when pigs flew." His grin was unnerving. "Then lo and behold, a pig flew. One of those moments a man cherishes." His face moved a bit closer.

Bree knew all the way down to the very marrow of her bones that he was going to kiss her. She wasn't ready for this! She had enough on her plate without adding a man to the list. The last man to kiss her was Fitz. Could she allow another man to do so?

And if she was so concerned, why was she tipping her head to one side, closing her eyes slightly and parting her lips just a bit?

She felt his breath warm on her skin before she felt his mouth dancing lightly across hers. Then his lips pressed firmly. A streak of electricity seemed to make its way through her body, starting where his mouth touched hers.

It had been so long since a man kissed her this way. Kissed her as if he wanted her. Kissed her so that she felt desired. It felt much too good.

"Cole." She pulled away before it got to feel so good that she'd be thinking about going a step further.

"Bree." He smiled at her. He rubbed a stray strand of hair between his fingers before tucking it behind her ear. "I always did like redheads."

"Redheads have nasty tempers."

"Then we'll just have to find a way to redirect all that negative energy."

Bree opened her mouth, even though she had no idea what she was going to say. At that moment, a scream ripped through the house.

"Damn." She shot off the couch and up the stairs, with Cole hard on her heels.

Cody sat up in bed, his face awash with tears as he cried so hard he was choking. Bree gathered him up in her arms as she sat down on the bed.

"Bad." He choked out the word. "Bad, Mommy."

"I'm here, sweetie," she soothed, rocking him gently back and forth. "It's okay, Cody. No one bad will get you. You know I won't let that happen."

"Big noise, lots of blood." He hiccuped between the words. "Mommy!" he wailed.

Bree looked over her son's head at Cole. *I'm sorry,* she mouthed.

"Will he be all right?" he asked softly.

"Does he look all right?" Sara demanded from behind him.

"Enough." Bree kept her voice low, but the authority remained.

"I can see you have enough going on without having me in the way. I'll talk to you later. Thanks for dinner."

She nodded. "Thank you for understanding."

Bree couldn't release Cody's stranglehold on her for almost ten minutes as he cried himself out.

"Would you feel better if Jinx slept in here?" she asked.

His eyes, the same startling emerald as her own, were blurred with his tears. Bree reached over to pluck a tissue out of the box by his bed so she could dry his face.

"He sleeps by your room," he mumbled.

"I'll have him stay in here with you tonight," she told him. "He'll sleep in the doorway and you know he'll make sure no one will come in to make any more bad dreams for you. Would you like that?"

"Uh-huh." His head bobbed up and down. "Can't he sleep on the bed with me?" His lower lip trembled.

"Sweetie, you know that Jinx is a working dog, not a pet," she said gently. "He'll be nearby and he'll protect you."

"Okay, but a kitten would protect me, too." He allowed himself to be tucked under the covers.

Bree called Jinx and ordered the dog to guard Cody. He laid down in the doorway and settled his face between his paws.

Bree checked the kitchen. She was gratified to find it clean. She picked up the cups and carafe from the family room and rinsed them out.

"You know why he had a nightmare, don't you?" Sara tracked down her stepmother. "Because you brought a man here. It upset him. Cody feels that he's losing you."

"Forget the psychotherapy, Sara. It wasn't because Mr. Becker was here," she stated. "The dreams just happen. You were there when the therapist said they wouldn't go away by a set time, but they would diminish over time. We will do whatever is necessary to make Cody feel safe and loved. That's the important thing."

The girl's delicate face tightened. "And what about the rest of us? He was our dad, too."

Bree grabbed Sara's hands and held on tight when she tried to pull away. "Yes, he was, and because you're older there may be things I'll expect of you that I won't expect of Cody. We'll do what we've been doing. Take it day by day."

Her expression was stormy and sullen. "Out here, that's all we can do." She tore away and ran off to her bedroom.

"Don't worry, I won't tell you what a horrible person you are," David said. He stood in the doorway of the kitchen.

"Thank you for being willing to wait at least until tomorrow," Bree replied.

She headed for her room with the intention of taking a nice long, relaxing bath. When she stepped inside, she'd started to finger the light switch when she felt that eerily familiar sensation of the hairs on the back of her neck standing straight up. Following a gut instinct that had protected her more than once, she crossed the dark room until she reached the window. By standing to the side, she could look out between the partially closed miniblinds. Her gaze swept the area beyond the backyard, tracking each shadow and mentally identifying it. Then she reached what she was looking for.

Once her eyes grew accustomed to the darkness outside, she could see the shape of a large vehicle—either a pickup truck or one of the larger sport utility vehicles. There was no way she could identify the driver.

Bree decided to forget the bath. She swiftly unlocked her gun safe and loaded her weapon. She stealthily made her way through the house to the back door and eased it open. When she looked in the direction of the shadowy vehicle, she found nothing but empty space.

She looked right and left as she crossed the backyard to the dirt area. Once there, she cursed herself for not thinking to bring a flashlight with her. With the ground so hard, she doubted she'd find any tire tracks, anyway.

She decided to come back out in the morning.

"Mom?" David stood in the open doorway. "Is everything okay?"

"Fine," she replied. "I thought I heard an animal."

"Big surprise when you're living out in the wild," he muttered, turning away.

Once back in her bedroom, Bree quickly undressed in the dark. Before she climbed into bed she tucked her weapon in the bedside table drawer. As she curled up in bed and opened her book, she wondered why someone would be out there watching her.

She was angry with herself for being unaware of being watched.

Even more so, she didn't like that someone dared to park on her property and watch the house.

The next morning, Bree's fears were realized.

The earth was hard because the area had had no rain for more than nine months. She found nothing to indicate that a vehicle had been there last night.

After Bree watched David drive off with Sara and Cody, she headed for the backyard and walked past Cody's tree house. She stopped at the area where she'd seen the truck the night before. Broken branches weren't a clue since there was nothing to guarantee they were broken the night before. No damn business card, cigarette butts from cigarettes only found at one store in the entire state, not even a discarded candy wrapper.

She muttered a few choice curses under her breath as she squatted by the trampled branches, where she knew the truck had parked. Easy enough for it to back up and head back down the dirt trail that eventually wound around to one of the back roads. She turned her head one way, then the other. She turned around so she could see what her observer had.

The windows along the rear of the house looked into the kitchen and family room downstairs, Sara's bedroom and her own upstairs. A chill ran through Bree, although the morning air was warm.

She decided she wouldn't tell anyone about her find. But she would make sure Sara kept her blinds closed at night. Until Bree could find the person who thought she needed to be watched, she would keep her weapon close at hand.

She sighed as she looked around in the futile hope of finding anything to help her figure things out.

"And here I thought moving here would be safer for the kids."

"Detective Fitzpatrick!"

Bree turned when she heard her name called. She could see Renee Patterson leaving a building across the street and coming toward her.

"Mrs. Patterson, how are you?"

"Renee, please." She smiled warmly. "How are you settling in?"

"All the boxes are unpacked and I can find everything. I see that as a plus," she said.

"Josh was in the army for the first twenty-two years of our marriage," Renee said. "I always felt a house was mine once everything was in its place. So I know what you mean. By the way, I want to thank you again for coming to talk to our group. They enjoyed it immensely."

"I'm glad they did. I've always felt more talks about street smarts and safety are needed with our senior citizens, since they've become more of a target."

Renee looked around her. "Yes, it is a shame that people our age have so much to fear," she murmured.

Bree wondered why the older woman chose that particular word. If she'd known her better she would have questioned her about it. She already noticed that while Renee's smile was warm and friendly, there was a hint of strain around her mouth. Even her eyes betrayed a hint of shadow.

"I'm surprised you have all those worries, since this area has such a low crime rate," she commented.

Renee's smile slipped a bit before she recaptured it. "The center sets up group trips to San Diego for plays and concerts and to Laughlin for gambling and shows. Talks like yours help us remember to be alert when we're away from Warm Springs. As you said, we have a low crime rate here, so we don't need to worry. Would you have time for a cup of coffee?" she asked suddenly.

"I'd like that," Bree replied.

"If I know Greta, she has just what we need."

Greta welcomed them with steaming cups of coffee with the rich taste of hot buttered rum, and freshly made caramel rolls. Not wanting to miss out on anything, she poured a cup for herself and joined them.

"Now tell me what you think about Cole," Renee said.

Greta grinned. "Yes, Bree, please tell us."

Bree could feel a faint blush staining her cheeks. "I don't know the man well enough to say too much."

"He had dinner at your house the other night." Renee chuckled at Bree's surprise. "Mamie, his assistant, said she was glad to see him getting out more. He tends to hole up in his office. For a man who's traveled all over the world and met world figures, he's practically turned into a homebody."

"Excuse me?" Bree said, putting down the roll. "What do you mean?"

The two women looked at her strangely.

"You can't tell us you don't know?" Greta asked.

"Know what?"

"Before Cole took over his uncle's newspaper, he was a journalist for *Today's View*." Renee named a well-known news magazine.

"C. Becker," Bree murmured. "A few years ago, there was an article about the leader of that new oil-rich nation in the Middle East. The man refused to be interviewed, but somehow C. Becker got the story of how the man came into power." She felt a falling sensation in the middle of her stomach.

"I gather he never mentioned it to you," Greta said, exchanging glances with Renee.

"No," Bree said calmly. "In fact, he let me believe he'd always been nothing more than a small-town news hack." She picked up her roll and bit down, tearing off a bite in a savage motion.

"Obviously, she spoke the truth about not knowing him well," Renee said to Greta. A smile played about her lips, as if she knew something Bree did not.

"He let me think he was a two-bit hack who had crazy ideas

about..." Bree halted. Both women looked expectant as they leaned in, eager to hear more.

"Crazy ideas about what?" Renee probed.

Bree thought about telling her exactly what. With Renee being such an active member at the senior center, she might have her own opinion about the high number of deaths. But Bree didn't want to start gossip. And she especially didn't want Roy Holloway knowing Cole was trying to interest her in his conspiracy theories. So far, she was getting along with her boss, and she wanted it to stay that way.

"Cole is a charmer few women can resist," Greta said when Bree didn't answer. "I swear he's like a lovable disease."

"Sounds as if a vaccine is in order," Bree stated dryly.

"Oh, hon, no one cares that there isn't a cure." Greta laughed. "They'd rather let it run its course."

"I always wondered why his wife left him," Renee mused.

Bree's ears perked up at that piece of information. "He's been married? He seems like the confirmed bachelor type." Admittedly, she didn't expect to know everything about the man, but it seemed she knew absolutely nothing about him.

Renee shook his head. "He got his divorce about eight years ago. His uncle, who owned the newspaper before him, said it wasn't easy on Cole. Following that, he went after the most dangerous stories he could find. Not so much as a death wish, but to keep himself fully immersed in his work, so he wouldn't have to think about anything else."

Bree had trouble equating the cocky man loaded with charm who filled her thoughts more than she liked to the man Renee and Greta talked about.

"So now he plays the field and breaks more than a few hearts along the way," she said.

"I'm not sure he breaks them," Greta told her. "Cracks them a little is more like it. They always seem to heal, because he keeps the ladies as friends. More than one of them has shown up here in hopes of running into him. Probably thinking the relationship can be rekindled."

"They've come to understand it's easier to be his friend than hope for more." Renee added her opinion.

"I've met a few reporters like C. Becker. Going after that next story is an addiction for them. They're adrenaline junkies. Without it, they can't function." Bree shook her head.

"Cole used to be that way. Then he changed. Came out here after his uncle's death and decided to take over running the newspaper," Renee said. "I don't think he's looked back since that day."

Bree glanced from one woman to the other. They both gazed at her speculatively.

"Oh no," she protested. "I have enough trouble in my life, thank you very much."

"Easier said than done," Greta teased.

By the time Bree left the shop she felt as if the other two women were planning her love life for her.

Cole Becker was an award-winning investigative journalist. He'd gone after stories braver souls would have turned down.

Cole Becker was divorced. He rarely dated a woman more than three times, and most of those dates were with women out of town. And the women he'd dated in the past remained friends with him.

According to Greta and Renee, the man was considerate of others, was a great listener, never did anything wrong, was beloved by all, and for all Bree knew, he probably helped little old ladies across the street. In general, the perfect man.

Damn if that didn't make him more appealing.

"Your son has a problem with his temper, Mrs. Fitzpatrick," Principal Vickers said, sounding as pompous as he looked. "I'm sure you understand that if something isn't done about it as soon as possible, it can only get worse."

There were few things Bree hated. Brussels sprouts headed the list and men who felt they could patronize any member of the opposite sex ran a close second.

Principal Everett Vickers was a good two inches shorter than Bree, and she silently bet the man had a Napoleon complex to go along with his less than engaging personality. Right now, he was edging out brussels sprouts.

Receiving a call from the high school with the message that

David had been fighting wasn't her idea of fun. She'd spent the past hour seeing if there was anything written up on the deaths Cole's notes listed. It hadn't been easy for her to do this since she didn't want Sheriff Holloway to know what she was doing. She didn't think her superior would be happy she was investigating cases not in her care.

Receiving the call merely increased her frustration.

She stared at her stepson, who sat slumped in a chair. David's shirt was torn and there was a nasty-looking bruise on his cheek.

"Who started it?" she asked David.

He shrugged.

"Does it matter who started the fight?" Principal Vickers asked. "It doesn't detract from the fact the boy was fighting. We have zero tolerance for fighting in our school. Naturally, David will be expelled."

"No way!" David snarled, starting to jump up out of the chair.

"Shut up and sit down," Bree ordered. She didn't bother to see if he obeyed her command as she turned back to the principal. "What about the other boy? Have his parents been called? He will also be expelled, won't he?"

The man looked away. "The matter is being dealt with. He will be suitably disciplined."

Bree's temper started to rise. "Disciplined? Are you telling me he won't be expelled, while David will be? Who is the other boy?"

"That has nothing to do with this matter," Principal Vickers argued.

"It has everything to do with it." She spun around, bearing down on her stepson. "Who was the other boy?"

He knew her temper well. Bree could flay strips off his hide with words alone. He raised his head and kept his gaze trained on her.

"Tim Holloway," he said sullenly.

"Holloway," she murmured. "As in—?"

A bare nod of the head was his answer.

Bree turned back to the principal. "I appreciate that you have a zero tolerance policy, and it's understandable in several situations. Fighting, for any reason, is not good. It does nothing but promote violence, which we're trying to get out of the schools. But there's something just as bad, and that's citing policy for one student and not for another. I have never believed kicking a child out of school was a suitable punishment. Not when kids could see it as a reward. I would think it would be more beneficial to keep them under your thumb, so to speak. True?''

The man realized he didn't have a chance with her.

''Perhaps.''

''What used to be the punishment for fighting?'' She kept her voice low, which didn't diminish any of its power.

''Five-day suspension and two months detention,'' the man muttered.

Bree nodded. ''That sounds adequate for a first offense. I'm sure both boys will be better behaved when they return after their suspension.'' She jerked her head in David's direction, indicating he should follow her. ''Good day, Principal Vickers.'' With her stepson in tow, she left the office.

''You sure haven't lost your touch. He's probably in there singing soprano,'' David muttered, following her outside.

Bree looked around. ''Do yourself a favor and don't say another word. I want you to drive straight home. Once you're there, I want you to start clearing out the bushes from the backyard that have been affecting Sara's allergies. If you get right to it, you'll probably have the job done by the time the five days are up. You'll also have to be back here in time to pick up Sara and then Cody.''

David's jaw dropped. ''What the hell?''

''And five dollars in the Cuss Jar,'' she stated. ''You don't fight. You know better.''

''I had a good reason.''

''There is no good reason for fighting.'' She noticed that the anger written on his face warred with sorrow. She knew better than to hug him. She knew he'd only reject any comfort she offered. Her voice softened. ''Whether you believe me or not, I do know where you're coming from. You're still angry with your dad for dying.''

He pulled his keys out of his jeans pocket, acting as if she hadn't spoken. "Since I have five days of work ahead of me, I better get to it." He walked off toward the school parking lot.

"Damn," she murmured, watching him leave. "It's days like this I hate being a mother. No matter what I do or say, I'm automatically wrong."

When Bree arrived at the house, she found Cole seated on the front steps. She ignored the little thrill she felt at seeing him. The silent reminder that a good cop wouldn't have this reaction was completely ignored. It was easier when she recalled everything Greta and Renee had told her.

She parked in the driveway and got out. She opened the back door and signaled for Jinx to jump out. She stayed by her vehicle with the dog by her side and waited until David drove into the garage. He didn't speak a word as he pulled off his jacket and threw it on his truck's hood. He gathered up a rake and hoe, tossed them into a wheelbarrow and pushed it toward the backyard.

"I see David came up against the school's zero tolerance policy regarding fighting," Cole said.

Bree looked amused. "What was your first clue?"

"Torn shirt, beginnings of a black eye. Pissed-off look when he got out of his truck. Takes me back to my high school days," he mused. "'Course, I didn't have Principal Vickers to make my life miserable. I had Mrs. Benjamin. Some of us swore she was a drill instructor in the marines. Even the toughest guy in school was afraid of her."

"I'm sure there are many people who would enjoy your trip down Memory Lane," Bree said sarcastically. "But I have things to do. Why don't we get down to why you're here?" Her voice turned silky smooth. "Or did you decide you wanted to work up a more comprehensive story about me? Isn't that what you top investigative reporters do? Gee, I bet that gives the ladies a thrill once they've learned they're with a man who's interviewed most of our world leaders."

He cocked an eyebrow at the silk covering the steely tone. "I prefer to keep a low profile."

"Yes, so I've learned. So tell me, why is a hotshot reporter such as yourself out here running a small-town newspaper?'' Bree asked. ''It must be tough for a man with your talent to live in a town where your biggest story is Mattie's feud with Teresa.''

''There's a bigger story here.'' He pulled a packet of papers out of his back pocket.

She looked at them warily. ''What are those?''

The smile left his face.

''There's been another questionable death.''

Chapter 7

"Tell me why you think this man was murdered," Bree said, dropping the papers onto the kitchen table in front of Cole after she'd perused them. "He had an allergic reaction, which sadly turned fatal. It happens."

"Yeah, it says he died from a bee sting and his Medic Alert bracelet stated his allergy to bee stings. How much do you want to bet the coroner won't find a bee sting on his body?" Cole's movements were leisurely as he settled back in the chair with his hands behind his head. "That would be an easy death, wouldn't it? Just make sure the victim gets hold of bee pollen and no easy access to help."

Bree threw up her hands. "You're thinking way too much like a murderer," she told him. "Can you give me a good reason why he would have been killed?"

Cole looked grim as he slowly shook his head.

"Then let's wait until I can see an autopsy report," she suggested.

He watched her fill two cups with coffee. He smiled his thanks when she handed one of the cups to him.

He really liked watching her. Not that he'd admit it to her.

With his luck, she'd tell him to forget it or even shoot him with that sweet little Glock she carried. Knowing her, she would not only be a crack shot, she'd make sure to shoot something vital.

Which was another reason why he didn't ask her if she'd like to borrow his reading glasses. The way she squinted as she looked over the typewritten pages told him she probably used them any other time.

He settled for studying his surroundings to get more of an idea of the woman Bree Fitzpatrick was when she wasn't on duty. An idea of what her home life reflected.

He hadn't gotten a good look at her kitchen when he was here last. Now he took closer note of his surroundings. The room was warm and homey, with touches of green and white in the wall-paper echoed in the place mats left on the table. Even the dog dishes set in a corner were green. Two drawings sketched with brightly colored crayons were fastened with magnets on the re-frigerator door, along with a magnet in the shape of a candy bar with You Can't Go Wrong with Chocolate printed on top.

He could hear the tinkling sound of the wind chimes through the open window.

He noticed the mug she gave him boasted the Los Angeles County sheriff's insignia, as did the one she drank out of. Her way of reminding him what she did for a living?

He would have enjoyed watching her more if he didn't have the uneasy sensation of being under observation himself. Her K-9 partner sat on his haunches, his dark eyes never leaving Cole.

"He's looking at me as if I'm the main course on the menu."

"He looks at everyone that way." Bree held up the top page of the report. "Care to tell me what makes you believe this wasn't an accident?"

"Gut instinct," Cole said promptly.

She looked up. "I see." Her tone spelled danger for Cole.

He felt as if she was preparing to sic the dog on him.

"Even a noncop can have gut instincts," he added.

She didn't blink. "So can award-winning investigative re-porters such as yourself."

Uh-oh.

"So your hot-shot reporter's gut instinct told you this man's death was murder, not an accident," she said in a sarcastic voice.

"That was another life."

"Funny you never mentioned it." Her voice was as smooth and deadly as a laser.

"As I said, another life. I run a small-town newspaper and am content doing just that," he replied.

"I came to this town because of its low crime rate and because it seemed so normal. Hell, if I wanted this kind of trouble, I could have stayed in L.A." Bree got up and refilled her coffee mug. She glanced at Cole and lifted the pot. He nodded and she brought it over to the table.

"I'm the only one who sees all this, remember," he pointed out.

"Let's wait and see what the autopsy shows," she said.

"Deal." He stared at Jinx, who stared back. "What happens if I don't agree with you? You'll sic your dog on me?"

"And have you claim police brutality? I don't think so." She got up and walked over to the sink. She looked out the window.

From where he sat, Cole could see David pulling weeds with a fierce determination he remembered from his own teenage years. The boy's movements were economical as he tossed the weeds into the wheelbarrow.

"Obviously, he's working off a lot of anger. Who'd he fight to deserve the hard-labor sentence?"

Her gaze followed his. Frustration crossed her face. "Sheriff Holloway's son," she said in a clipped tone.

Cole winced. "Damn, when he wants to get into trouble, he goes all out, doesn't he? I can already guess the rest. David's expelled, while good ole Tim gets disciplined with maybe a couple days detention or an admonition not to do it again. No wonder David's out there tearing up your backyard. But shouldn't you tell him to ease up? No reason to do it all in one day when he's going to have all that free time."

"You're right, five days suspension is a lot of time," Bree said dryly.

The look he shot her said he was impressed. "What'd you do

to Vickers for him to agree to only five days? He prides himself on his zero tolerance policy."

"Let's just say I pointed out to him that when kids are kept out of school they tend to view that as a reward, not a punishment," she said matter-of-factly. "It's the parents who are punished. We settled on five days suspension and two months detention."

"And Tim Holloway?"

"The same."

Cole didn't look convinced. "He'll get the suspension only if you scared Vickers more than Holloway can. Of course, Vickers is scared of anyone wearing a badge. By rights, Tim should be repeating his freshman year for the third time. The way he's going, he'll probably graduate valedictorian. Any reason why Tim picked on David?"

"So you don't think David started the fight?"

"If there's a fight in Tim's vicinity you can bet the farm he started it. But he always comes out smelling like that old rose. I always felt it had something to do with his name." Cole leaned back in his chair and surveyed her. "Are you this standoffish with everyone or am I the only lucky one?"

She ignored the last sentence. "So you're saying the sheriff knows his son is that way."

"Sure he does. I also think he has something to do with all these deaths. I haven't figured out how or why, but I will."

"That's a heavy accusation, Becker," she said in a low voice. "I wouldn't say anything more until you get some proof to stand behind it."

He nodded. "Fair enough, but if I find any proof, I expect you to help me nail the man to the wall."

"Fair enough," she echoed.

"So when are you going to let me take you out to dinner?" he asked in a quick change of subject.

Bree opened her mouth and suddenly closed it again. Cole grinned widely.

"Didn't dare try that when-pigs-fly-again routine, did you? Come on, Fitzpatrick. I'm harmless."

"So are flies. But when they've been around your face for a

few hours, you think about getting out some of that bug spray and doing something to them.''

''And you figure if I get you off to some nice place with tablecloths and a quiet atmosphere, I'm going to drag along my files and try to pound more theories into you.'' Cole shook his head. ''Not so. Come on, Bree. Go out with me.'' The last four words came out in a husky growl that skittered across Bree's nerve endings.

''The only reason you're pursuing me so ardently is because I keep turning you down. If I accepted, you'd lose interest real fast.''

''Then say yes and see what happens.'' He threw down the verbal challenge.

Her eyes gleamed brightly. ''See what happens,'' she repeated, tapping the center of her chin with her forefinger, as if she was giving his challenge a lot of thought. ''Let's see. What you're saying is if I say yes, we go out to dinner, and before I know it you're not returning my calls. I'm heartbroken, but gee, you're such an appealing guy, I decide it's better to be your friend than lose you altogether. Is that what you're talking about?'' She presented him with a wide-eyed look of innocence.

''Could be. Or, who knows, maybe you're the one who could change my mind.'' His smile could have been a choirboy's.

Bree looked at him and knew she was heading for trouble. She'd known she was on that road the moment she started checking into some of the reports. Damn him, he must have known that sooner or later he'd hit a chord. The man was trouble with a capital *T*.

And now she was considering going out with him.

Maybe it was because she was lonely for the company of a man who looked at her the way a man should look at a woman. As if she was beautiful. Desired.

Cole Becker looked at her that way. And more.

Maybe her putting him off for so long was a challenge. But what did that matter? It wasn't as if she was looking for another husband. Not even a relationship. She'd had a husband and love. She wasn't going to dare having it again.

Why not go out to dinner with him? She had been eating with

two teenagers and one small boy who weren't all that happy with her for moving them away from everything they considered necessary: the mall, skateboard parks, multiplex theaters.

"*If* I go out with you, we have to have a few ground rules." She fixed him with a steely eye. "There will be no discussion of the deaths."

"Not a word." He ran his fingers across his lips as if zipping them shut, locking them and throwing away the key. He got up and walked over to her. "Pick you up at seven."

She lifted her chin that extra fraction of an inch. "I didn't say I would go out with you."

Cole's grin was slow in coming, but when it happened, it was heart-stopping.

"You didn't have to." His touch on her cheek was feather-light and shook her all the way down to her toes. "And this time, I didn't have to worry about finding a flying pig or selling the devil a few snow machines to get you to say yes, either. See you at seven, Detective."

Even after he left, Bree still felt the touch of his hand against her cheek. She blew a gust of air between her lips and lightly pressed her hand against her stomach, which was still fluttering.

"I'm too old for this," she muttered, looking back out the window at David, who was tearing out weeds as if his very life depended on it.

"Mom, you have to tell him he cannot keep that—that thing!" Sara entered the kitchen with the haughty aplomb of a drama queen. She flicked her hair away from her face with a motion that Bree had seen her stepdaughter practice for hours in front of the mirror, until she felt it looked as if it was a natural movement.

"Mom, please, can we keep him?" Cody pleaded, running into the room with what looked like a scrap of fur in his hands. Mangy fur that let out a pitiful meow.

Jinx lifted his head, eyed the tiny bundle in Cody's arms and dropped his head back down on his paws.

"I better not find any fleas in my truck, squirt," David said, coming in last.

"Mommy, he needs me." Cody held up the kitten.

Bree plucked the gray-and-white animal out of his hands and looked it over.

"For one thing, he is a she," she told her son. "Poor thing. You can see every one of her ribs."

"She can eat tuna, can't she?" Cody scrambled onto the counter and opened a cabinet door. "And we can keep her? David almost drove over her, but I saw her and made him stop. Then Sara said she was ugly. She's not ugly, is she?"

Bree studied the cat, which was all skin and bones. It had a torn ear and the biggest eyes in history.

"We'll have to take her to the vet and make sure she's all right," she said.

"Why does he get to keep a ratty old cat?" Sara demanded. "And what are you doing?" She eyed the hot rollers on Bree's head.

"I didn't say he could keep the cat and I have a date. I ordered pizza for you kids and there's a salad in the refrigerator. I expect it to be eaten and not thrown down the garbage disposal unit like you've done in the past."

"You're going on a date?" Sara asked. "Why?"

"Because someone asked me," Bree said.

"It's with that reporter guy, isn't it?" David chimed in. "He was over here this afternoon."

Cody took the cat from Bree. "He can sleep with me, can't he?"

"*She* will sleep in a box. You can take a couple of old towels out of the box in the laundry room," she told him. "I'll see if we can get her in to the vet's tomorrow."

Cody cradled the kitten in his arms. The cat snuggled down and started purring.

"We have to name her. I wanna name her after the kitty lady on TV."

"Kitty lady?" Bree looked at the other two for help.

"Cat Woman on *Batman*," David explained. "Eartha Kitt."

Cody frowned. "No, she was Eartha Katt. I'll name her Eartha Katt."

Bree sighed. Past experience told her that once an animal was named, said animal never left the Fitzpatrick household.

"All you had to do was pick Cody up at soccer practice," she said. "And in the process, you managed to come home with a kitten. How?"

"I took a different route home." David poured milk into a glass and drank deeply.

"He was mad because everybody knows he fought with Tim Holloway because Tim said Lacey was using David to get Tim jealous. Then he said some really nasty things about Lacey, which got David mad," Sara declared. "Everybody knows Tim is a jerk. The only reason he doesn't get in trouble is because of his dad."

Bree turned and stared at her stepson. "You fought him because you were protecting Lacey's honor?"

"Sure, I did. I'm dating her and there was no reason for him to say what he did," he muttered, leaving the glass on the counter and walking out of the room. "Let me know when the pizza is here."

"Sara, help Cody make up a bed for the kitten, will you? I think there's a clean box in the garage that would work. What's one more animal in the house?" Bree muttered, returning to her bedroom to finish getting ready.

She was in the bathroom pulling the hot rollers out of her hair when she heard a knock on her open bedroom door. She looked out and saw David standing in the doorway.

"If the pizza's here, the money's on the kitchen table," she told him.

"It's not about the pizza." He walked in. "While driving home from Cody's soccer practice, I noticed a truck following us."

Bree felt her blood start to chill and the tingle along the back of her neck. It was never a good sign when it happened.

"Maybe it was someone going in the same direction as you were," she said casually, not wanting to think the worst.

He shook his head. "No, this was a definite tail. When I sped up, the driver did, too. When I slowed down, so did he."

"Did you see what kind of truck it was?"

"It stayed back far enough that I couldn't see it clearly. I couldn't even make out the make or color."

Her internal alarms started to go off one by one. She slowly set each roller down on the counter with careful precision.

She should call Cole now and tell him she couldn't go out.

"This is a small town with only so many roads going anywhere." She prayed that was the case, but that sixth sense of hers was saying different.

David gave her a knowing look that echoed the one Fitz used to give her. "Growing up around an FBI agent and a cop taught me what to look for. The driver kept too much distance between us. It was a tail."

"If that was the case, you know what you should have done," she said, not liking what she was hearing. If anything happened to the kids, she didn't know what she would do. She'd had one loss. She didn't want any more.

"If I thought there was any danger I would have called you while driving straight to the sheriff's station," he replied. "I wouldn't have put the others in danger."

"I know that, David," she assured him. "I guess I had to give the standard warning, anyway. Do you think it was Tim Holloway?"

"He drives a '67 Camaro that's all tricked out. I've never seen him in a truck." David searched her face. "When I was clearing out the backyard, I noticed some faint tire prints out near Cody's tree house. There's a connection there, isn't it? Between those tire prints out there and a truck following me tonight."

Bree breathed deeply through her nose. "There was a truck out there once," she admitted. "By the time I noticed it, he was gone in seconds. I don't think there's any danger."

"That night I saw you out there you were looking for something," he said. "It's because the sheriff didn't want you here, isn't it? Tim made that pretty clear while I was cleaning his clock."

Bree shot him her fiercest mother's glare. "You know my views on fighting."

David looked her straight in the eye. "All I did was tell him just what I thought of what he was saying about Lacey. But if somebody's fist comes my way, I'm going to do my best to make sure it doesn't connect.''

"Which is why you have a black eye, a cut lip and some painful bruises.''

"Yeah, but he's the one with a broken nose and a couple cracked ribs,'' he said with supreme male satisfaction. He watched his stepmother comb her fingers through her hair, tangling the curls. "Don't worry, I promise to stay out of his way from now on.''

"Good idea.'' She picked up her brush. "I honestly don't think there's any danger, David, but if there is…'' Her voice dropped off. No decision to make. She was going to cancel.

"You're still going out,'' David said, easily reading her mind. "We'll be fine. We've got Jinx, and I know your cell phone number. Besides, I can always take the perp down with my fists.'' He grinned, knowing that would get a rise out of her.

"In your dreams,'' she muttered.

"You've trusted me before, Mom,'' he said, suddenly serious. "Trust me now.''

Bree turned around and looked at him closely. She blinked her eyes to stop tears that threatened to fall. "Damn, you've grown up.''

David started laughing. "It took you this long to notice?'' he teased, effectively breaking the somber mood. "Just for that, I won't snitch to the others that you owe the Cuss Jar a quarter.''

Bree wrapped her arms around him, and realized sadly he was now a good four inches taller than her. "You know, when you're not being an idiot, you are my sanity,'' she told him. "I couldn't have made it through this past year without you.''

"Don't get all emotional, Mom.'' He sounded embarrassed as he patted her back. "Not when you were ready to throttle me this afternoon.''

"Yes, I was. For good reason. And if you do anything that stupid again, I *will* throttle you. And I know how to hide the body so it wouldn't be found for decades.'' She leaned back and patted his cheeks. Cheeks that were now rough with a beard that went along with the deeper voice and lean body filling out.

She knew with his good grades and extracurricular activities, David would have no problem getting into the college of his choice. And that he'd chosen to apply to the FBI after he graduated.

"The feds will be so lucky to get you," she said huskily. "I bet you'll be showing them a thing or two."

His face reddened. She wanted to smile at seeing the little boy still there with the emerging man. Then she glanced at the clock and winced.

"I've got to finish getting ready." She started to push him out of the room. "David, if anything happens, call 911 first, then call me."

He nodded as he obliged her by leaving her room.

Bree ran the brush through her hair, glared at the curls that refused to behave and wielded the brush with a heavier hand.

"I never remember dating being so hard."

Bree repeated that mantra as she pawed through her closet and realized that, except for styles used for court appearances, her wardrobe was practically nonexistent. In the end, she chose a knit dress in hunter green. The long sleeves were appropriate for the cooler evening, and the scooped neckline revealed the gold-and-diamond free-form pendant she wore.

"This is so sick," Sara announced, looking her mother up and down.

"I think I look pretty good." Bree carefully applied a rich bronze shade of lipstick.

"You're too old to date," she blurted.

"Excuse me?" Bree arched an eyebrow. "Sara, I hate to break it to you, but your grandmother Fitzpatrick has been leading an active social life for the past ten years. Her latest boyfriend is a retired Navy SEAL, if I recall."

Sara made a face. "Yeah, well, Grammy Fran's way too old to date guys."

Bree decided it was a good thing her stepdaughter didn't know that her grandmother was also enjoying a healthy sex life. Some things were better off left unsaid.

"Your day will come," she told her, as she dug out a smaller purse and dropped her cellular phone, wallet and lipstick inside.

Her weapon added a little bulge to her bag, but she was required to carry it off duty. "And I can say that with great authority, because my mother told me my day would come and I refused to believe her. Yet everything she told me came true."

"He's not Daddy." Sara stood nearby, with one foot balanced on the other. Years of dancing classes lent grace to all her movements. Bree was silently grateful that the girl never seemed to suffer an awkward moment, even when she'd shot up to five foot six inches when she was thirteen.

"Eartha Katt!" Cody's shout could be heard throughout the house.

Sara exhaled a deep sigh. "I'll go see what the problem is. He can have a cat, but you wouldn't let me get that rose tattoo I wanted."

"There's a big difference between a cat and a tattoo. You practically scream when you pluck your eyebrows. A tattoo would hurt a lot more." Bree sent a silent thank-you upward when she heard the doorbell peal.

"I'll get it!" David shouted.

She stopped long enough to study her reflection in the mirror.

"Not bad for thirty-something," she muttered as she adjusted her neckline.

When Bree entered the family room, she found David and Cole discussing the high school football team's chances for the state championship that year. David's demeanor was much better than that of a stormy-faced Sara who was standing nearby. Cody didn't look any happier. He had his hands wrapped around the kitten's middle. Bree was relieved to notice he wasn't squeezing the poor feline.

"Why do you have to go out?" he demanded.

"Because Mr. Becker asked me out to dinner," she explained, kissing the top of his head. "No arguments about a bath or when it's time for bed, and the kitten sleeps in the box in the laundry room. Understood?"

He nodded sullenly. The kitten let loose a plaintive meow.

"Did you feed her?" Bree asked.

"Yes." He didn't look up at her.

"Then why don't you and David take her outside so she can

go potty.'' She kissed him again. ''Sweet dreams, my baby boy,'' she whispered in his ear. ''I will come in and check on you when I get home.''

His lower lip trembled. ''Promise?''

As she looked at Cody's pathetic expression, she almost gave in and told Cole she couldn't go out. Almost.

''Come on, squirt, let's get the cat outside before he pees on the carpet,'' David said, heading for the back door.

''I promise,'' she vowed to her youngest as she wrapped the matching shawl around her shoulders and left the house with Cole.

''It looks like David's gardening chores took the fight out of him, so to speak,'' he said, as they walked to his vehicle.

''It usually does.'' She smiled as he assisted her into the truck. ''Beware of all that friendliness they show you. They're just waiting until you're off guard. You might want to start looking over your shoulder. They give no warning before they attack.''

''Glad to know my days are numbered.'' He started the engine and switched on the heater. Warm air soon drifted over their legs. ''Warm enough?''

''Fine, thank you.'' Out of reflex, Bree automatically glanced in the passenger side mirror, but saw only dark road behind them. ''Someone followed David after he picked Cody up at soccer practice.''

Cole glanced quickly at her, then back at the road. ''He see who it was?''

She shook her head. ''I asked if he thought it might be Tim Holloway, but he said this one drove a truck.''

''And Tim drives a tricked-out hot Camaro,'' he finished for her. ''Truck,'' he murmured. ''Like the truck you've seen outside your house?''

''No way to know without a positive ID.''

''Spoken like a true cop.''

Bree looked around when they reached the highway and Cole sped up.

''It's not paranoia,'' he said. ''There's just better restaurants farther down the road.''

''Where we might not run into anyone we know.''

He grinned. "That, too. It's about a half hour drive, but worth it."

"Sounds good to me," she replied, smiling at him.

Cole glanced briefly at her before turning his attention back to the road. "An evening alone with you sounds good to me."

"You're starting with that flattery again, Becker," Bree said, feeling a little uneasy.

"Just being honest, Fitzpatrick."

"Amazing after the evening you spent with my kids." She arched an eyebrow. "I've heard you don't spend your time with women who have children."

"I met you and decided it was time for a change." He inhaled the seductive scent of her perfume.

"Says the man who's never been a referee during dinner," she said.

"What? You don't use threats of jail?" he teased.

"I don't have to use threats that drastic. Agony for David is taking away the keys to his truck. For Sara, it's denying her a trip to the mall, and for Cody, it's taking away his computer games. That kind of punishment has been known to drive them to tears."

"I bet you would have been hell on wheels if you'd worked juvenile," he said.

"Juvie takes a special kind of person. That wasn't me." She looked out, seeing only a few flickering lights in the distance.

Cole glanced briefly at her. "Why did you choose homicide?"

"As opposed to something safe like vice or narcotics?" She chuckled, then sobered. "I guess I chose it because the victims aren't able to speak for themselves. I saw them needing someone on their side. To speak for them. I wanted to be that person." She absently rubbed her hands together, as if they were cold. "When I started out in homicide, I was partnered with this guy who'd been there for fifteen years. Before that, Danny had worked in narcotics. He used to say he'd never leave. That they'd have to carry him out. It was his life." She paused and softly added, "He died of a heart attack two years ago. Right after he informed a grateful mother that he'd arrested her daughter's killer. A serial rapist who had graduated to murder with his third victim. Danny forgot more about homicide investigation than many of us could learn in a lifetime,'' she said softly.

''That's what's needed now, Bree,'' Cole said quietly, with an intensity that struck her to the core. ''Someone to speak for people who have no one else to find out the truth. They need someone like you, because you honestly care.''

Chapter 8

The restaurant was a pleasant surprise to Bree. Nestled among the San Jacinto foothills, the rustic building boasted a stream that ran across the property, with a wooden bridge leading to the front door.

Inside, the dining areas were broken up into cozy niches where diners could enjoy their meal in private. Cole gave his name to the maître d', who led them off to one side toward a large fireplace. Bree sat down when the maître d' pulled her chair out for her. She unwound her shawl and dropped it behind her.

Cole conferred with Bree, then ordered a bottle of wine, which was promptly delivered to the table.

"This is lovely," she commented, looking around at the battered brass bed-warmer that lay against the wall and the antique fireplace implements. Shadow boxes and antique photographs decorated the walls, giving the restaurant the warmth and homey atmosphere of an old-fashioned parlor. "And very unexpected in an area that doesn't appear to be heavily populated."

"There's never been any worries about lack of business here. This building has an interesting history. Back in the late eighteen hundreds it was a very popular brothel, owned by an enterprising woman named Snub-nosed Sadie,'' he explained. ''Sadie ran herd over ten ladies, to use the term loosely—ladies who entertained men from the local army fort, and local cowhands who were always looking for some rest and relaxation on payday.'' His mouth tipped upward in a slow smile. ''Sadie died in 1910. Her daughter kept the place going until one of those ladies' temperance leagues had it shut down. She decided to turn Sadie's Place into a restaurant. Even then, more male patrons showed up than couples or families. The restaurant is still family owned. Sadie's great-granddaughter runs it now. Except now it's strictly a restaurant, so you don't need to flash your badge.''

''That's reassuring.'' Bree picked up her wineglass and sipped the liquid. It was slightly tart on her tongue, the flavor soothing as it slid down her throat. She took a second sip before setting down her glass. ''You don't like to keep promises, do you?''

She was surprised to see him look chagrined by her comment.

''I didn't plan on saying anything at all,'' he admitted. ''But then you started talking about your reasons for working homicide. How you seemed to see it as a calling. My uncle Charlie was that way. For him, the newspaper business was sacred. He felt the public had a right to know. He was never interested in the latest scandal, but looked for stories that got people talking. He liked nothing better than to run a piece on a topic that had people debating the pros and cons. He had a knack for finding and writing those kind of stories. Did it for more than fifty years.''

''If your uncle was so passionate about stories that would stimulate his readers' minds, why didn't he write for a bigger audience than Warm Springs?'' she asked.

''Charlie never cared for fame. He once told me he remembered times when a bunch of men would sit around the general store, talking. One day they might discuss politics. Another day they might argue about international affairs. Or maybe debate back and forth about when the next rainfall would come. That's what Charlie wanted with his articles—for people to stop and think.''

"Is your uncle why you became a reporter?" Bree asked, curious about the man.

"Yeah, I guess I'd have to say he's most of the reason. I spent a lot of summers with him," Cole replied. "My parents were divorced. My dad was an airline pilot and gone a lot, and my mom worked. When I stayed with Uncle Charlie, he'd take me to work with him, taught me everything I needed to know about running a newspaper, from finding a story to writing it and setting it up and printing it. But while he enjoyed looking at stories set close to home, I was more interested in finding stories that the world would read."

"If you loved it so much, why did you decide to quit and come back here?"

Cole chuckled. "It wasn't exactly my decision. I'd been working on a piece about a crime ring that specialized in stolen identities. They either stole or manufactured identities from scratch, and sold them to people who needed to leave the country in a hurry. I was confident I was getting close to breaking this story wide-open. I got proof of how close I was when someone planted a bomb under my car. Luckily for me, it went off too soon." He looked off into the distance, a wistful expression on his face. "Damn, I really loved that car."

Bree's mind's eye brought up a picture of Fitz's face at the exact moment he'd been shot. For a moment she wanted to tell Cole that nothing was worth a person's life. Whether it was a story or a car or a kid who thought he could escape arrest by shooting a federal officer. Nothing mattered more than life. She swallowed the words that threatened to spill out.

Cole already knew how lucky he was. She could tell by the way his hand tightened on the stem of the wineglass and the way he didn't look directly at her.

He had memories that haunted him, too.

"Better the car than you," Bree pointed out. "I've seen a few victims from car bombings. Not a pretty sight."

"Neither was my car." He drained the last of his wine and picked up the bottle to refill their glasses.

Further conversation was suspended as the waiter approached them.

Play
The

Lucky Hearts
Game

and get...
FREE BOOKS & a **FREE** GIFT...
YOURS to KEEP!

yes! I have scratched off the silver card.
Please send me my **2 FREE BOOKS**
and **FREE GIFT**. I understand that I am under
no obligation to purchase any books as
explained on the back of this card.

Scratch Here!
then look below to see
what your cards get you...

345 SDL DH4J   **245 SDL DH4H**

NAME   (PLEASE PRINT CLEARLY)

ADDRESS

APT.#   CITY

STATE/PROV.   ZIP/POSTAL CODE

DETACH AND MAIL CARD TODAY!

(S-IMA-02/02)

© 1998 HARLEQUIN ENTERPRISES LTD. ® and TM are
trademarks owned by Harlequin Books S.A., used under license.

The Silhouette Reader Service™ — Here's how it works:
Accepting your 2 free books and gift places you under no obligation to buy anything. You may keep the books and gift and return the shipping statement marked "cancel." If you do not cancel, about a month later we'll send you 6 additional books and bill you just $3.80 each in the U.S., or $4.21 each in Canada, plus 25¢ shipping & handling per book and applicable taxes if any.* That's the complete price and — compared to cover prices of $4.50 each in the U.S. and $5.25 each in Canada — it's quite a bargain! You may cancel at any time, but if you choose to continue, every month we'll send you 6 more books, which you may either purchase at the discount price or return to us and cancel your subscription.
*Terms and prices subject to change without notice. Sales tax applicable in N.Y. Canadian residents will be charged applicable provincial taxes and GST.

If offer card is missing write to: Silhouette Reader Service, 3010 Walden Ave., P.O. Box 1867, Buffalo NY 14240-1867

BUSINESS REPLY MAIL
FIRST-CLASS MAIL   PERMIT NO. 717-003   BUFFALO, NY

POSTAGE WILL BE PAID BY ADDRESSEE

SILHOUETTE READER SERVICE
3010 WALDEN AVE
PO BOX 1867
BUFFALO NY 14240-9952

NO POSTAGE
NECESSARY
IF MAILED
IN THE
UNITED STATES

"So you lost your beloved car and came back here to mourn," she said, after the waiter had taken their orders.

"Actually, I came back here because I had a wake-up call," he said. "A very noisy and messy wake-up call. Charlie died around that time and he left me the newspaper. At first I came out here to have some quiet time to myself. I'd planned on selling the newspaper. Then I found his files about these deaths. There weren't all that many then, but there had to have been something that caught his attention for him to keep them together."

"And you took up the cause," she said quietly.

"For good reason." He raised his eyes and looked directly at her. "He became one of those victims who shouldn't have died when he did."

Good going, Cole. First you take the lady to a nice restaurant. You even have the good sense to order a fine bottle of wine. So what do you do instead of telling her how pretty her eyes are? How good she looks in that sexy dress that hugs all her curves? How she's the best thing you've been around in a long time? You talk about the deaths. A subject you vowed not to discuss. You better do some damage control here.

Cole was used to these internal conversations. He had them all the time, a habit picked up when he was overseas and wanted another opinion. He could even debate with himself. This was the first time he'd had one in the middle of a date.

"So that's what started you on your quest," she guessed.

He shook his head. "Actually, not right away. It was a while before I found Charlie's notes about some deaths that weren't well explained. There was even mention about someone's wife knowing the truth and being too scared to say anything."

"No name or idea who the woman was?" Bree leaned forward, her eyes alight with interest.

"Nothing. Charlie wrote that there was an insidious going on that generated a lot of money for some people who were setting up deaths."

"Setting up deaths," Bree repeated. "Name one person who could set up deaths and pass any official investigation without sending out red flags."

Cole leaned across the table. "Has to be someone in the department."

"Whoever it is can't get away with it forever. No one is that smart," she declared. "All it takes is one little mistake. They always screw up."

"They haven't yet," he told her.

"We had a case where a man killed his wife. A pretty nasty way, too. He spent hours washing the blood off the walls and scrubbing the floor. He even shampooed the carpet. Once he'd finished, he remembered seeing a show on forensics that explained about Luminal, which detects bloodstains even after they've been washed away. He decided he wasn't going to take any chances. So he drove down to the neighborhood hardware store and asked for 'some of that Luminal stuff that shows where bloodstains are.'"

Cole laughed so hard he almost choked. "I can easily guess you can't buy Luminal at your local hardware store."

"No, but the store owner knew the guy and his wife had been having a lot of problems for quite some time. He guessed the worst had finally happened. He said he'd have to get it out of the back. He went to the storeroom and called the cops."

"You sure came up against some not-so-bright criminals in your career." Cole chuckled.

"For every stupid one, we had three dozen clever ones," she replied. She looked up as the waiter appeared with their dinners. "Some stand out more than others. You must have come across some pretty memorable people."

"More than I like to remember. I interviewed this desert sheikh who'd made literally a fortune in oil. He wanted to show off all his new toys, including his four new wives. He also wanted me to know his generosity, so he offered me my choice of one of his wives. He wanted me to be comfortable."

Bree rolled her eyes. "I've heard it's very bad form to turn down their offers."

"It is, but I found a way around it." He lowered his voice to a confidential level. "I explained I'd been injured as a young man, and it wouldn't be fair to any of his lovely wives."

She smiled. "Either very ingenious or very embarrassing for you to have to admit to any kind of failing."

Cole picked up his knife and fork. "I like the ingenious tag."

She stabbed one of her scallops with her fork. "*Sneaky* might have been a better word. You were trying to dig yourself out of that hole you dug when you brought up a forbidden subject. You did a pretty good job of it, too."

"I try," he said modestly. He sobered. "It might be forbidden, Bree, but it's not forgotten."

"Why do you think I called you the other night? I went over every one of those deaths, Cole. Yes, I understand your need to know the truth. I feel there's something wrong there, too, but without visiting the crime scenes, I don't have much to work with. There were hardly any photographs taken, and the ones in the file didn't show nearly enough detail."

"So we'll have to wait for another death?" He cut into his steak, his motions a little more savage than necessary for the tender meat.

"Unfortunately, yes. And then you'll have to hope I'm the one called out."

Cole looked off into the distance. "Okay," he said finally. "But I think I'm going to hope the deaths will stop first."

"I agree." She held up her glass in a silent toast.

Relieved she hadn't walked out on him for channeling the conversation in the wrong direction, Cole waited until their desserts arrived before he started coaxing information out of Bree. It was easy enough to get her to talk about her three kids, and in the process, he picked up bits and pieces about Bree herself. He made a mental note to make a point of catching some of the junior soccer games so he could see what she was like as a soccer mom. He had a pretty good idea that Norman Bailey, the referee, wouldn't know what hit him.

Cole was amazed that, considering Bree's workload, she made sure to attend sports games, and any other activities the kids were involved in.

He could also sense that she'd had a good marriage, and that if her husband hadn't been killed, she would have still been happily married and fighting crime in Los Angeles.

The realization that if her life hadn't changed, he never would have met her, came to mind. He didn't like that idea at all.

Not just because he wanted her to help him find out the truth behind the deaths, either. The lady was definitely growing on him. He hadn't enjoyed himself so much in a long time. Not like this. From the first moment he'd met her, he knew Bree Fitzpatrick was different.

Finding out about Bree, the person, was proving him right.

To be fair, he shared bits and pieces about himself at the same time. Not something he was known for.

Cole never thought there was anything to say. He didn't have much of a social life because of his work. Being ready to take off for a story at a moment's notice didn't bode well for any kind of a love life.

He revealed that once he'd settled down in Warm Springs, he had more than his share of local ladies wanting to set him up with daughters, nieces, granddaughters, along with female relatives of dear friends.

"Most of the time I'm told they're excellent cooks, have lovely personalities, plus other sterling qualities," he said. "There was once a woman whose sister-in-law's cousin's niece was an animal lover." He grimaced. "It meant that she was a vegetarian, and she believed that having pets was barbaric. I didn't mind the fact that she viewed me as one of those 'damn cannibals.' But our date ended abruptly when she refused to sit on the leather seats in my car. I wished her a nice life and got out of there fast." He savored his chocolate torte, which he felt was the absolute best in the world. "Any of your co-workers try to fix you up yet?"

"A few of them tried," Bree admitted. "Threatening to shoot them if they didn't stop didn't work, but threatening to return the favor got them to stop. And the married ones got worried I might divulge a few secrets, so they got smart and backed off before I hurt them. I've heard you now go out of town for your social life." She arched an eyebrow.

"Hell of a lot safer that way. I guess I won't have to worry anymore. They'll be busy finding you someone now."

"So you think my being here will take the heat off you?" she asked, amused.

"Sure it will, since I made certain they realized I wasn't a good candidate. Not to mention with the kids, you're the ultimate matchmaking challenge. They love that." He leaned across the table to advise in a low voice, "Run for the hills if they suggest Brad Grant. His idea of dinner out is the local fast-food restaurants. Or if he's got coupons for a buy one meal, get the second free, you'll get lucky and be taken to a nicer place."

"And here you take me to a lovely restaurant. I can't believe the ladies gave up on you."

"I had to do a lot of begging, and Mamie stepped in on my behalf. Told them I was the typical sloppy bachelor and would they really want to subject a nice lady to someone as bad as myself?" Cole said with false humility. "They decided it was best to leave me on my own."

"Living in bachelor squalor," she said.

"I do the best I can."

Bree shook her head. "Have you always been this incorrigible or was it just since you moved here?" she asked.

"I've probably always been this way."

"You don't win press awards by being a screwup. Nor do you work for some of the most prestigious magazines by running with the jet set and seducing women all over the world," Bree said. "You are one big fake."

"Don't let it get around." He grinned.

Bree wrapped her shawl more closely about her as they exited the restaurant and waited for the parking valet to fetch Cole's truck.

"I shouldn't have had that cheesecake," she mourned. "I'll need to run an extra ten miles to take it off."

Cole looked her up and down. "I don't think you need to worry."

"Easy for you to say. Jinx will love it, though. He's never happier than when he's running."

Cole tipped the valet and helped Bree into the vehicle. He got behind the wheel and immediately turned on the heater so the warm air would reach their legs. He paused before putting the truck in gear. "You have a curfew?"

She smiled. "Not really. Why, what do you have in mind?"

"A view you can't get just anywhere."

Bree noticed that when they reached the highway, Cole turned right instead of left to head back to Warm Springs.

"I would like to arrive home before dawn," she said, not sure if his idea of a view had anything to do with taking back roads to Mexico.

"It's not far from here, but when you get there, you'll think you're worlds away."

Bree looked out the window as he turned onto a side road that was nothing more than a dirt path. The headlights bounced off inky blackness before illuminating brush and rocks off to the side. It should have given her an eerie feeling, but she felt perfectly safe with him.

"Great place for a murder," she commented. "Nothing around for miles, probably no living things until the off-roaders show up on the weekends. By then a lot of trace evidence would be gone."

"Your mind must never leave the workplace," he marveled.

"I read murder mysteries for relaxation. Nine times out of ten I can guess the identity of the murderer before it's revealed," Bree said, echoing the false humility Cole had shown earlier. "Exactly how far are we going?"

"Afraid you'll run out of glow-in-the-dark bread crumbs before we get there?" he teased.

She chuckled. "I only have fifty pounds or so."

"Just be patient, Fitzpatrick. It'll be worth it. Trust me."

"Oh, I am," she said under her breath, noticing the road they were on was now rising upward.

When Cole rolled to a stop, he unbuckled his belt and opened his door. He walked around and opened Bree's door, helping her out. She almost stumbled on the rocky ground and grabbed hold of his arm to steady herself. He reached down and laced his fingers through hers, tucking her arm in his.

"I hate to tell you this, Becker, but I'm a city girl," she confessed. "The wide-open spaces aren't exactly my thing."

"That's because you haven't seen *these* wide-open spaces," he told her, keeping his steps slow to accommodate her stumbling gait in her high heels. When they reached an outcrop of boulders, he stopped. He waved his hand outward. "This is what I wanted you to see. The universe at your feet, milady."

Bree exclaimed in surprise as she looked down at strings of lights that glittered in myriad patterns before her.

"However did you find this?" she asked, unable to keep her eyes off the fairy-tale land below.

"Took a wrong turn one night and ended up here. Since then I've come up several times with a sleeping bag. The lights are almost hypnotic, aren't they?" His voice was low. "I like to come up here and just regroup."

She put her hand on one of the boulders as she leaned against it. The day's heat still radiated from the stone surface. She turned her head to look up at Cole and thank him for sharing this with her, but the words refused to move past her lips. Maybe there was still a sane part lingering inside her, after all.

"You're very welcome," Cole whispered, lowering his head to hers.

The man knew more than just how to kiss. He knew how to turn her sizzling hot from the top of her head all the way down to her toes. Even his tongue performed magic as it swept through her mouth, taunting her to enter into the sensual world he created. She gripped the top of the boulder, then slowly released it as she leaned closer to Cole. A lemony scent clung to his skin, while the sharp smell of desert brush surrounded them.

She dug her fingers into his shoulders as she felt his hands splay against her lower back, pressing her tightly against his aroused body.

His mouth was warm and seductive against hers, while his hands wove another kind of seduction. She closed her eyes to fight the dizziness that threatened to overtake her. A dizziness that she refused to admit was also due to what Cole was doing to her. The lemony scent she'd noticed before was around her. So different from Fitz, who preferred a spicy scent. The feel of Cole was different. His taste.

It was all too good. And too dangerous.

The need for air suddenly swamped her. She broke the embrace, stepping back. Her chest rose and fell rapidly.

Cole started to step toward her, but she held up her hand to stop him. "Okay, Becker, you've proved your point," she said, drawing in oxygen in hopes it would clear her brain. At the moment, she was sorely pressed to remember her own name.

In the light thrown by the headlights, which Cole had left on, she could see confusion and desire cross his face.

Oh my God. Their kiss had affected him as much as it had her. His world had rocked just as much as hers did.

"I've got to say, Detective, you pack quite a wallop," he murmured. "Right about now, I'm more than willing to confess to any crime you want to accuse me of."

"Give me time. I know I can come up with something appropriate," she retorted, still feeling the world sway around her.

She didn't like the slow grin crossing his face. The man was much too sure of himself. Much too sure of his charm on the opposite sex. She knew she'd seen a trace of surprise on his face after he'd kissed her. Surprise that meant she might have given him a shock, too. But all that was gone now, and he was back to his old self.

"Becker, the best thing for all womankind would be to list you as an illegal substance," she muttered, grateful when her equilibrium started to return.

"I'm flattered, Fitzpatrick. They always say forbidden fruit tastes the best," he said, drawing her back into his arms. "They're right."

Even with a scant second's warning, Bree barely had time to collect her wits before his mouth captured hers again. Her senses swam as the heat of his mouth sent images through her mind's eye that were decidedly X-rated.

If the man could do even a fraction of what her mind was projecting, he was one talented operator. She gripped his arms as she felt her knees buckle, and hung on as his mouth trailed up her jaw to nibble on her ear. He closed his fist around her shawl before it could fall to the ground.

"If I'd known kissing a cop could be this intoxicating I would have tried it much earlier,'' he muttered against her earlobe as he settled her shawl back around her shoulders.

"Wait a minute," she gasped.

"Bree." Her name sounded like a prayer. "Right about now, I'm wishing we were a lot closer to my place."

"And I'm glad we're not." She managed to pull away. She braced herself against the boulder purely because it was safer than holding on to him. Even if he felt so good. She turned around to face the lights flickering in the distance, but they did little to cool the hunger coursing through her veins. "I need to get home." They weren't the words she wanted to say, but she knew they were the ones that needed to be said.

"Bree," he murmured again as he rested his hands on her shoulders. He stood so close to her that she felt his arousal.

"Cole, this isn't a good idea," she lied. She closed her eyes as he began kneading the tension out of her shoulders.

"I don't know. I think it's a great idea." His breath warmed her nape.

She took a deep breath and moved away from the seductive feel of his hands on her before she gave in again. "Maybe you do, but I have to look at the complete picture here. I have a little boy at home who I'm sure is doing his best to remain awake until I come home so I can kiss him good-night." Her mentioning Cody was deliberate. She wanted to remind Cole, and herself, of her obligations. She doubted a seasoned bachelor would appreciate the reminder that she had children.

He flashed a rueful smile. "You're right, it's not fair to the little guy."

She didn't look back to see if he followed as she carefully made her way back toward the truck. She started to reach for the door handle, but the faintest of sounds reached her ears. She didn't react in any way as she waited for Cole to open the door for her.

"What is it?" he whispered.

Bree instinctively knew he wasn't thinking what she was. Or what she was really feeling. His question had nothing to do with the mixed feelings he'd stirred up inside her.

The back of her neck started to tingle as she walked back to the truck. She didn't want to think what it meant.

"It looks like your private little hideaway isn't all that private after all, Becker," she said under her breath. "Whoever it is must have been very quiet when they got up here. I didn't hear a thing, did you?" She deliberately rested back against his chest.

He quickly caught on to her intent. "Like you said, whoever it was was quiet as a church mouse." He played along, bending down and nuzzling her hair. "I guess we don't want our observer thinking we know he's out there."

Bree smiled. She kept her ears wide-open in hopes of hearing something. It wasn't easy with Cole standing so close against her. She tried telling herself they were doing this for the benefit of their watcher. "You guess right. Let's see if we hear anything else." She rested her hands on his wrists, which met at her waist.

Anyone looking at them would have thought they were enjoying a private moment. Bree kept a smile on her lips. She was aware of Cole so close to her, his breath warm on her skin, his lips moving as if he was saying sweet nothings in her ear.

Was this watcher indulging in some voyeuristic activity or was it something more dangerous?

Was there a gun trained on them this very moment?

She wasn't finding it easy to keep her mind on what she was doing when Cole was nibbling her ear erotically.

"Next time I decide to get romantic, I'm choosing the middle of a convention floor," he announced in a low voice. "We'd have a lot more privacy."

She felt a pull deep within her body. It was taking all of her self-control not to turn around and finish what they'd begun. The heat of his body was intoxicating. She could feel the tension, too. She didn't think it was all caused by whoever was spying on them.

Minutes stretched endlessly until she felt a slight relaxation in her muscles. It took her a few minutes more to recover her senses.

"Let's get out of here. Maybe we'll see something on the way back." She pulled open the door.

She doubted they would see anything. Not if the person was

able to get up there without being detected, and could escape unnoticed just as easily. But she was going to hope.

''There're any number of trails out here as long as you have an off-road vehicle.'' Cole helped her into the truck and closed the door after her. He walked around the front of the vehicle, passing through the glare of the headlights, and climbed into his seat. Nothing in his actions hinted that he felt they were under observation. He switched on the engine and turned the vehicle around to move down the dirt trail.

Bree pretended vague interest as she looked out the window.

Cole was right. Anyone with the right kind of vehicle could get up there.

She felt the watcher was still around, secure in his hiding place. And sure he hadn't been detected. She couldn't imagine it was a casual passerby who'd happened to see them, and play the role of Peeping Tom.

The tingling along the back of her neck told her she was right: whoever was up there had deliberately followed them.

As so many times before, she wondered why.

Chapter 9

"Any idea who it could have been back there?" Bree asked as Cole sped down the highway.

"Not a one. How about you? Any ideas come to you? Maybe a jealous ex-boyfriend?"

"Not a one," she parroted.

"Damn, I don't like it," he muttered. "Could we have been followed since the restaurant? Before then? I don't like to think someone's been tailing us all evening."

"I have trouble believing anyone followed us from the restaurant. I didn't sense anyone watching us while we had dinner." Bree searched her memory but came up a blank.

"We should have sensed something," he said grimly. He didn't need to point out that they'd been too occupied with each other to worry about any unwanted watchers. He cursed fluidly under his breath.

"Perhaps we both overreacted. For all we know it could have been a coyote or mountain lion or even a dog back there," she commented, unable to stop glancing in the sideview mirror. There wasn't even a hint of headlights along the flat road.

"Is that what you think?"

"No, but it sounds good." She wrapped the shawl around her even though the interior of the vehicle was warm.

"Let's say you were feeling paranoid about something and you happened to see the people who caused your paranoia. Would you try to creep up on them? Do whatever it took to hear what they were saying?" he asked.

"If I had the mind-set whoever is following us does. And if I had a chance, I'd do it."

He glanced up, looking at the rearview mirror for the same reason she'd checked the mirror on her side.

The road was as empty as it had been two minutes ago.

Cole felt uneasy. Tonight the traffic on the highway wasn't even sporadic. He pressed down harder on the accelerator. The big engine immediately responded and the speedometer needle moved upward.

"If you get stopped for speeding, don't expect me to intercede," Bree said.

"I won't worry if you won't." Cole silently damned himself. He'd wanted to show Bree something beautiful. He hadn't expected to kiss her and find himself practically knocked out of his socks.

What else could have happened up there was a moot point. Considering his reaction, it was probably a good thing it hadn't gone any further. With his luck, a sheriff's copter would have shown up at the wrong time.

He was relieved there weren't any headlights behind them. He'd hate to think he'd have to dig out his cell phone so he'd have it close at hand.

"You don't happen to have a gun in that tiny excuse for a purse, do you?" he asked half-jokingly.

"It's expected I carry a weapon when I'm off duty," she replied.

"Good. I hadn't anticipated running into anything out there, but if we had, it's nice to know one of us had protection."

"Now why doesn't that comfort me?" she asked out loud.

"I don't know. You're the one with the gun." He wasn't going to breathe a sigh of relief until he escorted Bree to her door.

The moment he pulled into the driveway, Cole started to feel the tension in his shoulders start to loosen.

"I don't even want to think what this means," Bree murmured, looking at the house. Not only was the light by the front door burning brightly, it looked like all the lights inside the house were blazing as well.

"Probably makes you want to come over to my place instead," Cole said, feeling his old self return.

She turned around and eyed him. "I don't think so."

He hopped out and walked around to her door. "Wild party? Long distance phone calls? Watching dirty movies?"

"You're talking about your idea of an evening's entertainment, Becker. Not theirs." She nudged him with her elbow as they walked toward the door. "I have to say you sure know how to show a girl a good time. Dinner. A nice view of the county. A Peeping Tom. A mad race back to the house. I can't imagine you'll be able to top this."

"I aim to please." He pulled on her hand to stop her from reaching for the doorknob.

She tipped her head back. "I'd invite you in, but I plan to kill my children for running the electric bill up a good thousand dollars, and if you saw me commit the murders, I'd have to kill you, too."

"Come on, Bree," he murmured, moving closer to her. "Danger's a great aphrodisiac."

"Not when there are three minors in the vicinity."

He didn't miss the sparkle in her eye. The lady could be convinced. He'd started to work on that when the sound of raised voices reached them.

Bree sighed. "Thank you for a lovely dinner, Cole," she said softly.

"You are very welcome." He smiled. "And I'd like to do it again."

"Next time we'll take Jinx. He can flush out the rabbits who might have been spying on us." She dug her key out of her purse. "Drive carefully."

"I will." He took a chance and dropped a light kiss on her

lips. "Good night, Fitzpatrick." He waited until she opened the door and slipped inside the house.

Cole sat in the truck. He drummed his fingers against the steering wheel.

"When I find out who was up there, we are going to have a serious conversation," he muttered as he started up the engine.

Bree was still smiling when she stepped into the family room. She was prepared to referee a battle between David and Sara about who handled the television remote control. She would even accomplish it without resorting to threats. Instead, she found Lacey and David seated on the couch, watching a movie, while Sara, cradling a bowl of popcorn in her lap, slouched in the big easy chair. She noticed her stepmother's presence first. She smirked.

"Hi, Mom," she sang out.

David and Lacey's heads swiveled around. Guilt crossed the young man's face.

"Hi, Mom," he said quietly. "Lacey's parents were gone for the evening and she felt nervous staying there by herself."

Bree mentally gave him points for meeting the problem head-on and not making excuses.

"Did you see or hear something that bothered you, Lacey?" she asked.

"It's not like I haven't been by myself at night before. I have," the girl replied. "I don't know why I felt nervous tonight, but I didn't want to stay there."

After the last hour, Bree could comprehend that feeling.

"Understandable." She unwound her shawl and dropped it on the back of the couch. She was tempted to wrap it around the young girl, who wore a red silk handkerchief halter top and black leather miniskirt. She wondered how Lacey managed not to freeze when she was out in the chilly night air. "Did you leave your folks a note in case they get back before you? I wouldn't want them to worry."

"I left a note, although I know they won't worry," she said with a wry twist of her lips. "Look, I'm sorry. I know you didn't want anyone over when you're not here.'' She started to rise to her feet.

"This is different." Bree gestured for her to remain seated. "Not to mention you two had the best chaperone around." She glanced at Sara, who was busy tossing popcorn into the air and catching it in her mouth.

"At least I let them sit together," she stated. "How was your evening?"

"We had dinner at a very nice restaurant out of town."

"You must have gone to Sadie's Place," Lacey said. "My parents go there a lot." She sat back and crossed her legs.

Bree silently prayed the skirt wouldn't go much higher.

"Yes, we did." She smiled at them. "And if you'll excuse me, I'm going to get out of these grown-up clothes." She shot David a telling glance. She gathered up her shawl and draped it over her arm.

"I'll be right back," he murmured to Lacey as he rose to his feet.

He followed Bree down the hallway.

"She was really scared, Mom," he said. "And with what happened here, I couldn't let her stay there alone. She said she knew it had to be her imagination, but she heard stuff out back and they don't have a dog or anything."

"David, you don't have to explain. I understand." Bree waved her hand dismissively. "Did anything happen around here while I was gone?"

He shook his head. "All was quiet. The kitten went to sleep after she ate a big can of tuna. She's in a box in the laundry room. Cody asked if Jinx could sleep in his room and I said it was fine. He said he was going to stay awake until you got home, but he conked out about fifteen minutes after going to bed." David stood in the doorway, his hands jammed in his jeans' pockets. "So, you like this guy?"

"Cole is very nice." She reached behind her and unfastened her necklace, placing it on her dresser top. "An interesting conversationalist."

"Does he have anything to do with the weird stuff that's gone on around here?" David asked.

"More like he's had some of it, too." She glanced at the clock. "If Lacey wants to use the guest room, she's welcome to as long as she calls her parents to let them know she's staying over."

He looked surprised at her offer.

"David, there is no way I would let you take her home if her parents still aren't there. I don't think she should be alone," she said. "Sara can loan her a nightgown."

"Thanks. I'll tell her. I'd feel better if she stayed." He turned away.

"David, do you think Tim Holloway could have been over there?" she asked.

His features tightened. "I thought of it. I don't care if he is the sheriff's son. He's a bastard who would do anything to get his way. Lacey said he wasn't happy when she broke up with him."

"Think of him as the walking plague and stay out of his way," she recommended. Then something occurred to her. "You said she broke up with him. Did she ever say why?"

He shook his head. "She never wanted to talk about it and I didn't push. I don't think it was good, though. She got really upset about my fight with him."

"Her hero." Bree's lips curved. "Don't stay up too late even if you don't have school tomorrow. And make sure Sara doesn't try to talk Lacey into loaning her that skirt."

"Good night. And thanks." He flashed her a smile.

Bree went into the bathroom and grabbed her robe. It didn't take her long to wash her face and change into her nightclothes. Then she moved quietly down the hallway.

Jinx lifted his head and promptly dropped it when he recognized the late-night intruder. Bree murmured a few words to him before she walked over to the bed, with its Dalmatians comforter hanging halfway to the floor. She straightened the covers and pressed her lips lightly against Cody's forehead.

He half opened his eyes. "Mom?" The word came out a sleepy croak.

"Go back to sleep," she whispered.

"Lacey came over," he mumbled. "Sara said David would

get in trouble cuz she was here. Lacey was nice. She told me Eartha Katt is really pretty. Then she made me hot chocolate and she put lots of marshmallows in it.'' He rolled over and promptly fell back to sleep.

''I'm glad to hear she knew how to get you on her side.'' Bree straightened the covers around his shoulder. ''May the angels come down and be with you through the night. And may they sing sweet songs to you while you sleep. And may you have happy dreams.'' She kissed him again before she left.

Minutes later, she was curled up in bed, tired but unable to sleep. The evening's events crowded her mind.

Not only that, but memories of Cole kissing and caressing her left her feeling unsettled. She told herself it was because it had been a long time since she'd been the object of a man's desire, and naturally, she would eat it up like a hot fudge sundae.

Which had her thinking about the way Cole looked at her. She'd swear it was the same way Eartha Katt had looked at that can of tuna earlier this evening. Bree felt as if she could turn into the main course on the man's menu if she wasn't careful.

''I don't need a man in my life,'' she told herself, rolling over and punching her pillow. She repeated that mantra until she fell asleep.

Bree had no idea how long she'd been sleeping, but the house was dark and quiet when her eyes snapped open.

Jinx had left Cody's bedroom and come into hers. His low throaty growl was her next clue something wasn't right. She slowly turned her head to see the dog standing at the window. Even in the dim light she could tell his body was tense and his fur practically stood straight up. He didn't move from his position.

Bree murmured Jinx's name as she slowly turned and reached into her nightstand drawer, pulling out her weapon. She stealthily made her way to the wall next to the window and flattened herself against it. She'd just started to part the miniblinds to look outside when she heard the distinctive sound of a truck engine growing fainter by the minute.

She knew Jinx would have been standing there from the moment he realized something was wrong. She cursed herself for sleeping so deeply she hadn't been aware sooner.

Not that it would have helped. She knew it had to have been the same truck that was out there before.

"What were you looking for this time?" she whispered. "Thought you'd find Becker's truck parked in my driveway?" She looked down at the German shepherd, who still hadn't relaxed. "Thanks, partner. Jinx, stand down."

He backed up a few steps and sat on his haunches. Bree went into the kitchen and returned with a training treat, which he inhaled.

"Do me a favor. Next time let me know when they arrive," she told the dog.

She climbed into bed again and settled back. Sleep refused to return. She replaced her weapon in the drawer and picked up the phone.

"Maybe I should put this number on speed dial."

"Yeah?" The sleepy growl sounded intoxicating to her still-heightened senses.

"Not a morning person, are we?" She settled the covers around her knees. "I had a visitor tonight."

"The truck?" Now he sounded more alert.

"Jinx let me know. It was leaving when I tried to get a look. Maybe I should set up a motion sensor light out there. Give my visitor a surprise next time. Do you think installing a thousand-watt bulb would be a bit too much?"

"Damn," Cole mumbled. "What the hell is going on?"

"That I figured out. Someone thinks you have me convinced of something. After this, I'd say we were wrong. There was someone at the restaurant, but there was nothing going on to alert us. Only when we were out in a place where there shouldn't have been any other human beings could we sense someone there. Just as there was no reason for anyone to check on me at—" she leaned over to glance at the clock "—four-thirty in the morning."

"Four-thirty?" Cole groaned. "You couldn't have waited a few hours before calling to tell me all this? What is it with you and middle of the night phone calls?"

"I wasn't going to wait until you were awake and alert, and I couldn't catch you off guard. I would have asked Jinx to make the call, but he always calls those psychic hotlines." She pulled out a notebook and began writing.

"What are you doing?" Cole asked.

"Talking to you."

"No, you sound distracted. You're doing something else at the same time." A rustle of sheets sounded faintly on his end.

"I'm writing down everything that's happened from the beginning. I should have documented this from the get-go."

"So when you got inside, did you have to break up any wild parties?"

"I guess they decided to behave tonight. What do you know about Lacey Danvers?"

"Ah, the lovely Lacey. She dated Tim Holloway for two years. Amazing they stayed together so long, since he treated her pretty lousy. Their breakup could have rivaled World War II for fireworks. Tim insists he dropped her. I'd hazard a good guess it was the other way around."

"What about her parents?"

"Her parents?" he repeated.

"Yes, parents," she said, losing her patience, but keeping her voice low in case anyone else was awake. She'd noticed Lacey had closed her door when she went to bed. "You know. The adults who supposedly are in charge of her."

"Ken Danvers is an extremely successful general contractor. Maria Danvers's major hobby is spending her husband's money. They like to party."

"And their daughter?" Bree already didn't like what she was hearing.

"Unlimited spending money, credit cards and next to no supervision. A year ago a kid made the mistake of calling her a slut. Tim practically turned the kid into hamburger. It was written off as self-defense."

"Is that all you know?"

"I told you gossip is almost as popular as cable around here. What I really think is that she's basically a nice kid who acts the way she does because she doesn't want anyone to know how hurt she really is.''

"Cody told me she made him hot chocolate with lots of marshmallows and she told him his kitten is pretty. He's now hers for life," Bree said. "She was here when I got home because she was nervous about staying home alone. I wouldn't be surprised if Tim hadn't been hanging around her place.''

"I wouldn't be surprised, either. He might have hoped she'd get scared enough to come running back to him.''

"I told her she could spend the night, since she didn't know when her parents would be coming home," she told him.

"You're really good at this mom thing," he said. "Did you always want to wrap up cop and mom into one package?''

"Not exactly. What about you? Were you practicing your reporter skills when you were a kid? Did you ask your third grade teacher how she felt when she found a frog in her desk drawer?''

"Nah. I would have been the one to put the frog in there. When I was a kid I wanted to be an astronaut," Cole confided.

His admission surprised her. "Really?''

"Yep.''

"What happened?''

"I found out I was afraid of heights.''

"Are you ever serious about anything?''

"Think about it, Fitzpatrick, and you'll know exactly what I'm serious about," he said quietly. "'Night.''

It took a moment for Bree to realize he'd hung up.

It didn't take her even that long to figure out what he was serious about. And that took her breath away.

Bree's next wake-up call was also animal related.

"Mom." The whisperer had cinnamon-and-milk-scented breath. "Mom, are you awake?''

She didn't open her eyes. "I'm sorry, Mom is not available to take your call. Please leave a message after the beep. *Beeep!*'' At the last word, she reached out and grabbed Cody, pulling him onto the bed.

Cody's shriek mixed with Bree's when she realized her son

was holding his kitten. The kitten meowed and dug in her tiny claws.

"Lacey made pancakes," Cody told his mother, moving off and bouncing up and down on the bed. "Cinnamon ones and they're really good. Come and have some."

"That I will do." She tossed the covers aside.

"Jinx got mad last night," Cody said, watching her pull on her robe. "He growled when he got up and left my room. So he must have heard something, huh?"

"Probably a rabbit," Bree said blithely, scooping the kitten up off her pillow before she could make herself at home. "Let's see if there're any pancakes left."

"Jinx doesn't chase rabbits. He knows he's not supposed to," Cody said, following his mother down the hallway. "He's a police dog," he reminded her unnecessarily.

"Even police dogs think about chasing rabbits." She circled his shoulders with her arm and hugged him.

"Mom!" Sara stormed down the hallway, her slim figure vibrating with fury, her brown eyes spitting fire. "She made breakfast."

"You make it sound as if she concocted some horrible poison." Bree kept her voice low. She could hear Lacey's and David's voices coming from the kitchen, although she couldn't make out actual words.

"I cook on Saturday mornings," Sara announced, crossing her arms in front of her chest.

"Lacey is our guest, and if she wanted to cook, I'd say you should graciously let her. And I also suggest you offer to do the dishes."

"It seems I had no choice."

"That's cuz you didn't want to get up and cook and Lacey did," Cody announced.

Bree glanced at one then the other. Sara looked as if she wanted to pounce on her little brother. Cody held Eartha Katt protectively in his arms and glared at his sister.

"No more battles," Bree said in a firm voice. "We will sit down and have a friendly family breakfast. Am I understood?" She made eye contact with each one to insure they got the message. Sara nodded reluctantly. Cody's head bobbed up and down. "Good. Now, I am going to try some of those cinnamon pancakes." She walked away, leaving them behind.

When she entered the kitchen, she found Lacey and David standing close together at the sink. Lacey looked over her shoulder, saw Bree and blushed hotly, moving away from David and toward the frying pan. The rich scent of cinnamon hung in the air.

"Good morning," she said awkwardly. "I hope you don't mind that I made breakfast."

"Mind? Cooking has never been one of my favorite activities," Bree admitted, as she poured herself a cup of coffee. "I'm sure the kids already told you that."

"There's been more than a few casseroles that are better left forgotten," David said, a twinkle in his eye.

"*Forgotten* being the operative word." Bree sat down as Lacey set a plate of pancakes in front of her. She noticed a covered plate in the middle of the table. Investigation revealed crisp bacon. A few bites of pancake and Bree knew she was in heaven. "These are fantastic," she declared.

"It's a recipe I made up when I used to fool around with different ideas. Like your casseroles, some of them weren't too memorable." Lacey smiled.

"More, please!" Cody hopped into his chair.

Bree noticed that Sara slipped into the kitchen. She poured herself a glass of juice before sitting at the table.

Bree concentrated on her food and listened to the conversation around her. She listened to David telling Lacey he'd run her home when she was ready and that he'd drop Sara off at the library.

"Lacey, you can cook here anytime you want," Bree told her. "Now if you all don't mind, Jinx and I are going for a much needed run."

"I have a soccer game this afternoon," Cody reminded her.

"And I will be there," she promised as she rose to her feet.

Ten minutes later, Bree adjusted the leash that attached to a special belt wrapped around her waist, along with her fanny pack, which held her cell phone and identification. Jinx's ears twitched and his body quivered in anticipation of one of his favorite activities. She started out at a slow lope along the side of the road. Jinx kept pace with her.

"I don't know, boy," Bree said. "It seems like there's a romance brewing. He's too young to get serious about a girl. Any girl. Even one who can cook." As her muscles started to warm up, she stepped up the pace. "And I'm not ready to think about romance. Even with a charmer like Cole Becker. He's got one agenda and I've got another. And never the twain shall meet."

Bree's first indication something was wrong was Jinx lifting his head and swiveling it to the side. His growl came a bare second before a large vehicle sped past them, so closely she barely had time to release Jinx's leash as she dove off the side of the road to avoid being hit. By the time she looked up, the truck was already racing out of sight, but the distinctive sound of the engine wouldn't leave her memory. She'd heard it last night.

"Damn!" She sat up, brushing dirt and pebbles off her hands. She winced as she felt a few aches traveling up her limbs.

Jinx whined and pawed at one of her legs. He cocked his head to one side as if asking if she was all right.

Bree got up slowly, noticing the scrapes along her legs and arms and the tear in her tank top. She could feel the imprint of her fanny pack against her aching side.

She looked down at the dog.

"If someone is trying to tick me off, they are sure going about it the right way."

Chapter 10

"What in the world happened to you?" Greta stopped and turned off the small vacuum cleaner she was pushing across the carpet. "Tell me the other guy looks worse."

"No such luck, considering he was inside a big truck and I was on the road. Are you telling me I look that bad? And here I thought I looked pretty good," Bree joked, walking slowly into the shop.

"You look as if you got into a fight at the playground." She moved behind the counter.

"More like a truck that wanted the strip of road I happened to be on. Could I get four large coffees to go?"

"Emerald Creme, French Roast or Sumatran Blend?"

"Make them all French Roast." Bree looked ruefully down at her legs, bare under her denim skirt. "I tried putting on jeans but the scrapes are too fresh. I feel like I'm ten years old."

Greta paused in pouring the coffee into large cups. "You look it, too. So you're telling me you were run off the road?"

She nodded. "Jinx and I went out for a run this morning and a big truck appeared out of nowhere. Came by so fast we had no option but to get off the road before we were tossed off. Jinx ended up better off than me.''

Greta clucked her tongue and shook her head. ''That's terrible. You could have been badly hurt.''

Bree had thought the same thing but didn't want to voice the thought.

''All I know is if I see that truck, the driver is getting more than a ticket for reckless driving,'' she muttered, laying money for the coffee on the counter.

''If he's cute, can I help with the strip search?'' Greta asked with a hopeful gleam in her eye.

''By the time I finish with him, there won't be anything left to search,'' Bree said grimly, opening a glass container and pulling out a handful of large cookies. She laid down money for those, too. ''This truck has haunted me long enough,'' she muttered.

Greta paused. ''Haunted you? Bree! What is going on? You mean you've seen the truck before?''

''I've only heard it a couple of times,'' she explained. ''It has a distinctive sound in the engine that you don't forget. Otherwise, all I know is that it's a dually, a dark color, and seems to like to hang out at my house late at night.''

''Maybe it's teenagers looking for a quiet make-out spot?'' she suggested, handing over a bag for the cookies.

Bree shook her head. ''No kid, no matter how desperate, would park practically in my backyard. Not with Jinx on guard. He knows the difference between friend and foe.''

''The difference?'' Greta immediately picked up on her tone and wording. She looked concerned. ''Bree, what's going on? And what about your dinner date with Cole? How did that go?''

Bree glanced at her watch. She wasn't sure she wanted to talk about either situation just yet. Although she was greatly tempted to talk about Cole. ''I've got to get to Cody's game.''

''You're off the hook. For now. Lunch on Monday,'' Greta stated. ''Be at The Eatery at one.''

''You're on.'' She grabbed the cookies and cups and almost ran for the door.

Bree raced over to the park where the junior soccer league

played, and quickly parked next to David's truck. She scanned the grassy area and found David, Lacey and Sara seated on folding beach chairs, with an empty one next to Sara.

"Anything happen yet?" Bree asked, handing a coffee cup to each before dropping onto the empty chair.

"What kind of cookies?" David almost pounced on the bag. He opened it and sniffed the contents.

"Citrus with white chocolate chips."

He made a face. "You couldn't have gotten oatmeal, chocolate chip or even sugar? You had to take citrus, didn't you? I'm buying some of those slice and bake cookies for the next game."

"Barbarian." Lacey grinned, taking one of the cookies and biting into it. "Thanks, Mrs. Fitzpatrick."

"Call me Bree," she told the girl. "I won't feel as old then." She stretched her legs out in front of her.

"The referee is a jerk," David announced. "But I heard he's an equal opportunity jerk." He slanted a look at his stepmother. "Cody begged me to make sure you don't do anything."

Bree rolled her eyes. "I already promised him I wouldn't pull my weapon out. Next time he'll want me to take a blood vow."

Lacey looked from one to the other in confusion.

"Mom gets a little overheated when the referee makes a bad decision," David explained. "Last year, they gave her a trophy for being the parent thrown out of the most games. She still holds the league record. No mother has been thrown out of more games than her."

"It wasn't that bad!" Bree held up her hand as she defended herself. "I behaved when you were in Little League."

David rolled his eyes. "The umpire threatened to get a restraining order."

"I merely suggested the umpire have his eyes checked," she said huffily.

"She was a lot more forceful than that," Sara interjected. "She told him to go back to umpire school. That's when she was banned from the rest of the season's games. Mom is the stage mother from hell."

"I sure wish I'd seen that." Cole dropped down on the grass next to Bree. He looked up and smiled.

"What are you doing here?" she crossly demanded, feeling that the world was picking on her.

"I always report on the games," he said amiably. "From what I've heard, I might have even more to report this time. My readers love human interest stories."

"Don't bet on it." She switched her coffee cup to her other hand when she noticed him eyeing it. "You should have brought your own."

"Didn't have time. Overslept. Got a crank call last night that kept me awake." He flashed her a wicked grin.

"I heard the newspaper business can be brutal to one's lifestyle." She jumped up when she saw that Cody had the ball and was guiding it toward his goal. "Go for it, Cody!"

"What happened to you?" Cole asked, noticing the cuts and scrapes on Bree's legs.

"I had a little tussle with a big truck on the road this morning when Jinx and I went out for our run. The truck won." She kept her voice low so she wouldn't be overheard.

He lifted an eyebrow. Her saying it was a truck piqued his interest. "Any truck in particular?" he murmured. "You didn't happen to get a license plate number, did you?"

Bree shook her head. "I was too busy rolling in the dirt and making sure I didn't get run over. I don't think he meant to hit me. I think he just wanted to give me a good scare."

Cole kept his gaze focused on her face. "Judging by that gleam in your eye, I'd say you weren't all that frightened."

"Too bad I couldn't have at least tried shooting his tires out." She kept her voice low and a smile on her face, but Cole couldn't miss the fury shooting out of her eyes.

If he was a nice guy, he'd feel real sorry for the driver when Bree caught up with him.

"Oh come on!" Bree leaped to her feet again. "There was nothing wrong with that goal!"

"Mom, you promised," Sara reminded her.

"I promised not to shoot anyone," she said. "But when referees are outright blind, I will point it out." She ignored a woman who glared at her.

"Blind referee's wife," Cole said under his breath. "She's also his biggest supporter."

"Then she should teach him the rules."

Cole watched with open amazement as Bree revealed her rabid soccer mom side. Sara and David tried to remind her of promises she'd made and, so far, had broken. Bree cheerfully ignored them, too.

"Is she always like this?" Cole asked David.

"This is actually a good day," he replied. "She's usually much worse."

"What did you do with her on the bad days? Put her in handcuffs?"

"Dad thought about it a few times. He explained to her she wasn't helping and she told him to stuff a sock in it."

"In other words, stand clear."

Both teenagers nodded.

Cole decided to sit back and enjoy the show. At one point, he happened to look across the field. A man stood at the edge of the parking lot next to the grassy field. Cole figured he stood there with the sun at his back so it wouldn't be easy to identify him. The man made doubly sure of hiding his identity by keeping his hat tugged down low on his forehead. His mirrored sunglasses obscured half his face.

"Think we're being watched again?" Cole muttered.

Bree heard him and turned her head just enough to see what he was looking at.

"An interested father?" she asked for his ears only.

"If it was, you'd think he'd be over on this side of the field. And his interest seems more in us than in the kids. Think I should go over and ask him what his problem is?"

"I doubt he'll be around by the time you get there."

Sure enough, a moment later the man turned and walked away.

Bree studied the man's build, the way he moved, but there was nothing distinctive about them. The bright afternoon sun didn't help, either.

She turned back with the intention of focusing on the game.

"Whoever it was knew enough to stand where the sun would be in our eyes in case we noticed him," she said quietly.

"Not to mention we were so busy watching the game we don't know how long he was there," Cole replied. "But I'd say he was there long enough if he wanted to make a point. What do you think, Detective?"

"He's thrown the ball into our court." She immediately spied a foul. She started to rise up out of her chair again, then dropped back down. "No, if I say one more thing, Cody will make sure they ban me from the field forever, and I couldn't bear that."

"Nothing more dangerous than a soccer mom," Cole quipped, quickly ducking to avoid Bree's playful smack upside the head.

"Okay, give," Greta ordered when Bree met her for lunch on Monday.

"Which part?" she asked with an innocent, wide-eyed look.

Greta held out her hands as if she was going to strangle Bree. "I don't care where you start, because I want to hear it all. Your accident. Your date with Cole. The more lascivious, the better."

"There's nothing lascivious to tell."

"Anyone who says there's nothing means the exact opposite. Why don't you start off by telling me about your date with Cole Becker? After that, you can tell me what turned you into a walking train wreck Saturday."

"I wouldn't call what we had a date. And I wouldn't exactly call what happened to me Saturday a battle with a train," she argued. She looked askance at the large bowl set in front of her. "Excuse me, but I ordered a garden salad."

"That's right. Enjoy," the waitress said cheerfully before moving off.

"I only wanted a salad, not the whole garden." Bree stared at the small scarecrow set in the middle of the bowl. "If a crow shows up, I'm out of here."

"Not a chance. I'm not letting you go anywhere until you tell me about your date with Cole."

Bree sighed. "I told you, it wasn't a date. All we did was go out to dinner Friday night. Two friends sharing a meal. That was all.''

"Did he pay or did you?"

"He paid."

"Then it was a date," Greta said triumphantly. "So tell me everything that happened."

"Let's see." Bree looked lost in thought as she tapped her forefinger against her chin. "I had scallops. He had steak. We also had a very nice wine. During dinner, we discussed our mutual work. After dinner, he took me home." Not for anything was she going to disclose that they'd gone for a drive, or what had happened. Or that she'd learned the man's kisses were not only highly illegal, but left her wanting a great deal more.

She felt there were some things that didn't need to be shared. Especially Cole kissing her and her kissing him back. She willed herself not to blush as the memories danced through her head.

Greta lowered her voice. "You discussed work? My God, you have been out of the dating arena too long. You can discuss his work by asking him about it and then listening as if it's the most fascinating subject in the world, of course. Cole did write some incredible stories from all over the world. And your work is fascinating. Speaking of which—" she arched an eyebrow "—what's the reason for your looking like a playground accident?" She picked up the shaker and sprinkled pepper over her salad.

"It wasn't anything unusual. In fact, it happens more than you think. A driver takes a corner too sharp and fast. Or he weaves across lanes. The runner is either hit, or if he's lucky, just run off the road. I was running against traffic, but this truck seemed to sneak up on me. Luckily, Jinx's reflexes are faster than mine and he realized what was going on. He caught my attention in time." She stabbed a romaine leaf. "It's just one of the hazards of running out in the open like that."

"You were running against traffic, so the driver would have seen you. There's no excuse for what he did," Greta guessed correctly. "It can't be deliberate because you haven't been in town long enough to make any enemies. Even though I understand David is now at the top of Tim Holloway's list. And not a list of his best friends, either.''

''All because David wanted to explain proper manners to the school bully. I can give you a logical reason for my accident. Someone I once arrested in L.A. was out this way for a drive. He happened to see me and saw his chance to get even,'' Bree said, tongue in cheek.

Greta's opinion of Bree's deduction was less than complimentary.

''Stranger things have happened,'' Bree countered. ''I heard of a burglary detective who was down in Texas on a fishing trip. One night in a bar, he gets friendly with this other guy who's also down there fishing. The other guy keeps insisting he knows him, just can't figure out from where. Turns out the detective had arrested him five years before for a rash of burglaries.''

''Sounds like some of my dates. And I don't think you're writing this off as an accident. I saw you when you came in Saturday and you seemed pretty angry at this guy.''

''Of course I was mad. I ended up eating dirt,'' Bree grumbled. ''Let me tell you, if I hear of it happening to anyone else, I'll track him down. Until then, it's just one of those things that can happen on country roads.'' Bree used her fork for emphasis.

Greta glanced to her left. ''Well, well, well,'' she murmured. ''Look who we have here. Think we should invite him in?''

Bree followed her glance, to find Cole standing at the window looking in at them. He stood in his usual semislouch with his hands jammed in his pants pockets. His head was cocked to one side, while his crooked smile was guaranteed to fan flames in more than one woman.

Right now that lethal smile was directed right at Bree.

Her stomach felt as if she'd suddenly fallen off the roof of a tall building.

''Just dinner, huh? Nothing special?'' Greta smiled and waved at him. She gestured for him to come in and join them.

''Don't do that!'' Bree muttered.

''Too late.'' She smirked.

"Ladies." Cole looked at Greta, then swung his gaze to Bree. "Hey there, Slugger."

"I did not hit that referee," she said between clenched teeth.

Greta's head swiveled from one to the other. Her eyes were alight with interest as she rested her chin on her laced fingers.

"He thought you were going to hit him, along with arresting him for giving bad calls."

"I have never used my position to intimidate someone," she insisted. "Especially an idiot like Norman, our so-called umpire, who wouldn't have appreciated the irony."

"I've got to tell you this woman has an incredible vocabulary," Cole told Greta. "And in deference to all the kids, she didn't use one profane word. I was impressed." Without waiting for further invitation, he sat down in the chair next to Bree.

"Hey, Cole, your cheeseburger will be ready in no time." One of the waitresses breezed by.

"Thanks, Diane." Still smiling, he turned to Bree. "How are your legs?"

"The usual. Healing and itching. How about you?"

"No one tried to run me off the road." He shot a quick glance at Greta, who unabashedly eavesdropped. "Any suspects in sight?"

"Not a one. Why, did you come up with any ideas?" Bree picked up her glass of iced tea.

"Nope." He sat back as a plate of food was deposited in front of him.

"Look at the time." Greta made a show of studying her watch. "I've got to get back to the shop." She pulled out her wallet.

Cole shook his head. "My treat."

"Thank you, darling," she drawled. She turned to Bree. "Keep me informed." With a wave of her hand she was gone.

"You going to have some free time anytime soon?" Cole asked, keeping his voice low.

"I just had some." Bree nibbled on her salad. "Why?"

"There's someone I'd like to talk to and I was hoping you could go with me. Do you mind?" He accepted the ketchup bottle she passed to him. "Thanks."

''Any reason why you feel you need someone with you, or are you hoping I can do something in an official sense?'' she asked, stealthily filching a French fry from his plate.

''I thought you might think of something I don't. Interested?''

She paused. ''I don't go on duty tomorrow until early afternoon, so my morning is free.''

''I'll even buy breakfast,'' he offered.

''How early are we talking about?'' she asked suspiciously.

''Eight.''

''Then I'll take the offer of breakfast.'' Bree stole another fry and dipped it in the pool of ketchup decorating a corner of Cole's plate. ''And brief me on who we're going to see.''

''Tomorrow,'' he promised. ''I'll pick you up about quarter to eight for breakfast and mission preparation.''

She smiled sardonically. ''Be still my heart.''

''I guess I should have specified I didn't want my breakfast served in a cardboard container.'' Bree glared at Cole.

''Are you kidding? It's the best place in town for that first meal of the day. I really like how they serve the hash browns as little cubes,'' he said, popping one into his mouth. ''And French toast sticks.'' He picked one up and dipped it in syrup.

She sipped her coffee. ''When I get up early when I don't have to, I expect more. But since you're paying I'll make sure to order seconds. So wipe the syrup off your face and tell me about where we're going.''

''We're going to visit Estelle Timmerman,'' he replied.

Bree recognized the name. ''I met her the day I gave a talk at the senior center.''

''Her husband died about ten months ago,'' he continued. ''Choked on a piece of liver.''

''I hate to tell you this, Becker, but it happens,'' she said. ''If no one in the vicinity knows the Heimlich maneuver, the poor person doesn't have a chance.''

''I agree with you but for some reason Estelle doesn't think so,'' he replied. ''She's positive something went wrong. She called me and asked me to check into it. She said if anyone would know what to do, I would. That's why we're going to talk to her.''

Bree shook her head. ''It doesn't make sense Cole. Unless,'' she paused, ''she's using it as an excuse to talk to us.''

He nodded. ''I thought that, too. That's why I told her we'd come by. If nothing else, maybe we can find a way to assure her her husband's death wasn't intentional.''

When Bree met Estelle Timmerman again she was once more struck by how sad she was.

And how tiny. The woman couldn't have hit the five-foot mark if she stood on her toes. She wore a flowered housedress and pink fluffy slippers, and had her gray hair pinned up in a bun. She said a few chirpy words to a parakeet housed in a cage, then led them into the living room.

''Are you certain you wouldn't like some tea?'' she asked them as they sat on a turquoise couch that Bree thought could have come straight off a 1960s movie set.

''No, thank you, Mrs. Timmerman.'' Bree smiled. ''We just finished our breakfast.''

The elderly lady's head bobbed up and down in understanding. ''I always enjoy a few cups in the morning,'' she confided, holding a paper-thin china cup.

''Mrs. Timmerman, you said you wanted to talk about your husband,'' Cole prodded.

''Yes, my Bernie.'' She turned misty-eyed. ''We were married for fifty-six years. I still miss him.'' She pulled a handkerchief out of her sleeve and dabbed her eyes.

''I understand.'' Bree reached across and covered her hand. ''I lost my husband a year ago.''

''Ah, then you do know what I feel.'' She smiled sadly. ''And you're so young.'' After a moment she continued. ''Bernie didn't want me to worry, you see.''

''Worry about what, Mrs. Timmerman?'' Cole asked gently.

''Please call me Estelle. He didn't want me to worry about a thing,'' she replied. ''Bernie always took care of everything. He said that was his job, while mine was to take care of the house and our children. We have three. Two daughters and a son. But Bernie started to worry about things.''

"What type of things, Estelle?" Bree pressed. "Did he ever tell you exactly what worried him?"

Estelle lowered her head and stared into her teacup for a long time. "I wasn't supposed to say anything," she whispered. "It was a secret."

Bree and Cole exchanged glances.

"I understand you feel uncomfortable revealing a confidence," Bree said slowly. "But sometimes it's good to talk about things that might bother you. And this secret bothers you, doesn't it?"

Estelle looked off to the side, as if she was listening to someone else.

"It does bother me," she whispered finally. "I had to promise not to tell anyone. But now, I feel I did wrong in making that promise. That's why I called Mr. Becker. He writes lovely editorials, you know. I particularly enjoyed the one he wrote saying that just because people were over the age of sixty didn't mean they couldn't be active. That's when I decided to go on a cruise. I'd never been on one before, but my neighbor, Katherine Carter, had and said they're lovely. I took one to Alaska and I thoroughly enjoyed myself."

"I'm glad to know my editorial helped," Cole said sincerely. If he was impatient for the elderly woman to impart her information, he didn't show it.

Bree silently congratulated him on his forbearance. She decided he must have come up against subjects who weren't easy to interview, ones who needed to be coaxed a word at a time. A bare nod of his head told her to continue.

"Have you done anything else other than the cruise?" she asked.

"Oh yes. I take classes at the senior center," the elderly woman replied. "And I've gone on a few day trips to Laughlin. Renee is always after me to go with one of the groups."

"I'm sure Bernie would be glad to know you keep busy," Bree told her. "I can't imagine he would want you unhappy."

"It was just that Bernie worried what would happen to me when he was gone," Estelle explained. "That's why it happened."

Cole leaned forward. "Why what happened, Estelle?"

Her head snapped up as she heard the phone ring. "Would you excuse me? That could be my doctor's office about a prescription I need." She got up and walked into the kitchen.

Bree and Cole exchanged glances as they heard Estelle's chirpy greeting, then silence. When she returned, her expression was stiff.

"Was it your doctor?" Bree asked.

"No, it was a wrong number," she mumbled, sitting down.

Bree leaned forward and picked up the elderly woman's hand. She worried when she found it ice-cold to the touch.

"Estelle?" she gently prompted, rubbing her hand between her own. "Are you all right? Is there something we can do to help?"

"No, I'm fine." Estelle licked her lips. "I'm sorry, I forgot what we were talking about." She touched her forehead with her fingertips. "I forget so many things nowadays," she tittered nervously. "Old age, I guess."

Cole started to say something, but Bree shook her head.

"Estelle, are you sure you're feeling all right?" she asked softly. "Do you need me to call anyone?"

"No, but I do think I need to lie down." She refused to look at them. "I hope you don't mind."

"Not at all." Bree's warm smile belied the frustration she felt inside. She'd hoped for something. Even a tiny hint. "You still have the magnet I gave you, right?" She noted the woman's nod. "Then if you ever feel the need to talk to someone, please don't hesitate to call me. No matter what time of day or night, no matter what you need to talk about, call me. Will you do that, Estelle?"

The woman's lips were pursed together as if she was afraid they'd tremble and reveal her agitation. She nodded but said nothing.

Bree touched her shoulder as she and Cole left the house.

"You know what happened in there, don't you?" he said, as he held the truck door open for Bree. "Estelle lied to us. That wasn't a wrong number. Someone found out we were here and called her with the intention of scaring the hell out of her." He looked up and down the street, as if he was hoping to see the culprit. "Dammit!" He pounded the top of the vehicle with his fist. "There's no denying Bernie's death was an accident. So why all the secrecy?"

"Because something has made her afraid," she said. "Talk about lousy timing. For all we know, she could think his death was an accident, but she used it as an excuse to get us to come here. Then she goes into the kitchen to answer the phone. When she comes back, she's so afraid she tells a blatant lie and asks us to leave. Which means she knows something important. And now we won't know what that is," she murmured.

Cole's expression was somber as he slid behind the wheel. "I don't like it, Bree. There was no reason to frighten a sweet lady like Estelle."

"Yes, there was, Cole," she said quietly, turning to him. "An excellent reason. Why would someone call her and spook her so much that they knew she wouldn't say anything more to us? They're afraid we're getting too close to the truth."

Chapter 11

"Tell me something, Fitzpatrick. Do we not give you enough work?" Sheriff Holloway stood at her desk. "Now I realize we're not a super crime capital like L.A. We don't get all that many big-time felonies like the ones you've investigated in the past. But I figured our little misdemeanors would be enough to keep you occupied."

Bree experienced a sinking feeling as she looked up into the face of her fierce-eyed superior. He looked as if he was ready to throttle her. She issued a hand command to Jinx, who'd straightened up the moment Roy's harsh voice washed over them. The dog lay back down, but his gaze never left the man looming over Bree.

She had only to look at her superior's face to know she was in big trouble.

"Actually, Sheriff, I'm able to keep myself more than occupied," she said, mentally wondering what sin she was allegedly guilty of.

He leaned over, planting his palms on the top of her desk,

not caring that papers shifted every which way. Bree grabbed a few pages before they fell to the floor.

"Then why don't you tell me something? Why don't you tell me why you're wasting your time studying closed cases when you already have more than enough to do?" he demanded, leaning down until they were almost nose to nose. "I don't know about you, but I call looking through old cases a waste of taxpayers' money. Don't you?" His words washed over her like acid.

Several curses flew through Bree's head. This was the first time she'd seen the sheriff angry. That she was his target wasn't pleasant.

"I don't believe I have ever wasted taxpayers' money, Sheriff," she said carefully. "I was merely familiarizing myself with past cases to get a feel for what's gone on in the county. I also did it on my own time. I can't imagine why this was even brought to your attention."

Roy straightened up. "Maybe that's why I check every officer's computer log. To make sure they're not getting on the Internet for other purposes or to play games. When yours shows you going through closed cases instead of open ones, I have to wonder why you're bothering with them. If you need to familiarize yourself with what goes on in the county, look to current cases. Maybe you can see something others haven't and we can get those cases closed. Wouldn't you agree that's a better plan?" he growled in her face. "I gotta tell you, Fitzpatrick, the last I looked, we have plenty of open cases you can deal with. Hell, the next thing we know you'll be turning molehills into the freakin' Swiss Alps!"

Bree stiffened. The sparks in her eyes would have quelled many a man.

"One thing I pride myself on, Sheriff Holloway, is my professionalism," she stated in a hard voice. "I was curious as to the large number of seniors' deaths in the past few years. Looking at the cases showed me how they were handled."

Roy's jaw seemed to have been carved from stone. "If I were you, *Detective,* I'd use your extra time to work on your family life. It seems your stepson has a hot temper. It's not good for a kid to act out so violently. I wouldn't like to see things happen here the way they have in other high schools.''

There were a lot of things Bree wanted to say at that moment. All of them would have bounced her out of the department without further ado. She dug down deep and drew on every ounce of self-restraint she possessed.

''I always thought it took two to make a fight, Sheriff,'' she said quietly. ''From what I've heard, your son has been in trouble like this before. I've had a talk with my stepson and we agreed the best thing he can do is stay out of your son's way. I'm sure your boy will do the same. Was there anything else you needed to discuss?'' She refused to back down.

His jaw worked furiously. ''Not at the moment.'' He pushed himself off the desk and walked away.

''It would have been easier if he'd just skinned you alive,'' Don, one of the deputies, muttered as he walked by. ''At least it would have been a hell of a lot easier on the ears.''

''Don.'' Bree waited for the man to turn around before she spoke again. ''Has the sheriff always been this sensitive about so many deaths around here that were not natural?''

''I think Roy's sensitive about any case he can't close. He takes his work seriously. But nothing ever turned up wrong. If anything had, you can be sure he wouldn't have stopped until he found the culprit and hauled him in to jail.''

''Thanks,'' she murmured, settling back in her chair. She replayed both conversations in her head. Roy's obvious hostility. Don's explanation that should have made everything clear and logical. Should have settled things in her mind.

The funny feeling in the pit of her stomach said otherwise.

She looked up and noticed Roy leaving the station. She picked up the phone.

''We need to talk.''

''Am I supposed to give you a password?'' Cole asked, when Bree opened the front door and gestured for him to enter. Jinx stood by her side with his ears cocked forward and his eyes fastened on Cole.

"It might not hurt." She walked down the hallway. "Want something to drink?"

"What you got?"

"Wine, coffee, Coke, milk," she said over her shoulder as she walked into the kitchen.

"Something tells me I'd be better off with the wine."

"Go on into the family room. I'll be back with the wine."

"Where are the kids?" he asked, walking into the room. He glanced warily at Jinx, who followed him.

"I asked David to take them to the movies," Bree said from the kitchen. "Since it had to be G-rated, I'm sure he'll expect me to owe him and Sara big time. Especially since Cody chose one of those animated films with some weird characters that morph into something else when they want to save the world. Funny thing. Cody would have preferred staying home and playing in his tree house with his friends than going to the movies. That's a new twist."

Cole settled onto the couch, while Jinx sat back on his haunches a few feet away.

"If I promise not to jump your partner's bones, will you promise not to tear my throat out?" he asked the dog.

He decided the canine's silence was a yes.

Cole glanced at the pile of file folders scattered across the coffee table, and was about to open one when Bree entered the room carrying two glasses and an open bottle of wine.

"It's that bad, is it?" he said wryly, taking the glasses and the bottle out of her hands. He poured the wine and handed a glass to her.

"It seems Holloway found out I was looking into old cases," she told him as she sat down on the couch next to him. She lifted the glass to her lips and drank deeply.

"Good thing we're not drinking the hard stuff," Cole muttered, watching her. "You'd be on the floor in no time if you downed it like that."

"Don't tempt me," she said tightly, setting the glass down.

"I've got some good single malt in there." She shook her head. "The man was furious with me for studying those cases. He accused me of wasting taxpayers' dollars." Her upper lip curled.

"How did he know what you were doing?" he asked.

"He said he looks at his officers' computer logs. He likes to make sure we're not playing on the Internet."

Cole shook his head. "Do you think he's suspicious?"

"I'm sure he is. We've already figured out he investigated most of the accident cases that were suspicious."

"Warm Springs doesn't have a large department, so it's not unheard of for him to handle many of them," Cole pointed out. He held up his hands in a gesture of surrender. "I'm just playing devil's advocate here."

"And sherifs don't usually come out in the middle of the night for a straightforward accident unless there is an excellent reason for doing so," she pointed out.

Cole slowly lifted his head and looked at her. "Late-night accidents mean fewer witnesses."

She nodded.

"We've had our differences in the past, but he's always cared about the community. He's always helping out at the senior center," Cole mused. Then it hit him. "Seniors are dying and he's always there."

Bree nodded again. "A good reason why he wasn't happy I was looking over the reports. There's something missing from those files that I'd like to see—the coroner's reports. We really need them. I'd also like to see if any toxicology reports were run. All of that is missing. Which could be intentional. I doubt all the victims were autopsied, but some had to be. After Holloway's diatribe today, I don't think he'd be too happy if he found out I was still looking into these cases."

"I'd offer to see what I can do, but Holloway and the coroner are golfing buddies," Cole admitted.

Bree stared at the papers. "I'll get them."

Cole sipped his wine. "You play golf? Because that's the only way you'll make friends with the coroner."

"No, but I know people who can get them for me without

having to spend the day hitting a little white ball around.'' She picked up a notebook and wrote in a looping scrawl. ''Or raise any red flags in case Holloway does have something to do with the deaths.''

''I guess you know those unsavory types who understand the terms breaking and entering,'' he said glibly.

Bree shot him a look guaranteed to slice him in half. ''If I thought it would work, I'd do just that. But if there's something illegal going on, I want to make sure our butts are covered. I'm not allowing anything to get thrown out of court because we didn't go by the book.''

He muttered a grim curse that echoed their moods. ''You're right. If these are murders, we can't let the killers get away with it.''

Bree nodded as she kept writing.

''Any way this could go federal?'' Cole asked, looking over her shoulder as she wrote down names and other notes to herself.

She shook her head. ''Not unless the crime has crossed state lines or a federal officer was involved. I don't need the feds to figure this out for me.''

''I forgot that locals don't like feds interfering,'' he muttered. ''How did you handle being married to a fed?''

''He kept to his side of the street and I kept to mine.'' Bree's head was down as she continued scribbling in her notebook.

Cole topped up their wineglasses and sipped at his while watching her work.

He likened her focus to his own. When he was working on a story, he was like a pit bull: he'd dig in and refuse to let go. He easily guessed Bree was the same way.

He didn't feel sorry for anyone who came up against her. She'd make sure justice was done.

''Senior citizens are the perfect targets,'' she said suddenly.

''That's nothing new. Why do you think I was looking into the deaths?''

She nodded. ''The death of a senior citizen is easier to cover up, because they're expected to die, rather than someone in, say, their twenties. Seniors are more prone to accidents.''

"Keep going," he urged, following her line of thought.

She tapped her pen against the edge of her notebook. "We've already decided that someone is targeting senior citizens. When you first looked into this, why didn't you talk to Joshua and Renee Patterson? From what I've seen, they're very active at the senior center. And well respected in town. It stands to reason they'd know everything that goes on in the senior community. It also stands to reason they would know something about this."

Cole shook his head almost violently. "No way," he argued. "I refuse to believe they would have anything to do with this." He held up his hand to indicate Bree should remain silent. "I've always prided myself on my gut instincts. Not Josh and Renee."

"Did you ever talk to them about any of this?"

He looked away for a moment before replying. "No," he finally admitted. "And I should have. They practically built that center from the ground up. They know everyone involved with the place. If anyone knows if anything is going on, it would be them. If they thought something was wrong, why wouldn't they have said something to Holloway or even me?"

"Because they know too much?" She didn't back down from his glare. "I'm a cop, Becker. Suspicion is my business."

"And finding the truth is mine," he insisted.

"Then let's agree to do just that. Find the truth. Did you ever talk to Holloway about this?"

Cole nodded. "Once. I thought he might have overheard something when he was helping out at the center that might not have meant anything at the time. He said that as sad as it is, we have to expect people in a certain age group to die sooner rather than later. He didn't want me to start a witch hunt."

"He's right, in that respect."

"And after the way he reacted when he found out you were looking into those cases, you're not going to be able to speak to anyone in an official capacity," Cole said.

She nodded. "Not if I want to keep my job. I've got to keep a very low profile in this."

"Then we won't do it officially. I'll talk to Josh and Renee.

See about getting together with them for lunch or something. Keep it all casual.''

"Good idea. In the meantime, I'll make some calls and see if there's a way I can get copies of the coroner's reports.'' She began writing again.

"Bree.'' He said her name quietly.

It took her a moment to register the fact that he'd spoken. She looked up with an inquiring expression.

"Thank you.''

A faint smile touched her lips. "I wanted to believe that nothing bad could happen in a small town.''

"It would be nice to think that way, wouldn't it?'' Cole set his wineglass down and turned to better face her.

He figured once she'd gotten home, she'd changed out of whatever she'd worn to work. Now she wore a knit tunic the color of paprika and dark tan leggings. Her feet were bare, with the nails painted a deep russet. He'd noticed a pair of fuzzy rabbit slippers lying near a chair. He hid a smile. They looked to be her size.

The hard-nosed sheriff's detective who once primarily dealt with corpses had some interesting curves, sported painted toenails and smelled like sin.

Memories of that night out in the desert foothills, when she'd been in his arms, swept over him.

She'd felt damn good. Tasted even better.

The desire to repeat those moments came through so strong he felt as if it was written across his face.

He'd already broken his personal rule about not dating anyone who lived in Warm Springs. There was no reason to stop now.

"We through with business matters?'' he murmured.

"I'd say so. Why, you have a hot date?'' Her lips curved upward.

The reply she didn't expect was his mouth suddenly pressing against hers.

Bree's lips instantly softened under his gentle assault. She lifted her arms to loop them around his neck.

Their mouths couldn't seem to get enough as they hungrily feasted on each other.

He slid his hand under her top, splaying his fingertips against her midriff. He felt her sharp indrawn breath. In seconds, he had her top off and dropped it to the floor.

"Gorgeous," he muttered against her mouth. "I did tell you you're gorgeous, didn't I?"

"Yes, but don't stop," she whispered, as she unbuttoned his shirt. He drew back long enough for her to pull his shirt off.

"I always believe in doing what the law tells me to do," he whispered back as he cupped her breast, using his thumb to tenderly caress the taut nipple. He dropped his head to lave it with his tongue. The dark rose tip pebbled under his touch. Encouraged, he drew it into his mouth and sucked gently.

"Cole!" she gasped, pulling on his shoulders. She arched against him. She blindly sought his mouth, which he brought down to hers with a hunger that wasn't about to be denied.

Muttered words between them were raw, aching with need.

"I lose any good sense I have when I'm around you," he murmured, as he hooked his thumbs in the waistband of her leggings and started to pull them down. A faint tan line from her bathing suit bottom teased him as he lowered the skintight fabric. He leaned over to caress the tiny freckle on her hip with his lips.

"*Oh no!*" Bree jumped up so fast that Cole was neatly clipped in the chin. He fell backward, landing painfully on the floor.

"What's wrong?" he asked, startled and puzzled by this sudden change.

She looked around wildly, spied her top and snatched it up. She pulled it on over her head. After that, she ran her fingers through her hair and jumped up off the couch.

"Pull your shirt back on," she ordered. She looked at him, her dropped eyes downward, then lifted them. "You have to do something about that!" she hissed.

He didn't need to look down to know what she was talking

about. "It's not like I can think it down," he said mildly, even though his nerve endings were screaming for relief.

"The garage door went up two seconds ago, which means my kids will be coming in here in another five seconds. Cody asks enough questions now without him coming up with a few more I really don't want to answer just yet." She looked down, realized her top was on inside out and quickly pulled it off and then on again.

Cole buttoned his shirt and tucked the tails back into his jeans.

"It was a lame movie, Cody!" Sara shouted, as the trio tramped into the kitchen.

"You're just mad cuz that boy from your school saw you," Cody yelled back. "Lacey didn't care."

"Of course she didn't. She was playing snuggle up with David all through the movie."

Bree and Cole caught a glimpse of the teenager as she swept down the hallway. A moment later, her bedroom door slammed.

Bree winced. "I really need to add door slamming to the list of sins to be paid into the Cuss Jar."

"I'm not taking Sara again," David announced, appearing in the doorway. Lacey stood just behind him. "She's the one who acted like a six-year-old. Hey, Cole," he acknowledged the man, spearing him with a hard gaze.

Cole noticed Bree's smile wasn't as natural as it normally would have been as she faced her stepson.

"Dare I ask how that happened?" she inquired.

"She didn't want to see the movie and I told her she couldn't see a different one," he stated. "She pulled a major pout all through the film." He lowered his voice. "Okay, it wasn't meant for anyone over the age of seven, but it wasn't totally bad, either. At least, not as bad as she made it out to be. I told her to knock off her attitude or she could walk home. Lacey and I are going to listen to CDs in my room."

Bree nodded. "Okay."

Cole waited until he figured the teenagers were out of earshot. "You're a trusting mom. I know mine wouldn't have let me take a girl into my bedroom to listen to music."

"There are three reasons why it's allowed. One, his door has to remain open at all times. Two, the music can't be so loud it deafens the household. Three, and most important, is that privacy is not in the vocabulary of a six-year-old boy. Their virtue is as safe in there as it would be in church."

"Not like yours a few minutes ago."

"Oh, Mom." David peeked around the corner. "You might want to fix your shirt—it's on backward. If the drama queen notices, there'll be hell to pay."

Bree gasped and spun around, piercing Cole with a look that should have left him on the floor writhing in acute pain. His silent answer was an expression of angelic innocence and his hands held up in a helpless gesture.

"Sara's at that horrible age where she thinks everything she does is right and everything I do is wrong," she whispered furiously as she tugged her top around until it was on correctly.

She'd barely set things to right before Sara appeared in the doorway. She ignored Cole as she looked at her stepmother. "I gather the smell coming from the kitchen is dinner?"

"Stew in the crockpot," Bree clarified. "It should be ready in about an hour."

Sara glanced at Cole, then turned back to Bree. "Is he staying for dinner?"

"How sweet of you to suggest it, dear. Why don't you set the table?"

"She didn't notice a thing," Cole said in a low voice once they were alone.

"That's what you think," Bree mumbled, walking over to the bunny slippers and pushing her feet into them. "She can see a hair out of place at a hundred yards." She glanced down at her watch and headed for the cordless phone resting in a cradle near the couch. "Might as well start on those calls right now."

Cole sipped his wine and listened to Detective Bree Fitzpatrick work her magic. He heard snippets of what must have been old war stories, her murmured words of yes, the family was doing fine and no, working in a small town was not petrifying her brain. By the time she'd finished, she was assured copies of the reports she'd requested and no, her name would never come up. Not once did she say exactly why she wanted the reports nor why she didn't request them through local channels.

"Something tells me you've done this before," he commented after she'd finished her last call.

"I take the Fifth." She added a few more notes. "Hope you don't mind stew."

"Anytime I eat something I haven't cooked means I won't suffer food poisoning."

"Just be prepared to hear all about the movie," she warned him. "Cody will give us a detailed review."

"Hey, Fitzpatrick." He smiled at her. "Your kids don't terrify me."

"They should. There are days when they completely paralyze me." She chuckled. "There's a reason for those T-shirts saying You Can't Scare Me. I Have Teenagers."

"Mom!" Cody ran into the room and leaped into his mother's arms. Only her quick reflexes kept her on her feet as she swept him up. "You shudda come with us. It was neat."

"It was, huh?" She glanced sideways at Cole. "All sorts of cool fighting machines?"

"Yeah, and really yucky aliens. Sara said they were stupid." He wrinkled his nose. "And you know what? When the movie was over and we were going out of the theater, we saw the sheriff."

If Cole hadn't been watching Bree so intently, he would have missed the slight stiffening of her body.

"Really?" she said casually as she set her son down on his feet. "Did he see you?"

"Yeah." Cody picked up a robot and started rolling it across the coffee table. Bree took it from him and set it on the floor. "But he looked mad."

"Did he say anything to you?" She glanced at Cole, her expression now unreadable.

Cody shook his head. "Can I have Coke with dinner?"

"Did you have any at the movie?"

His hesitation told her the truth before he revealed it. "Yeah."

"You know the rules. You have Coke at the show, you have milk for dinner."

"Okay." He ran out of the room.

"Coke and, I'm sure, candy that David bought him will have Cody riding a sugar high all evening." She breathed a deep sigh. "I need to go in and finish up a few things for dinner. Turn on the TV if you want. Being a man, you'll have no problem finding the remote, I'm sure," she said with a teasing smile as she left the room.

As predicted, Cole easily found the remote control among magazines and puzzles on the coffee table, and switched on the news. Even with the commentator droning on about world events, he could hear a low-voiced exchange between Bree and Sara.

"There was no reason for me to go with them to see that movie!" Sara's furious whisper easily reached his ears.

Bree's murmur was less distinct, but he guessed she was warning her daughter to be more discreet.

"—never do anything!" The last part of Sara's retort was full throttle.

"Sara's on the rampage," David said, walking into the room. He fell back into a chair with the practiced slouch of a teenager. But his probing gaze was one Cole was familiar with. He'd seen more than one cop sport that look. "If we're lucky, she'll only pout during dinner."

"Not having a sister, I guess I missed out on all that fun." He pressed the mute on the remote.

"What do you want Mom to do for you?" David asked suddenly.

There were a variety of answers Cole could have given him. None of them true, but plausible enough that the kid would have believed him. Except David Fitzpatrick wasn't just any kid. He'd grown up in the law enforcement world. Cole doubted these kids were completely shielded from the darker side of life.

"Some local deaths listed as accidents or by natural causes don't strike me as that. I asked Bree if she'd be willing to look into them," he replied.

David nodded in understanding. "So that's why Sheriff Holloway is mad at her. He said there's nothing wrong there. You're saying there is and she's thinking the same because of you. You trying to get her fired?"

"Not at all. I just want some answers."

David's gaze never left his face. "Mom's good at what she does," he said bluntly. "She once said her rabbi told her open cases were an insult to the investigator. Not rabbi in the religious sense. A rabbi in the police world is a mentor."

Cole nodded. "Is law enforcement what you plan to do?"

David smiled. "The FBI and I have talked. Same with the DEA and CIA. But I have college ahead of me. We'll probably talk again in three or four years and I'll make my decision then."

"They'll never know what hit them." Cole chuckled. "My money's on you."

"Then think about what you're putting Mom through. We've got somebody watching the house. I felt like we've been watched other times."

Cole's interest sharpened and a chill slithered down his spine. "When?"

"At some of Cody's soccer games. A few times when we've been in town after school. Nothing definite. Just a feeling."

"I trust your feelings more than I'd trust most peoples'. Does your mom know?"

David nodded. "For the time being, Sara and Cody don't go anywhere without Mom or me or a trusted adult with them. They're not allowed to go anywhere even with friends. Cody doesn't care much. Sara's the problem. She doesn't like the restrictions, but she doesn't like much of anything lately. I guess it's all due to you. She has trouble with Mom dating."

"Then I guess I have to say I'm guilty as charged."

"Come on in for dinner," Bree called from the kitchen.

David pushed himself out of his chair. "One other thing you might want to consider," he said. "Mom's a crack shot. She's won awards."

Cole followed him out of the room. "I'll see if I have a Kevlar vest in the closet."

His previous time with the Fitzpatrick family hadn't prepared him for this evening. They didn't believe in standing on ceremony during dinner.

Cody chattered about the movie, while Sara sighed dramatically and David alternated bites of dinner with knowing glances at Bree and Cole. Bree noticed her stepson's attention directed at her, and flashed him a pointed look of her own, but he refused to back down. Cole had to give him a lot of credit. At the young man's age, Cole might have thought twice about standing up to Bree, who looked her most formidable at that moment.

He was so engrossed watching them, he didn't notice Sara lean over and whisper something in Cody's ear.

"No!" the little boy wailed. He shot an accusing glare at Cole. "I don't need a daddy!" He jumped out of his chair and ran out of the room.

Bree didn't waste any time before turning to her daughter. "Good going, Sara," she said tightly. "Two dollars to the Cuss Jar." She held up her hand to halt the expected protests. "Your behavior warrants a little loss of money. You will go in there and apologize to your brother for whatever you said to him, and you have dish duty all week. And you *can't* use the dishwasher."

Sara's face tightened. "Are you sure you wouldn't rather have me flogged?"

"Don't tempt me."

"Then excuse me. It appears I have amends to make." With her head held high, she left room.

"And to think my mother complained about having three boys." Cole was the first to break the silence.

"Must be that time of the month," David muttered, then winced when he encountered his stepmother's eyes. "Sorry."

"Damn straight, you're sorry." Bree turned to Cole. "And I'm sorry you had to see them like this."

"Don't worry, I won't write one of those stories on life with a sheriff's detective's family for the next issue." He forked up his last bite of stew.

Bree turned back to David. "Cody said he saw Sheriff Holloway when you came out of the theater."

He shrugged. "I think he's pissed at me for getting his son in trouble. I guess he thinks he's intimidating me."

"Just don't do anything to get him really angry," she warned.

David gathered up plates and carried them over to the sink.

"Don't worry, I'm leaving them for Sara," he said as he left the room. "I've got a paper to finish. With my suspension over, I don't have a decent excuse for it to be late," he joked. "'Night."

"David, don't forget David Boa needs to be fed," she reminded him.

"Yeah, yeah, I'll do it tomorrow when Cody isn't around."

Cole lifted a brow. "David Boa?"

"Boa constrictor," she explained. "Cody thinks the snake is cool, but he doesn't like to think what D.B. eats. I don't blame him. I'm not too keen on it, either. As long as I don't have to feed it or handle it, I'm fine."

"You're one cool mom," he complimented her.

She smiled. "Let's sit outside. Coffee?"

"Sounds good."

Jinx walked out in front of them, his ears twitching forward and head lifted as he sniffed the air.

"Most dogs race around the yard," Cole commented.

"No, he'll patrol the perimeter." She led the way to the patio table. "Once he's reassured everything's all right, he'll settle down." She looked up when the patio door opened. Cody walked out, holding the kitten in his arms.

"Eartha Katt has to go potty," he announced.

"Sweetheart, we have a litter box for Eartha now," Bree reminded him.

"Sometimes she wants real grass." He walked over to a corner of the yard and set the kitten down.

"He's a lot like his dad," she said softly, watching her youngest. "Analytical, studies things from every angle before making his decision. They're all like Fitz. Even Sara." She laughed softly.

"Are you still mourning him?"

Cole's question had Bree's head snapping upward. The only light was the spillover from the kitchen window and patio door. Cody's whispered conversation with his kitten warred with the cicadas singing in the distance.

"Would another guy ever have a chance with you?" Cole murmured.

She didn't answer right away. Both adults were so intent on each other, they were barely aware of Cody picking his kitten up and going back into the house.

"Fitz will always be in a special corner of my heart, but my mourning him is over," she said finally. "As for anyone else, I honestly haven't given it a lot of thought. I have enough going on in my life without adding too much more to it."

Cole sat back, one ankle resting on the opposite knee.

"Then I guess I'll just have to do what I can to change your mind."

Chapter 12

Bree hadn't expected to get lucky when she took some personal time to do some quick grocery shopping. Running into Renee Patterson made her feel as if she'd just won the lottery. She couldn't have asked for a more positive sign.

"Renee." She greeted the woman with a warm smile. "It's good to see you. How are you doing?"

"Bree, I'm doing fine, thank you. It's good to see you, too." Her smile was faint. She gestured toward Bree's navy pants and cream-colored blouse. A cell phone was clipped to her belt, along with her weapon. "You look very official today."

"They still wouldn't let me cut to the front of the line," Bree joked. She studied the shadows under the woman's eyes and the lack of color in her face. "Do you have time for some coffee?"

Renee hesitated. "I really shouldn't," she murmured.

Just at that moment, Bree looked up and saw Cole coming out of the dry cleaners with a handful of plastic-covered shirts draped over his shoulder. She willed him to look her way. As if he heard her, he did just that. He stowed his shirts in his truck and started walking toward her.

"There's Cole." Bree infused surprise in her voice. "Cole! Hello. Care to join Renee and me for coffee?"

"Sure," he said, not missing a beat. "Hey there, gorgeous. How's my second favorite woman?" He draped his arm around Renee's shoulders and kissed her on the cheek. "Where's Joshua? I've been trying to get hold of you for two days now. Bree and I were hoping you'd double date with us one night," he joked.

"Where else would he be on a lovely day like today but at the golf course?" She patted his shoulder. "Why aren't you at the office?"

"I'm out here getting the impressions of the people on that new bond issue," he said glibly. "Do you have anything inspiring to tell me? So far I've only heard negatives about the bond."

"Don't get old," Renee said.

At first Bree thought she should smile, as if the older woman had just made a joke. But something in Renee's eyes told her that wasn't the case.

"I don't think we have an option. My kids are already convinced I'm older than dirt," Bree said. "I'm just biding my time until it's their turn."

"Best thing to do," Cole agreed, steering Renee and Bree toward the Coffee Spot. "If we're lucky, Greta has some of her great pastries left."

If Renee thought of protesting again, she didn't have a chance as Bree and Cole sandwiched her between them. Cole waved at Greta and herded the women toward a small table in the rear.

"What will you have, ladies? My treat," he declared with a winning smile.

"I'll have a latte," Bree decided.

"I'll have one, too," Renee said.

Bree noticed Renee nervously twisting her shoulder bag straps. She stared toward the counter, where Cole stood talking to Greta. She turned back to Bree.

"Have you and Cole been dating long?" she asked brightly.

"Longer than I expected," Bree replied, looking up when

Cole said something to Greta that had her laughing. "I think he's beginning to grow on me. Like a fungus," she said wryly.

"That boy is the salt of the earth," Renee murmured. "He cares about people. Probably cares about them too much." She suddenly reached across the table and grasped Bree's hand in a tight grip that was almost painful.

Bree was stunned to find the woman's fingers ice-cold to the touch.

"Please, dear, do whatever you can to keep him safe," she said fervently. "Cole tends to jump in without any thought of the consequences. I can tell you have a level head. You have to, with your work, don't you, dear? You'll make sure he doesn't do anything that could get him hurt, won't you?"

"Of course I will," Bree replied, startled by the older woman's plea. "But I can't imagine that Cole would do anything that would get him into trouble." She prayed this lie wouldn't come back to haunt her.

Renee laughed softly. "I'm afraid I know Cole better than you do in that respect. The man dodged bullets for so many years he doesn't know how to act unless he's in some sort of danger." She lowered her voice to a conspiratorial whisper. "Right now, he's looking into something that could get him badly hurt." Her gaze burrowed into Bree's eyes. "And I think you know it."

The hairs on the back of Bree's neck stood up. Her favorite barometer for trouble hadn't let her down.

"Renee, what is going on?" she asked, keeping her voice low. "Please, tell me. Let me help you."

The woman looked around, then straightened up and reverted to the bright voice she'd used before. "I am so glad I ran into you today. So many people at the senior center have commented on the safety speech you gave. I'm hoping you can come speak to us again sometime in the near future."

"I would be happy to speak to them again," Bree replied, smiling her thanks at Cole as he set cups down in front of them. He set a plate filled with a variety of cookies in the middle of the table.

"You had to, didn't you?" Bree groaned, even as she picked

up a cookie and bit into it. She murmured appreciatively as the rich flavors of chocolate, pecans and walnuts mingled in her mouth. When she looked at Cole, he shot her a silent question. She gave him a slight shake of the head.

"I'm surprised you let Joshua head for the golf course without you," he commented to Renee. "Used to be you had your clubs in the back of the car if he even whispered the word *golf*."

"I had things to do today, so I thought I'd let him go on his own." Renee sipped her latte. "I doubted he would have a problem finding someone to play with him."

"Not around here, where golf clubs are found in just about every household," Cole joked. "Except mine. I never had the patience to learn."

"Joshua and Cole's uncle tried to teach him some years ago," Renee told Bree. "It wasn't a pretty sight."

"I told them I'd rather watch paint dry," he said.

As Bree listened to Renee, she noticed the woman seemed more animated, more relaxed than she had been before. But there were still shadows in the back of the woman's eyes. Bree felt that if Cole hadn't returned when he had, she might have been able to learn what had upset the older woman.

At Cole's appearance, Renee's demeanor had changed to that of a smiling woman without a care in the world.

"Have you and Joshua lived in Warm Springs a long time?" Bree asked.

"We moved here a little over ten years ago." Renee's fingers lingered over the cookies before she chose one. "We'd come down one weekend to visit friends, and liked the area so much that when Joshua retired, we decided to move down here."

"When did you get involved with the senior center?" she asked.

"About six months after we moved here. Joshua was asked to give a seminar on financial planning. The center was in a small storefront then and not very well attended. I talked to several women who wanted to get more going on in there, and we started working on setting up various classes, day trips to Laughlin. We even arranged shopping trips and theater jaunts to San Diego. At the same time, we worked to find the proper building for our new center. We moved into our present accommodations three years ago," she said proudly. "We offer at least ten different classes or workshops a week."

"It's about Estelle Timmerman," Bree said.

Renee looked wary. "What about Estelle?" She looked from one to the other. "What are you trying to find out?" Her hand trembled as she pushed her cup toward the middle of the table.

"What exactly is Estelle afraid of?" Cole said. "A week ago, she asked Bree and me to come over because she had something to tell us. Except while we were there, someone called her, and after she took the call, she suddenly clammed up. Bree told me how you'd talked to her about Estelle. What else can you tell us?"

"Good going, Becker," Bree muttered, as the older woman's expression abruptly shut them out.

Renee groped for her bag. "I have to go," she mumbled.

"Renee." Bree reached out for her, but she shrugged her off. When the older woman turned to look at her, her eyes glistened with tears. "You don't know, do you?"

Bree and Cole shook their heads.

"Estelle passed away last night. She had a heart attack." She moved jerkily as she swiftly left the shop. The bell over the door tinkled merrily.

Cole muttered an expletive that Bree softly echoed.

"I hadn't heard a thing at the station." She pressed her fingertips against her forehead, where a headache was winding its way around her skull.

"None of my sources told me anything, either." Cole slumped in his chair. "She asked us to come over. Someone frightened her and now she's dead."

"Is everything okay over there?" Greta called out.

"Just fine," Cole said glumly.

"Then do me a favor and look as if you're enjoying my coffee and food. People will run the other way if they see the two of you look as if someone just died."

Bree closed her eyes at Greta's inadvertent choice of words.

"I'll get over to the office and see what I can find out," he muttered.

"I don't dare ask around the station right now," she said. "Not unless it's related to a crime. Holloway's just looking for an excuse to put my head on a platter for any imagined infraction."

Cole picked up his cup and finished his coffee. "Think you can get away tonight? My place for dinner?"

She kept her eyes closed as she rubbed her fingertips across her brows. "What time?"

"Six-thirty?" He rattled off an address.

"I'll be there."

Cole pushed himself out of his chair. He leaned over the table and kissed Bree, lingering for a moment.

"If chocolate tastes that good on your mouth, I wonder how it would taste other places?" he murmured, before he took off.

The bell over the door seemed to echo inside Bree's head.

"Wow, whatever did the man say?" Greta dropped into the chair Cole had vacated.

"What do you mean?"

"If you saw your face, you'd know exactly what I mean. Anyone looking at the two of you would think you are having some hot sex. Are you?" she probed.

"I wish," Bree said fervently.

"Then do something about it, girl! You don't use it, you'll lose it," she insisted.

"I imagine you're not asked to teach sex education."

"Of course not. I'm a bad influence." Greta slid the cookies from the plate into a bag. She handed them to Bree. "Tempt Cole with them."

"I don't think I need to tempt him with cookies." She smiled, accepting the bag.

Greta's own smile dimmed. "What's wrong, Bree?"

She shook her head. "More than you can imagine." She stood up. "I'll see you later."

"I'm always here," she called after her, injecting extra meaning into her words.

Bree tried to still the voices in her head as she walked to her vehicle.

It wasn't easy to shut them out when they were pleading with her to help the senior citizens of Warm Springs.

Cole spent the next couple hours in his office making phone calls and trying to act as if nothing was wrong, when he felt the exact opposite.

He blamed himself for Estelle Timmerman's death. In his mind, the news that the woman had died in the hospital hadn't made things better.

He slumped back in his chair, tapping a pencil against the desk edge.

Mamie stepped inside his office and closed the door behind her. The sorrow darkening her eyes told him she knew.

"She wasn't a well woman, Cole," his assistant told him, as if guessing the direction of his thoughts.

He shook his head. "Dammit, Mamie, why can't you find out anything?" he snarled.

"You really want to know why I can't find out anything? No one will talk to me because I work for you," she said bluntly. "You haven't exactly made it a secret that you feel Sheriff Holloway knows something about the deaths you've labeled wrongful. And gee, Cole," she said sarcastically, "some people are afraid of the man. I think you should be, too."

"No way. If the bastard is behind these deaths I'll do whatever is necessary to take the man down." Cole continued with his pencil tapping, increasing the tempo.

Mamie shot him a dark look. She reached across the desk and snatched the pencil out of his hand. He looked up, puzzled by her action.

"Do you realize how annoying that is?" She dropped the pencil in the coffee mug he used for a pencil cup. "What are you and Bree Fitzpatrick going to do next?"

"I don't think I should tell you, Mamie. After all, no one will talk to you." Cole's smile was without guile. Innocence personified.

Mamie didn't buy it.

"Fine, but if I learn anything I *will* come to you first."

The moment she left the office, he dug the pencil out of the cup and started tapping it against the desk edge.

There was nothing better than an annoying sound to help him straighten things out inside his head.

Cole's idea of preparing for Bree's visit was to toss his dirty clothes in the closet and make sure the toilet seat was down.

He set the containers of Chinese food in the oven, set the temperature on low and opened a bottle of wine.

"What did you find out?" Bree demanded, when he opened his front door. She swept past him. She'd obviously been home before coming over, since she was wearing trim-fitting jeans and a mustard-colored, long-sleeved T-shirt.

"That no one will talk to Mamie because she works for me, and she inferred I'm treading on dangerous ground." He headed for the kitchen. "Want some wine? I hope Chinese food is okay."

"Yes and fine." She followed him.

He set the cartons on the table and laid out paper plates. "Kung Pao chicken, broccoli beef, orange chicken—which is spicy but really good—barbecue pork fried rice, shrimp in lobster sauce." He pointed to each carton.

"Exactly how many people were you expecting for dinner?" She spooned a little out of each container.

"I want to have leftovers."

Bree nodded. "Ah, your dinner for the next week."

"And breakfast, too. Chopsticks or forks?"

"Chopsticks." She made a small sound of approval when he handed her delicately carved eating instruments.

"Picked them up during one of my trips to China," he explained. "You get a chance to find out anything?"

Bree shook her head. She expertly manipulated the chopsticks as she picked up a piece of orange chicken.

"I checked our logs at the station, but there was nothing there. Probably because she died in the hospital." She laughed as the spices exploded through her mouth. "This is really good."

"Shay's Chinese Pagoda." He gave a wry shrug. "Yeah, the

name doesn't work, but everyone knows he serves the best Chinese food around.''

''Did I tell you that not only did Holloway lecture me big time, but he also accused me of turning a molehill into the freakin' Swiss Alps?'' she asked. ''His words, not mine.''

Cole cocked an eyebrow. ''Really? And why would he say that?''

''Because he knows something we don't,'' she said smugly.

''I knew you'd help me figure this out.'' He gave an admiring shake of the head. ''So how do we prove he does?''

''Hell if I know, but with some luck we'll find out everything we need to know.'' She tried the shrimp next. ''Unfortunately, I don't think he keeps a diary or computer file we can hack into.''

''Too bad.'' Cole munched on a chow mein noodle. ''Villains don't make it easy anymore.''

Bree stared off into the distance, one chopstick waving in the air to a tune that only played in her head.

''It's getting bad, Cole,'' she said grimly. ''Estelle died because of us.''

Equally serious, he grabbed her free hand. ''We're going to nail the son of a bitch, Bree.''

''I know we will.'' There was no doubt in her voice. She took a deep breath. ''All right, let's finish the food before it gets cold. I tend to think better when I'm fed, anyway.'' She stole a water chestnut off his plate.

''Our business will be tabled for the time being.'' In return, he swiped a piece of chicken.

It wasn't easy for them, but they managed to turn the conversation to other subjects.

''Exactly how many of Cody's games have you been thrown out of?'' Cole asked.

''Not as many as he tries to make it sound,'' she replied. ''I used to make jokes about stage mothers and fathers, not to mention the radical parents at sports games. I saw them at Sara's dance recitals and when David played Little League and Pee Wee football. Then, at one of Sara's recitals, I listened to a mother try to psyche her out. She insisted Sara was doing the steps wrong. Poor baby was only nine and I could tell she believed the woman. I didn't stop to think, I waded in and took the woman off into a corner. She was advised to worry about her own kid.''

"Man, you don't fool around, do you?" He held up the wine bottle in a silent question. She shook her head.

"Holloway would have a litter of kittens if I was stopped for Driving Under the Influence.''

"Litter of kittens," Cole repeated. "You do have a way with words." He watched the deft way she handled her chopsticks.

He tracked the faint smile touching her lips and the way her eyes crinkled a bit at the corners. She didn't seem to worry about the fact that she was over thirty. He couldn't remember the last time he'd met a woman so comfortable in her own skin.

He watched her sitting in the chair, one arm resting on the table as she plucked bits of barbecue pork out of the rice and popped them into her mouth.

"Do you realize how much I want to make love to you?"

By the startled look on her face, he guessed he'd scored a direct hit.

She chewed slowly and swallowed before answering.

"I've thought that way about you," she admitted in a low voice. She tipped her head back, looking up at the ceiling instead of looking at him.

Cole was surprised, since Bree never seemed to have any problem facing him squarely.

She took a deep breath. "When I changed my clothes, I made sure to put on new underwear.''

He stilled, not sure what she meant and not daring to hope. "And this is a good thing?"

Bree laughed. Her earlier unease seemed to be disappearing fast.

"Oh yes. It's a very good thing. You see, through the ages, we girls have been told by our mothers to always wear nice underwear when leaving the house. That way, if we get in an accident, we won't be wearing something old and faded.''

Cole swallowed. The idea of seeing Bree in that new underwear was a tantalizing thought. "I don't think this was the kind of situation your mother was thinking of when she passed out that advice.''

Bree stood up. She carefully closed the tops of the food cartons and gathered them up. She put them away in the refrigerator, then carried the paper plates to the sink. When she turned around and leaned against the counter, a devilish gleam in her eyes warned him what was coming next.

"Okay, Becker, I've had my say. Now it's your turn," she challenged. "Put your money where your mouth is."

He wasted no time in abandoning his chair.

"We will not act like teenagers and make out in the kitchen," he said against her mouth, as he pulled her against him.

"Of course not." She nipped at his lower lip. "After all, we are responsible adults. We can restrain ourselves. Just how far is your bedroom from here?" Her fingertips brushed across his fly.

Cole groaned. He grasped her fingers before they went any further. "Right now, it seems like a thousand miles." He kept his arms around her as he guided her out of the kitchen and down the hallway.

"If I find one centerfold on the walls..." Her warning came out more as a tease.

"Don't worry. I'll save you the aggravation and shoot myself," he vowed, fumbling for the light switch. In seconds, a soft glow bathed the room.

Bree peeked over Cole's shoulder. "No centerfolds. No dirty underwear or socks on the floor. I'm impressed, Becker." She laughed throatily as he tried to silence her with kisses.

"Dammit, woman, there are times when you talk too much," he growled as he reached for the hem of her T-shirt. She obliged by lifting her arms so he could pull it off. In turn, she dispensed with his polo shirt.

Their fingers worked in unison as they unbuckled each other's belts and unzipped zippers. Even their mouths refused to leave each other, their tongues tangling. The soft rasp of Cole's beard against Bree's skin was a delicious sensation.

Cole looked at Bree wearing a bra the color of candlelight and matching bikini underwear. Her daily runs gave her a lean look, with just the right amount of healthy curves. A round patch of puckered skin was a sad reminder of the pain she'd suffered a year ago.

He pursed his lips in a low whistle of appreciation. "Right about now, I am so glad you listened to your mother."

"So am I." She gave him a less than gentle push that dropped him backward onto the bed. She followed him, straddling his hips. She bent forward, planting her hands on the bed on either side of his shoulders.

"Tough guy," he taunted, gripping her hips.

"Tough guy? Oh, Becker, we have a lot of work ahead of us. And here I thought you were so observant." She dropped her head to trail kisses along his jawline. "Some investigative reporter you are if you can't tell the difference," she breathed into his ear. At the same time her tongue curled around his earlobe.

Wanting much more, Cole framed her face in his hands and brought her mouth to his. The tension and hunger that had built up between them exploded in a cataclysm of need as they feasted on each other.

Cole practically tore off Bree's bra and panties even as his mouth refused to leave hers. He uttered a supremely male growl as he cupped her breasts in his hands. His thumbs pressed lightly against her nipples until they pearled, a deep dusky rose.

"They're not young and perky." She chuckled against his lips.

"Like a fine wine, they just get better." In return, he gently nipped a corner of her mouth.

"I'm not perfect." She breathed a sigh against his skin, drawing in his musky scent.

Cole rested his fingertips against the puckered scar from the gunshot wound. "A badge of honor," he murmured just before he trailed his mouth across it in a loving caress. "Ah, Bree, we should have gotten naked and rolled around on the bed a lot sooner."

"You're not naked yet," she reminded him, running her fingers around the band of his briefs.

He obliged by lifting his hips so she could slide them off. She purred as she encircled him with her hands.

"Are you the typical male with supplies in the nightstand drawer?" she asked as she continued a slow up-and-down massage with her fingertips.

"Yeah." He figured the one-word answer was coherent enough, since there wasn't enough breath in his body to say anything more.

It was.

When she slid down on top of him, Cole felt as if he'd died and gone to heaven. Bree's slow and leisurely movements soon left both their bodies sheened with perspiration. It wasn't enough for either of them, but neither wanted to rush the moment. By unspoken agreement, they alternately teased each other with words and caresses as the heat between them built up until they could take no more.

Cole turned the tables by rolling until he was on top. His hips rocked against hers, accelerating until they moved in a frenzied rhythm.

He looked down and saw her eyes blaze with an emerald fire as she tipped over that ultimate edge. He blindly followed.

Bree felt boneless and so relaxed she didn't think she'd move for the next year.

Since the air was cool, Cole rolled them enough to pull the bedspread out and cover them with it. Bree curled her body against his as he wrapped his arms around her.

"Wow," he murmured in her ear. "Detective, you are one hot number."

She smiled against the curve of his shoulder. She inhaled the warm musky scent of his skin, knowing it was imprinted on her own.

"You're not so bad yourself."

He rolled over onto his side until he loomed over her.

"You better understand this ain't no one-night stand," he rumbled.

Her smile grew even wider. "I'm glad to hear that."

"Good, because I bought a new box a week ago." He kept his eyes on her as he reached blindly into the nightstand drawer.

Bree thought sneaking into the house so she wouldn't wake the occupants had ended when she finished high school.

At the late hour of two in the morning and at the ripe age of thirty-five, she found herself whispering a command to Jinx as the dog greeted her with his cold muzzle against her hand.

She'd almost made it to her bedroom when David's door opened.

"About time you got home." He uttered words parents all over the world were familiar with. "Do you know what time it is?"

She clenched her teeth before a curse dropped from her lips. She could tell he'd been sleeping. His hair stuck out in all directions and his T-shirt and pajama pants were rumpled.

"Shouldn't you be asleep?" She countered with a question of her own.

"I was until I heard the garage door go up." He lifted an eyebrow.

"David, when you enter the FBI Academy, you think you'll be going in there as an adult. I'll make sure every wall in that building has a copy of one of your baby pictures on it." She uttered the threat in a pleasant voice. "Along with some of those oh-so-cute stories your father told me. Running outside naked so you could play in the mud. Things like that."

"Don't let Sara see all that guilt on your face or you'll never hear the end of it, since you won't let her date unless it's with a group," he warned her.

"I'll stand on the Fifth."

David grinned. "I figured you would."

Chapter 13

Bree felt as if she'd just crawled into bed and fallen asleep when the telephone rang. Which turned out to be true. The clock showed it had been only twenty minutes since she'd crawled under the covers.

"Fitzpatrick," she mumbled into the receiver.

"Detective." Randy Larkin's nasal drawl, tinged with something more serious, chased away the lingering bits of sleep still trying to hang on. "I'm sorry to wake you up."

"That's all right," she assured him. "What's up?"

"I'm afraid we've got a bad situation here," he said in a low voice, as if he was afraid he'd be overheard.

She sat up and switched on a light. "What kind of situation are we talking about?"

"Ma'am, there's been a bad accident out here on the highway. I tried calling Sheriff Holloway, but he ain't answering his cell phone or pager. Joe at Dispatch said to call you." He still sounded apologetic. "That it'd be better if I got you direct rather than going through him."

Bree bit back the curse that threatened to erupt. She knew she was on the list to be called in the event of an emergency. She also knew the young man had been with the department for only a few months. His shaky voice told her he'd found something a hell of a lot more traumatic than anything he'd come up against in his short career.

"Were there any fatalities?" she asked crisply.

"Yes'm. The driver is dead. Looks like she lost control of the car and ran off the road. No other vehicles were involved."

"Tell me where you are." Bree jotted down the location. "You're sure the driver is dead?" She stood up and pulled her nightshirt off over her head, then put the cordless phone against her ear again.

"Ma'am, Detective, there's no way anyone could have survived. It was a bad crash."

"No other vehicle, you say?"

"No, ma'am."

She breathed a silent prayer of thanks that there weren't more victims.

"No witnesses? No one taking a late-night walk? Anything?"

"No, Detective."

Her mind started to run in high gear. She ran for the bathroom. "Okay, I'll be there in fifteen minutes."

"Yes'm. Detective."

Bree pulled on the clothing she'd worn to Cole's house and took enough time to brush her teeth and run a comb through her hair. She knocked on David's door.

"I thought you were going to bed." He gave a jaw-cracking yawn.

"There was an accident out on the highway," she told him. "I don't know how long I'll be." This was always the part she hated. Having to leave them in the middle of the night.

He nodded. "Gotcha. I'll take Cody to his soccer game, drop Sara at the library, since she has that project for history class and she's supposed to do her research the old-fashioned way with books and not the Internet. No prob." He yawned again.

She reached out and touched his shoulder. She hadn't noticed until now how much it had broadened in the past year. Her boy had grown up. "I'm sorry I've had to count so heavily on you this year."

"Hey, better me than Sara." He grinned. "Don't worry, we'll be fine."

Bree called to Jinx and quickly drove out of the garage. Because of the late hour, there was no traffic on the highway and she reached the accident scene in no time. As she parked behind the patrol car, she noted with approval the flares the deputy had laid out on the road.

In the glare of the headlights, she could see the young man's face was a faint shade of green. She looked at him and felt a hundred years old, while he looked not much older than David.

"You okay?" she asked, walking swiftly toward him.

He nodded. "Sorry, it's my first..."

"Just tell me you didn't throw up anywhere in the vicinity."

"No, ma'am, uh, Detective."

"Try Bree, it's easier." She patted his shoulder.

"It doesn't look like an accident, ma'am. I called the crime scene investigator, along with the coroner's office, and asked for a tow truck to come out," he told her.

"Good. I'm going to go down and take a look. Jinx, stay." She switched on her flashlight, then adjusted the small headset for her voice-activated microphone and the tape recorder in a small fanny pack she'd secured around her waist. Bree discovered that tape recording her impressions gave her immediate access to her thoughts without having to stop and write everything down. She also found it more helpful when she filled out her reports.

As she made her way down the steep side of the ditch, she noted the car headlights were still burning, but the engine was switched off. She called up to Randy and asked if he'd turned the engine off and learned he hadn't.

"It wasn't running when I found it. I think the engine died when the car crashed," he explained.

She looked around at the dry brush surrounding them and breathed a sigh of relief that the crash hadn't started a fire. "Probably a good thing it did."

Bree flashed her light around, dictated the make, model and estimated year of the car.

"Driver appears to be female. Age—" She stopped stockstill

when her light reached the front seat and struck the driver. "Oh my God." Bree felt the breath leave her body in a rush.

"Detective, uh, Bree, is everything okay?" Randy called out.

"Yes," she called back, even as her senses screamed *No! Everything is all wrong! This shouldn't have happened!* Speaking in a monotone, she finished recording her observations and slowly climbed back up to the road. She was barely aware of the Crime Scene Unit van and the coroner showing up, or the blinking lights of a tow truck in the distance.

"Hey there, Bree." Will Gregory, the crime scene investigator, greeted her. "You got the lucky call, huh?"

She nodded. "Victim is a resident of Warm Springs. Her name is Renee Patterson."

Will's shock told her he, too, knew the woman. "Renee? What the hell was she doing out here at this hour?"

Bree shook her head. "I don't know." She looked back at the car.

"Damn, I'm glad I don't have to give the news to Joshua," Will muttered, as he pulled on latex gloves. "I'm surprised he hasn't called the station about her, what with her being out at such a late hour."

Will went down with the coroner, who officially announced Renee deceased. After that, Will went to work taking photographs and searching for any evidence that might indicate foul play.

Bree remained on the highway, watching Will work his way around the car. She spoke in monosyllables to the coroner and tow truck driver as they waited for Will to finish his work.

When he finally returned, he carried several evidence bags, which he stowed in his kit. One he held up in front of Bree.

She flashed her light on the evidence bag to better read the note written in a graceful script.

"No," she said decisively. "There is no way I will believe that Renee committed suicide. I didn't know her all that well, but she didn't seem the type to want to kill herself."

Will glanced toward Randy, who was smoking a cigarette and talking to the tow truck driver. Will lowered his voice. "Then you noticed the inconsistencies, too."

She nodded grimly. "Why would someone as levelheaded as Renee want to kill herself? Would she want to leave Joshua, who she loved so deeply, behind? Know that her death in this manner would cause him so much pain?

"And if she was going to do it, why try something as risky as crashing her car into a ditch? There's the chance of only ending up badly injured or, God forbid, paralyzed. No one desiring death would take that chance. And what about all those cuts on her palms? Those kind of cuts would only show up if, by reflex, she threw her hands up to protect her face when the car hit the bottom of the ditch." She held her arms up, crossed at the wrists, to demonstrate.

"Yeah, they don't want their faces messed up," he agreed.

"Exactly. Something deep inside me doesn't want to believe this was a suicide," she stated. "She loved her husband too much to leave him this way."

"It sounds good but we have evidence that says otherwise. We have a note allegedly written by the victim which pretty much seals the case. Maybe at the last second she regretted what she was doing and put her hands up in some futile hope of protecting herself."

Bree looked at him. "Renee Patterson wears glasses. Where are they?"

Will shook his head. "Maybe they flew off. I'll check under the seat when I get the car back to the garage."

She stared down at the crash scene. "Will, does it seem odd to you that so many senior citizens die in accidents?"

"I guess I haven't thought about it too much," he admitted.

"I've been wondering about it," she said in a low voice. "That maybe not all these were accidents."

Will shook his head. "I sure hope not. Because if you're thinking murder, you know what you have to do. This kind of death, it's usually the spouse the investigator looks at first. I'll be honest. I wouldn't like to see Joshua as the prime suspect," Will said.

She stared down into the ditch, where the taillights still glowed red.

"Damn, it's never easy."

* * *

When Cole stumbled into his kitchen he didn't expect to see a familiar SUV parked in his driveway. The driver's seat was empty.

He opened the front door and found Bree seated on the front steps.

"The doorbell still works," he said, stepping outside and dropping down beside her. He winced as the feel of ice-cold cement seeped through the lightweight cotton of his pajama pants. One look at her set features told him that whatever reason brought her here, it wasn't for a repeat of last night. "What happened, Bree?"

She shook her head as she continued to look off into the distance. He took her hand, nestling it between his two. He hoped his touch, and his silence, would soothe whatever demons haunted her.

"I just left Joshua Patterson's house," she said finally.

Now he knew it wasn't good.

"Barely a half hour after I got home I was called out to an auto accident on the highway," she continued in a monotone. "A car ran off the road into a ditch. Driver was dead when the deputy found the wreck. I went down to check it out and discovered the driver was Renee." She took a deep breath. "Crime Scene Unit discovered a note allegedly written by Renee. She didn't want Joshua to suffer the indignity. What indignity she meant we have no idea."

Cole tightened his grip on her hand as he swore long and colorfully.

"Why didn't I hear about this on the scanner?" he asked himself, referring to his police scanner. Then he remembered he'd been having problems with the electrical connection. Something he'd meant to replace and hadn't yet.

Bree shook her head. "Do you have any coffee?" she asked in a voice hoarse from lack of sleep.

"Brewing now." He stood up, gently pulling on her hand to urge her to her feet. He didn't put his arm around her, because he knew the last thing she needed was any semblance of comfort. But he didn't release her hand.

The rich aroma of coffee filled the house as they walked back to the kitchen. Cole filled two cups, handing one to Bree.

"I thought Holloway handled all the accidents," he commented.

"Dispatch couldn't get hold of him, so they called me." She rubbed her eyes before she drank down half the cup. She didn't wince as the almost scalding liquid slid past her tongue.

Cole noticed her eyes were bloodshot, her lips unadorned and slightly chapped. Her hair was windblown and she hadn't bothered to push it back behind her ears. She wore the same clothing she'd worn to his house.

Now that was a nice memory.

What she had encountered later on wasn't even remotely nice.

He ran his palm over his hair. "Dammit, there was no reason for her to die. I should have tried harder to set up a meeting with them. Maybe we could have learned something." He verbally beat himself up.

"She lost control of her car, Cole." Bree's voice bore no expression, nor did her face. "As far as the crime scene investigator is concerned, it's an accident."

Cole refilled her coffee cup. "What did Joshua say?"

She shot him a harsh look. "I'm not going to have you print his words."

He lost his temper at her assumption. "What the hell kind of person do you think I am? Dammit, Bree, I'm not asking as a newsman. I'm asking as a friend of the Pattersons."

Bree rubbed her eyes. Weariness seemed to take over her bones. "How do you think he took it? I had to go over there and tell him the woman he'd been married to for over fifty years was dead. He didn't take it well at all. I don't like it when the victim is someone I know," she whispered. She glanced at her watch and pushed herself off the chair. "I need to get back to the station. I've got reports to write." She picked up her cup and drained the contents.

Cole risked rejection then by standing up and gathering her into his arms. She dug her fingers into his shoulders as if using him as her anchor.

"There's been enough death," she whispered against his neck.

"What can I do?" He felt helpless. And he knew Bree felt the same way. An emotion he knew was as alien to her as it was to him.

"You might want to go over to Joshua's." She leaned back so she could look into his face. "But say nothing about my telling you about it. Let him assume you heard it another way. The way this town's grapevine works, half the population probably knows by now. He's a shattered man. He's going to need his friends."

"I'll go over there as soon as I've showered and dressed," he promised. "What about you? Are you all through with everything? You going to have a chance to sleep? You're more than welcome to stay here."

She shook her head. "I have to go to the station and write up my report," she repeated grimly. "The thing that bothers me the most is not knowing the reason behind these deaths." She turned to go.

He wasn't about to just let her leave. He pulled her into his arms and kissed her in a way that left him hard and aching and her completely dazed. She muttered something about having to go as she made her way back to her vehicle.

It wasn't until Cole was stepping into the shower that he realized the slight taste of salt from Bree's lips had to have come from tears.

What had he gotten her into? Was there a chance she would be the next victim if they got too close to the truth?

"Damn printer," Bree muttered, resisting the urge to give the equipment a good swift kick. She stabbed the print button with her forefinger, but received no results. She knew she should at least get a sign that the office-shared machine was spitting out her report. She spat a curse at the printer, its manufacturer and anyone else who had anything to do with the technology in general. As if sensing doom was at hand, the printer began whirring, shooting papers into the waiting tray. She picked them up and skimmed the words.

She knew at first glance there was nothing unusual about her report. The facts listed were succinct: the driver intentionally ran her car into a ditch. The suicide occurred sometime between 1:00 and 2:00 a.m. The vehicle's air bag did not inflate upon impact and the driver did not survive the crash. Evidence as to the victim's mental state before the accident was a note left on the passenger seat. It detailed her sorrow and her wish to end her life. The writing and signature were confirmed to be the victim's own. Because of the note, the crash would be listed as a suicide. Case closed.

So why didn't Bree feel confident about it being a closed case, when the facts pointed to it being a cut-and-dried suicide?

She signed her report and carried it into Holloway's office. He looked up. A scowl marred his features.

"That the report for the Patterson suicide?" he asked crisply, holding out his hand.

She nodded as she passed him the report. "To be honest, I don't think it was a suicide. You'll see that I noted my thoughts in the report."

"Really?" He cocked an eyebrow. He nodded toward the chair across from him before settling back in his seat and perusing the report.

Bree dropped into the chair and waited.

Holloway finally leaned back and tossed the report on his desk. "You've decided she didn't commit suicide because she tried to protect her face. What about the handwritten note left on the passenger seat? Or are you going to have the handwriting analyzed to ensure it was written by the victim?"

Bree ignored his sarcastic jab. "She wore glasses. They were nowhere to be found," she explained. She was aware she was probably making a major mistake in lecturing a man whose law enforcement experience exceeded hers by a good twelve years. In other words, she could be the one committing suicide—political suicide.

"True." He surprised her by replying amiably. "But women are also known to change their minds at the last minute. Renee Patterson had been under a doctor's care for the past few years because of health problems. A toxicological screen is being run, right?''

Bree nodded, wary of saying too much. She wondered if he was setting a trap.

''Do yourself a favor, Fitzpatrick. Don't let your boyfriend's paranoia interfere with your police work,'' Roy affably suggested.

Bree felt her hackles rise. ''Nothing interferes with my work,'' she replied in a level voice. ''But I have this problem. When something doesn't seem right, the back of my neck tingles. Funny thing, boss. For the past few hours, my neck has been tingling nonstop. No matter what her problems, I can't see Renee leaving Joshua of her own volition.''

That he didn't like what she said was evident in the slight tightening of his facial muscles. Roy remained silent as he rocked back and forth in his chair.

''I've known the Pattersons a hell of a lot longer than you have, Fitzpatrick,'' he finally said. ''If you had the health problems she had, you'd probably do whatever was necessary to spare your family any future pain.'' He kept his eyes leveled on her. ''There are some people who deserve to rest in peace, Fitzpatrick. Renee Patterson's never wanted people to know just how bad she felt most days. I think her pain finally caught up with her. It's unfortunate she chose a nasty way to die. I only hope no one else will decide to take their life in such a horrible way.''

Bree's gaze didn't waver from his. ''I agree.''

He waved at her in dismissal. She stood up and headed for the door.

''Fitzpatrick.''

She stopped and turned around.

''You didn't talk to Cole Becker about any of this, did you?''

''No, sir, this is strictly department business,'' she lied, without batting an eye.

''Mommy, I don't feel good,'' Cody muttered, injecting just enough whine into his voice to make sure he'd be heard. He walked up to his mother and leaned against her.

"Are you sure you don't have a reason for not going to school today? Because it's Monday. Do you have a test today?" she asked, brushing his hair away from his face. Her fingertips lingered when she encountered skin much too warm to the touch. "Where don't you feel good?"

"My ear feels bad." He wrapped his arms around her hips. "It feels like it did before."

Bree grimaced. She knew Cody was speaking of the time when he'd had a nasty ear infection.

"I'll call the doctor's office and see if I can get you an appointment today." She picked up the phone and called the department.

"I'll let the sheriff know, Detective Fitzpatrick," Irene told her. "Don't worry about anything except getting your little boy well. We're a lot more relaxed here than in L.A."

"I have someone lined up for days like this," she replied. "It's just a matter of getting Cody to the doctor."

"If you don't already have a doctor, call Dr. Warren's office," she suggested. "Mike treats just about everyone here. And he always has some same-day appointments set aside for last-minute emergencies like this."

"Thanks, I will." She jotted down the phone number Irene recited.

Bree uttered a silent prayer of thanks when the receptionist at Dr. Warren's office informed her they could squeeze Cody in later that morning.

She tried to keep him occupied with a coloring book and crayons as she made a few phone calls. She hoped her contacts had news about the autopsy reports she was trying to get. She was assured the papers would be faxed to her home that day.

"Does this doctor have an aquarium like Dr. Brian did?" Cody asked on their way into town.

"I don't know, sweetie," she replied, searching for a parking space and finding one in front of a two-story building.

Cody looked disappointed when he discovered there was no aquarium in the reception area, but he brightened up when he saw a room off to one side set up with toys. Lured by the sight of toy cars, he abandoned his mother. Bree signed Cody in and sat down, picking up a magazine.

"Detective?"

She looked up and saw Leo standing over her. The elderly janitor smiled at her.

"Hello, Leo." She returned his smile. "Are you feeling all right?" She chuckled. "I guess most people would assume the worst when you're in a doctor's office."

"No, just came in for my checkup," he explained, taking the chair next to her. His gaze seemed pleading. "You know something, don't you?" he said in a low voice so he wouldn't be overheard.

"Know what?" She kept her voice equally low.

"That things aren't what they appear to be," he replied. "Some may think there's a good reason why people die, but it's not always so."

Bree put her magazine to one side. "What do you know, Leo?" she demanded.

Sorrow seemed to wrap itself around him. "I shouldn'a done it, ma'am. It was wrong."

"What was wrong?"

"Leo, the doctor will see you now."

He hesitated as if he feared he'd said too much. Or was it that he felt he hadn't said enough?

"Just be careful," he whispered, as he slowly rose to his feet and made his way to the waiting nurse.

Bree hoped to catch him when he left, but Cody was called next. Instead, she sat impatiently with her son while the nurse took his vitals and asked a few questions, then told them the doctor would be in directly.

Bree felt the vibration of her pager against her waistband. She glanced down and read the phone number. Cole.

"Do you have to go to work?" Cody asked, watching her with anxious eyes.

"Not yet," she assured him. She looked up when she heard a crisp rap on the door and it opened.

A man she guessed to be in his early forties walked briskly into the room. He had blond hair that looked styled, without a strand out of place, a blue polo shirt probably chosen because it matched his eyes, and a lean body thanks to the gym.

Bree didn't feel the slightest tingle.

He flashed a brilliant smile at both mother and son. "Mrs. Fitzpatrick, I'm Mike Warren." He held out his hand.

"Dr. Warren." She returned his smile.

The man turned to Cody. "So, young man, you're not feeling so hot."

"Uh-uh," he mumbled, not looking up at the doctor.

"Can I take a peek in your ear?" he asked.

Cody gazed imploringly at Bree. She gave a barely imperceptible nod.

She watched the doctor talk to Cody in a low voice meant to soothe as he examined the ear.

"Definitely a flare-up there," he said. "I'll prescribe some drops for the ear and antibiotics he'll need to take for the next ten days." He pulled out his prescription pad and began scribbling. "Don't worry, he'll bounce back in no time. Kids generally do."

"He's allergic to penicillin," Bree said.

"Yes, I see that." He tapped the chart. He finished writing and held out the prescriptions to Bree. "If he's not showing any improvement in five days, bring him back in."

"I'll do that." She reached for them. "Thank you."

He held on a beat too long before he released them. "Maybe sometime we could get together for dinner," he suggested. "I'm sure you've noticed that there's not too many single adults under the age of seventy in this town."

Bree couldn't believe she could feel immune to what was probably a smile that made most women's knees turn to jelly. What exactly had Cole done to her?

Maybe the good doctor didn't have that devil-may-care attitude Cole Becker sported.

"I have too much going on in my life right now, Dr. Warren, to think about a social life," she replied. "I'm still taking things one step at a time."

He lifted his brows in question. "Does that mean I can ask again?"

She smiled. "We'll see."

Bree left the office with Cody trotting alongside her. She stopped at the reception desk to inquire if Leo was still there, and was told he'd left fifteen minutes ago.

"You're not going to go out with him, are you?" Cody asked, as he hopped into their vehicle.

"I hadn't planned on it," she replied. "Why? Do you want me to date him?"

He screwed up his face. "No way! I don't have to go back to see him, do I?" He fiddled with the vent levers until Bree stopped him. "I don't like doctors, Mom."

"And this is a new thing?" she teased, well aware of his dislike of the medical profession. She never told him she was positive he would grow up to be a doctor because of his empathy with the human race.

As her cell phone rang and she switched it on, she noticed Cody rubbing his ear. "Don't rub your ear, hon," she chided. "Hello?"

"Your phone tells you what I'm doing?" Cole's voice rumbled in her ear.

"Cody and I just left the doctor's office. He has an ear infection." She settled the phone more snugly. "I made a call about those reports. We'll have them by the end of today."

"Which doctor did you see?"

"Dr. Warren. Cody's pediatrician was out of the office on an emergency."

"He hit on you?" Cole asked, sounding suspicious.

"Oh yeah." She reached out and gently brushed Cody's hand away from his ear. "Big time."

"Does this mean I need to beat him up on your behalf? I've never defended a woman's honor before, but for you, I'll give it a whirl. Of course, that will probably mean he won't play basketball with me anymore. But for you, I'd do it."

"Thanks a lot, Becker. I'm so glad I have you on my side," she said in a sarcastic voice. "But you were safe. If there had been a problem I could have easily taken him down. Is there anything else?"

"Will you call me when you get the reports?" he asked. "Or

better yet, wanna come over tonight and we'll study them together?''

She could feel the warmth flood through her body as she heard the hidden meaning in his voice. They would definitely do more than read through autopsy reports.

''I'll call you later,'' she said crisply, while she could still function.

''Mom, you didn't answer my question.'' Cody demanded her attention. ''I don't have to see that doctor again, do I?''

''Not if you don't want to go back to him. We'll see what other doctors we might like in the area. However, that means you have to take all your medicine and not complain when I put the drops in your ear,'' she told him. ''But why don't you want to go back to Dr. Warren? He seemed nice,'' she lied.

Cody gave that little-boy shrug that could mean so many things. ''I just don't like him.''

Bree hid her grin as she thought of Cole's typical male comments at the thought of competition. ''I don't think you're alone.''

Chapter 14

Bree had barely crossed Cole's threshold before she snatched the glass of wine from him and jammed a sheaf of papers into his now-empty hand.

"That bad?" he asked.

"When men are sick, they turn into little boys," she informed him, dropping down onto the couch. "When little boys are sick, they're worse. The baby-sitter who'd always told me she could look after Cody if he had to stay home from school couldn't do it today. It seems it was her spa day and she was heading for San Diego. Cody didn't want to color. He didn't want to watch cartoons. He didn't want to play any of his video games. He wanted to follow me around the house. He hasn't been this clingy since he was two. I got a twenty-minute break when his medication kicked in and he fell asleep." She downed her wine like water.

"Another?" Cole held up the bottle.

She shook her head. "No, that did it for me."

"Have you looked these over?" He sat down beside her.

"I only had time to skim them." She set the empty glass down.

He began reading the top page. "Anything reach out and grab you?"

"A few things, but I wanted to wait until I brought them over here. I want to see if you notice the same things. But there's something I want to tell you first." She relayed her conversation with Leo in the doctor's office.

Cole's brow furrowed with thought. "He knows something."

"I agree. The question is what. He looked scared, Cole. Whatever he knows has him pretty frightened," she pointed out. "I think it took a lot of courage on his part to tell me what little he did. I think he wants to tell me more, but he's afraid to."

"Afraid you have something to do with it, too?"

She shook her head. "No, I think he's afraid I might say something to the wrong person. I need to talk to him more. Assure him that he has nothing to be afraid of. Whatever he knows has been bottled up inside him and he needs to get it out. He must feel he can trust me. The problem now is getting him to talk freely."

"Anna's death," Cole mused. "It could be tied up with that."

"For now, let's see what we can do with these." She gestured to the reports.

Cole picked up one of the reports and began reading. He murmured a few curses under his breath. "All so impersonal. As if they were never human beings."

"Keeping it impersonal makes it easier to handle. You can't lose your objectivity or it gets too difficult to remain on track." She took a deep breath. "There's something really funny about the doctors' signatures."

He turned his head. "Funny how?"

Bree sorted through the papers and pulled three sheets out. She placed them side by side on the coffee table. She picked up a pen and used it as a pointer.

"I'm no handwriting expert, but while the names on these reports are different, I'd swear the handwriting is the same. It just goes to show that no one ever really read the names or checked them out."

"How can you tell?" he asked. "I haven't met one doctor yet who can sign his name so it's even slightly legible."

"One thing I've been told is you search for constants. They're here if you look closely enough," she said. "Not to mention this." She unfolded a pink sheet of paper and laid it next to the others. "Dr. Warren's signature from Cody's bill," she said smugly. "Perfect for comparison, and you can see the similarity in handwriting."

"One more piece to the puzzle," he said.

"And more questions," she said. "But I think one important one is answered as to why some of the deaths weren't questioned. When I took Cody to the medical office, I could see that the doctor is kept busy. A lot of senior citizens were in there. It's the perfect place to determine who will be next."

Cole shook his head. "A vulture preying on the weak. No one else would have the resources Michael has." His face darkened with anger. "I play basketball with that bastard a couple times a month. I've seen him in pain because he's lost a patient."

"Who better than your typical nice guy to plan murder," she said flatly. "The kind of man who shows the world how much he cares about his patients. Who would dispute it? The deaths weren't the kind that would raise enough questions to prompt further investigation."

"I have a friend who's a handwriting expert," Cole offered. "He can confirm all those signatures are from the same man."

"I have one, too. Want to pit my expert against yours?"

"Mine's good enough to be used when historical documents are in question." He chose several pages and placed them to one side. "I'll send him several examples, along with the sheet you got today."

Bree nodded. "All right."

Cole slumped back against the couch. "All for money."

"Anything like this is always for the money." She slid off her loafers and tucked her bare feet up under her body.

"Joshua," Cole said suddenly. "We need to talk to him. He has to know something about this." He turned around and snagged his phone, but Bree stopped him.

"You can't talk to him tonight. Renee's funeral is tomorrow," she reminded him.

"But if we catch him off guard we could find out something," he insisted.

"That's the hard-core reporter talking. Listen to the hard-nosed detective. No." She exaggerated the word.

"He might be able to fill in the missing pieces," Cole argued.

"I'm sure he can, and if this was part of a sheriff's investigation, I would call him and do this the right way," she said. "But it's not. In many ways my hands are tied."

Cole nodded. "I had no idea it would grow into this. You came here for a quieter way of life and I'm dragging you into something that's threatening you and your family. I'm sorry."

"Don't be sorry," she argued. "You saw a wrong you wanted to make right. Which we will do."

Bree swiveled around when she heard the doorbell ring.

"That's our pizza," he explained, getting up.

"There better not be any mushrooms on it," she called after him. "And there better be extra cheese."

"There aren't and there is."

Cole sat on the floor in front of the coffee table watching Bree easily demolish half a large pizza.

"Hungry, were you?" he said mildly.

"With three kids, I'm usually lucky to get one slice," she explained. "Not having to grab for food or referee battles is nice."

"Bree, how long are you going to hide behind your widow-hood and your kids?" he asked suddenly.

She stopped, her slice of pizza halfway to her mouth.

"I'm not hiding behind anything," she muttered, refusing to look at him.

"Then why can't you look me in the face and say that? Look at me. Come on, Bree, what are you so scared of?"

She did as he requested and looked him square in the eye. "Don't you know you can't scare a person when they have teenagers?"

"See? You're doing it right now. Invoking the *mother* word as if it's some kind of shield to keep you safe." He pushed their paper plates and pizza carton to one side.

Bree again refused to look at him. "I have responsibilities," she said flatly.

"That doesn't mean you can't open yourself up." He grabbed hold of her chin and brought her around to face him.

"Look who's talking," she sniped. "The man who makes sure any woman he's with knows there are no strings attached."

He took a deep breath. "Yeah, well, things can change."

She arched an eyebrow. "Really?" Skepticism colored her voice. "In what way? You'll date them more than once?"

"I've seen you a hell of a lot more than once," Cole snapped.

"There's that warm and fuzzy feeling."

"You're afraid," he accused. "You're afraid of allowing yourself to feel. Would he want you doing this? Would he expect you to wear virtual mourning for the rest of your life? Would he want you to use his death as an excuse for not living your life to the fullest? From what I've heard about the man, he wouldn't. Which means you're doing it to yourself."

"This from the man who goes out of town for his social life," she retorted, pulling back from him. He tightened his grip.

"Yeah, I did," he said honestly. "But the minute I met you, the idea of seeing anyone else went right out of my mind. You don't think this isn't scary for me, too? The idea of falling in love is about as scary for me as the prospect of, well, I can't think of anything that scary just now, but I know it's out there."

Bree's face crumpled in confusion and pain. "No." She batted at his hands as he again reached for her. "No, don't talk about love," she mumbled, clumsily getting to her feet. She rooted around for her shoes and slid her feet in them. "I had love. I don't need to have it again."

"And you think I intended to fall in love?" He shot to his feet. "Bree, this hit me fast and hard." He followed her to the door. "I'm still trying to get it straight in my head. I was the guy who wouldn't date a woman with kids because we'd be ruled by a baby-sitter's curfew. I screwed up my marriage because I cared more for my work than I did for my wife. Let me tell you, lady, I'm no longer that guy, and it's all because of you."

"They all say that," she muttered, snatching up her jacket off the table near the door. "I have to go. Let me know when you hear something from the handwriting analyst."

"Dammit, Bree!" He was hot on her heels. "Talk to me about this!"

She kept shaking her head as she practically ran to her SUV, activating the door locks at the same time.

"Bree!" Cole shouted after her, uncaring if the entire county heard him.

All he received was dust in his face.

He muttered more than a few choice curses as he returned to the house.

"I guess I should be grateful you didn't use your damn gun on me," he muttered, pushing the door open.

Bree forced herself to focus on the road. The cop in her knew it wasn't wise to drive while in this kind of emotional state. The woman in her said to get the hell out of Dodge.

Using Fitz like some shield against his so-called charms, she thought angrily. *Hiding behind the kids, my butt. Who the hell does he think he is to make those accusations? He's the one who doesn't date a woman more than a couple times, and even then finds them out of town, so he doesn't have to worry about running into them.*

"I'm not hiding behind anyone," she said out loud. "I just don't feel the need to make any kind of commitment."

It's not every day a man tells you he's falling in love with you, a sly voice whispered in her ear. *Especially when that man knows you have three children. Do you know how many women would kill for someone like him?*

"I don't need a man," she argued with herself.

I don't recall you thinking that when you were in the man's bed and he was rocking your world.

"Someday, I need to get a conscience that agrees with me."

Without warning, a blinding light bounced off her rearview mirror.

"Take off the high beams, buddy," she grumbled, reaching up to adjust her mirror to deflect the light. When it didn't work, she glanced into her sideview mirror and saw the reason why. The truck behind her moved closer. "Sorry, sweetheart, but you're not my type.'' She pressed down on the accelerator. At the same time, her brain registered a distinctive, familiar sound coming from behind.

With the other driver's headlights on high beam she didn't have a chance of reading the license plate. It looked like she wouldn't have a chance of outrunning him, either.

As she increased her speed, she ran through a list of possibilities. In the end, she went for the best chance. She snatched up her microphone and keyed it on.

''Dispatch, this is K-nine-one,'' she said crisply, while keeping one eye on her pursuer. ''I've got a joyrider on my tail. Large pickup, dark color. I think it's a dually. No way to read the plate. I'm out on Canyon Ridge Road about two miles before I reach Spinning Wheel Road. I wouldn't mind someone meeting up with me to have a chat with this guy.''

''Got it, K-nine-one,'' the night dispatcher replied. ''I'll be sending you a solution.''

''Thanks.'' She keyed off.

The moment she dropped the microphone, she felt a jolt go through her body. She gripped the steering wheel to keep the vehicle on a straight path. She'd barely recovered when another jolt sent her bouncing against the seat.

She wasn't sure if it was her imagination when she saw the familiar flashing lights in the distance.

''Okay, jerk, you are going down,'' she muttered, just as the truck rammed into the back of her vehicle so hard she swerved off the road. She relied on memories of defensive driving as she twisted the wheel so she could avoid a tree that suddenly appeared in front of her. The SUV bounced over rocks, sending her thumping painfully against the top of the truck. All she was aware of then was the air bag exploding in her face at the same time the front end collided with something unforgiving. After that, her world turned black.

''Detective. Ma'am. Are you okay?''

Bree moaned as she opened her eyes. For a moment, she was positive stars danced in front of them. She turned her head and moaned again as pain shot through her head. Randy had opened her door and was leaning forward, with one hand braced on the top.

"Please tell me you got the number of that truck," she said feebly.

"Sorry. When I got here, all I found was you down here," he said, sounding apologetic. "For a minute I was afraid I'd find you like…"

Like Renee Patterson.

She easily read his meaning. She lifted her hand to her head and brought it back. Dampness stained her fingertips.

"I called for an ambulance," he told her, putting both hands out when she started to unbuckle her belt. "No, Detective, you need to stay there until the paramedics can check you over."

She took a quick mental inventory. "Nothing's broken." She started to get out, but fell back when her spinning head refused to allow her to go any farther. "Okay, not a good idea." She closed her eyes as nausea threatened.

The piercing scream of a siren cut through her aching head like a laser.

"How bad does my vehicle look?" she asked.

"Pretty bad," he told her. "The whole back end is caved in. Must have been a big truck. Not to mention what you did to the front when you hit the tree."

Bree fought the pain so she could concentrate. "Which means the other guy must have some damage to the front of his truck. Somebody needs to check body shops."

"Ma'am. Detective. We'll get on it. Don't you worry," he assured her. "But you need to stay still until they check you over."

She noticed the worried look on his thin features and realized she'd better do what he suggested. It was easy to listen to him, since she felt as if she could throw up without a second's notice.

By the time paramedics appeared, she almost embraced them.

"How do you feel, Detective?" one of the men asked, shining a penlight in her eyes, then moving it away.

"As if the world is spinning around me at warp speed after a steamroller ran over me."

He asked her a few more questions as he checked her head wound.

"We're taking you to the hospital, Detective," his partner told her. "What with you losing consciousness and experiencing nausea, you need to be under observation."

"I don't need—" The nausea hit her full force the moment they helped her out of the seat.

"My kids," she said weakly, once they strapped her onto a gurney. "I need to call my kids."

"Someone can call for you once we get in there," the paramedic told her.

"I'll go by your house and tell them, ma'am," Randy offered.

"No." She unsuccessfully fought the dizziness. "If they see you drive up, they'll think the worst." She felt a soft thump as her bag was set on the gurney beside her.

The next thing Bree remembered was opening her eyes and staring into a pair of puppy dog brown eyes. The stark white of a doctor's lab coat hurt her own eyes.

"How are you feeling?" the doctor asked.

"Like I ran into a tree," she said truthfully, trying to sit up.

But the emergency room doctor held her down. "If I were you, I wouldn't try sitting up just yet," he advised. "I'm going to order some X rays, but I'd say you have a nasty concussion. Had to stitch up a cut on your forehead and you've got a cut lip."

"My kids," she moaned. "I've got to get home."

"Sorry, Detective, but you aren't going anywhere except to a bed upstairs."

"Calls, I need to make calls," she babbled.

"One of your people is here. I'm sure they know who to call."

The next few hours were a blur for Bree as she was wheeled to the X-ray department, then taken to a room, undressed and put into bed.

"Why am I being put to bed when you're just going to wake me up later to make sure I know what day it is, what my name is and who's the president of the United States?" she argued.

"Fine, I'll ask you who the vice president is," the nurse said cheerfully as she left the room.

"I won't sleep, anyway," Bree grumbled even as her lids drooped down.

Squeaky wheel. Definitely a squeaky wheel. There shouldn't be anything like a squeaky wheel in a hospital. Weren't there rules about that kind of thing?

"Would you be happier if I found some oil and took care of it?" A familiar male voice rumbled comfortably.

Bree opened one eye. A disheveled Cole sat slumped in the chair by her bed. His face was dark with beard and his eyes were bloodshot, as if he hadn't gotten much sleep the night before. She thought back and vaguely remembered the nurse waking her up several times. Bree had thought there was someone else in the room at those times, but she hadn't realized it was Cole. Or maybe a part of her did know he was there with her and that was why she slept so peacefully.

"What are you doing here?" she croaked, trying to lick her dry lips.

He reached over for her cup of water and handed it to her. She drank thirstily.

"Mamie's son is the night dispatcher. He told her you were in a car accident on Canyon Ridge Road. She assumed you were leaving my place and thought I should know," he said. "I stopped by your house first. I'm afraid they're not taking it well."

"Of course they wouldn't take it well. Why should they? They lost their father a year ago." She combed her fingers through her hair and encountered gauze. She noticed even her fingertips hurt. Then she remembered she'd put her hands up in front of her face to protect it. The air bag must have burned them slightly.

"I heard a truck ran you off the road." His gaze was troubled.

She started to nod, then decided against it. "It was our old friend. Big truck. There was no missing the distinctive sound in the engine. He decided to cream the back end of my Expedition.

Good thing I didn't have Jinx with me or he'd be in the next bed.''

"Actually, he'd be at the veterinary clinic down the road,'' Cole pointed out.

"He's a cop. He'd be with me.'' She mentally checked herself over. "Have they served breakfast yet?''

"Not yet.'' He took her hand and brought it up to his mouth. The rasp of his unshaved face was like sandpaper against her skin and all the more welcome. "I'm sorry, Bree.'' His breath was warm against her skin. "If I hadn't picked a fight with you, this wouldn't have happened.''

"It still would have happened. Just at another time. Maybe a time where I wouldn't have had backup so quickly. Cole, you were right.''

He leaned forward. "Excuse me?''

She managed a weak smile. "You're excused.''

"Come on, Fitzpatrick, no jokes.'' He kept her hand resting against his mouth. "If anything had happened to you…'' His voice trailed off.

"Now you know why I drive a tank.'' She rested her free hand on his head, feeling the springy crispness of his hair. For a moment, she thought there were more gray hairs than there had been the night before. "I don't want to fight with you,'' she whispered.

"Good, then we won't.'' His eyes deepened in color.

"And I won't hide.''

Cole immediately understood her meaning.

"I'm glad you're here,'' she admitted.

"We've got to find this truck, Bree,'' he said.

"They'll be checking body shops. Ramming me had to do some serious damage.'' She winced.

He was instantly standing over her. "How's your head?''

"Like Woody Woodpecker is tap-dancing on my forehead,'' she replied.

"I better call a nurse. They only let me stay in here as long as I promised to let them know when you woke up.'' He leaned down, kissing her gently on the lips. "Damn, Bree, I don't know what I would have done if I'd lost you.'' He turned around and left the room.

Bree breathed in and out deeply.

What are you going to do now, Bree? The man has pretty much laid his heart on the line. Now it's up to you.

''Shut up,'' she muttered to the nagging voice.

''So you decided to wake up,'' the nurse said cheerfully as she entered the room. ''How do you feel?''

''Ready to leave.'' She waited while her temperature and blood pressure were taken.

''We'll see what the doctor says.''

''Do I get breakfast?'' Bree asked the nurse as she was departing.

''Soon.''

''At least she didn't use that medical 'we,''' she said sarcastically, and plopped back against the pillow.

''You're one of those cranky patients, aren't you?'' Cole walked back in. He gave an exaggerated sniff. ''Um, disinfectant number five. My favorite.'' He leaned down and kissed her gently on the lips. ''I hate to tell you this, Fitzpatrick, but you look like hell.''

''Thank you so much. Hospitals have never been my favorite place,'' she admitted crankily. ''Cole, I've got to get my kids out of this town,'' she said in a low voice. ''Deep down, I don't think this creep would go after them, but what if I'm wrong? I couldn't live with myself if anything happened to them.''

''Is there anyone you can send them to?'' he asked, dropping back into the chair and taking her hand, keeping it warmly clasped between his.

Bree nodded. ''I can call my sister.'' She looked around at the blue-painted walls and the window that overlooked a parking lot. ''I've spent too much time in hospitals in the past year what with the surgery after I was shot.'' Her eyes glistened with tears as she looked at him. ''Not that Fitz made it to one. He was pronounced dead at the scene.'' Her smile wobbled. ''You were right, Cole. I was hiding behind him and the kids. I saw the man I thought I would be spending the rest of my life with shot down. Before I lost consciousness, a part of me knew he was dying.

There was no chance for me to say goodbye. No chance for the kids to say goodbye. I didn't want to experience that pain again. I was afraid if I got too close to you I would leave myself open for that. The best way to make sure it didn't happen was to wall myself off. Those walls are falling because I want to see what I can have with you.''

Cole leaned forward, bracing his elbows on the side of the bed. He kept her hand between his.

"Does that mean you won't run out again when I tell you my feelings?''

She started to shake her head and instantly realized it wasn't a good idea when her world started to tilt. "No more running.''

"I understand someone in here wants to leave our happy place.'' A man wearing a white lab coat entered the room.

"Someone very much wants to leave,'' Bree said with feeling.

"Better do what she says, Doc,'' Cole recommended. "She's a highly trained law enforcement officer. She can take you down in ten seconds.''

"Not today she can't,'' the doctor said, flashing a warm grin. "I don't think our detective here could take down a teddy bear.''

"If you'll sign my release papers right now, I promise not to hurt you,'' she told him.

"I'll look after her,'' Cole offered. "I'll make sure she follows any directions you give.''

Bree breathed a sigh of relief when, after the doctor examined her, he pronounced she could go home as long as she took it easy for the next twenty-four hours.

She wasted no time changing into her clothes. She winced at the bloodstains on her sweater and jeans and the slight smoky smell of her clothing. She knew her first task when she got home would be to take a long hot shower.

"I will be a happy person if I never have to enter a hospital again,'' she said, collapsing into the passenger seat of Cole's truck.

"Anyone from the station try to contact you?'' he asked, driving slowly through the parking lot.

"Not that I know of. I'll have to call in when I get home. They'll need a statement from me.'' She pulled her sunglasses out of her bag and slipped them on. "I also need to call the insurance company about my truck."

Bree immediately smelled the lemon scent of furniture polish when she entered the house. Bare floors sparkled and a look inside the family room showed all of Cody's toys had been picked up.

"Are you sure this is my house?"

"Mom!" Cody ran down the hallway and launched himself into her arms.

"Whoa, kid." Cole scooped him up before he could reach his objective. "Your mom's kinda sore right now."

David appeared with Lacey and a wide-eyed Sara on his heels. He came forward and carefully put his arms around her.

"From now on, you're on a curfew," he muttered, stepping back so Sara could hug her, too.

The girl uttered a soft cry of dismay when she saw the gauze patch on Bree's forehead and the bloodstains on her clothing.

"I'm all right," Bree assured her, wrapping her arms around her.

"Did they feed you?" Lacey asked. "I could make you an omelette."

"Her omelettes look like omelettes," Sara said. "And they're good."

"They gave me something called oatmeal, and yes, Lacey, I would love an omelette," Bree said gratefully. "But first I'd like to take a shower and get into some clean clothes."

She headed for her bedroom. The moment she closed the door behind her, she began shedding her clothing, dropping it on the floor behind her as she headed for the bathroom.

Mindful of the stitches, she directed the shower nozzle at her chest. As she allowed the water to run down her body, she did a self-examination of various bruises caused from her bouncing around. She took care in washing her hair and, once finished, felt a little more human.

When she walked into the kitchen, she found everyone but Lacey sitting around the table. The teenager was busy at the stove.

"It's just about ready," she announced, sliding the egg creation onto a plate.

"I poured juice for you," Cody said, bouncing up and down in his chair.

"Sara's right. Lacey knows what she's doing," Cole said around a mouthful of his own omelette.

Bree decided to wait until she'd eaten before she made her announcement. She enjoyed the cheese omelette flavored with herbs much more than the oatmeal she'd been given in the hospital, and she was quick to tell Lacey so. The girl blushed hotly at her praise.

"I'm hoping to attend a culinary academy and start up a restaurant," she replied.

"Count me as one of your first customers," Bree stated.

She looked at the group seated at the table watching her finish her last mouthful.

"I'm calling your aunt Wendy to see if she can put you three up for a while," she announced. "After what happened last night, I can't afford to take any chances."

"No!" Sara and Cody cried.

"You can't do this, Mom," David argued, a steely glint in his eye.

Bree turned to him first. She smiled as she saw even more traces of his father in the stubborn look she was receiving in return.

"Yes, I can," she said softly, but firmly. She already knew she would be truthful with them. She always had been and wouldn't lie to them now. "I am investigating something that's proving to be dangerous. I don't want anything to happen to any of you."

"I don't want you to die," Cody declared, his lower lip trembling.

She held out her arms. He wasted no time crawling into her lap.

"I don't intend to," she assured him, moving her gaze from one child to the next. "I just would feel better if you'd stay with your aunt Wendy right now." As she said it, she noticed the look that passed between Lacey and David. *Uh-oh.* It was not a look she wanted to see between two teenagers.

Something else she'd have to worry about.

"It was a warning, Mom," David stated. "Nobody wants to actually hurt us. Whoever it was just wanted to give us a good scare. They want you to back off checking out those past cases." The expression he shot his stepmother told her he didn't expect that to happen.

"I wanted us to go to the carnival." Cody spoke up with a mournful air. "It's only here for this weekend." He caressed his mother's cheek. His gaze silently pleaded with her.

Bree had thought the same thing as David. Running her off the road was a warning. She didn't want to think whoever was behind this would stoop to terrorizing children. But there was always a first time. She didn't want them to end up victims because she didn't do everything possible to protect them.

"We could all stay together," David said. "We'll be in a crowded place. No one would dare try anything."

"Power in numbers." Cole backed him up.

Bree looked from one to the other.

"Tell you what. Let me take a nap this afternoon and we'll go tonight as long as you all follow my rules," she told Cody. "But tomorrow you go to Aunt Wendy's."

"At least she lives near a mall," Sara muttered. She turned a bright red when everyone turned to her. "I'm trying to look on the bright side, okay?"

"A carnival sounds good," Cole said. "Lots of junk food. Loud music. Bright lights. Rides that go so fast you want to throw up. Just the thing."

Bree turned to Lacey. "You don't think your parents will mind?"

She shook her head. "They went to Las Vegas for a week or so."

"Just be prepared to watch David turn into a total carnival animal," Bree teased, looking at her stepson. "All those midway games make him crazy."

"I win my fair share," he said defensively.

Bree gazed at each one, ending with Cole. He smiled and sent her a look that spoke volumes.

Taking down those shields proved much easier than she thought.

Chapter 15

The large fields on the other side of town had been transformed into a noisy, multicolored world filled with a number of rides, games and every kind of junk food a kid would want.

Bree assured Cole she was feeling better after resting all afternoon, but he couldn't help noticing she walked slower than usual. He wouldn't be surprised if she hadn't popped more than her share of aspirin since arriving home. She'd refused the prescription for painkillers the doctor had offered.

The moment they arrived, Lacey and David took off, after promising to meet up with them in two hours. Sara complained about staying with the adults, but Cody was only too happy to stick close by when Cole offered to go on some of the more stomach-churning rides with him.

"Better you than me," Bree murmured, squeezing Cole's hand.

"I'll be honest. I haven't had a lot of experience with humans his age, so it's a good chance for me to see how I do," he told her, keeping an arm looped around her neck. He brought her closer and kissed her temple. "Be good to me and I'll win you one of those huge stuffed animals."

She laughed softly. "Sure, after you drop at least fifty dollars."

"I think I can succeed before I go broke."

Cole didn't miss that Bree's gaze swept all around them. He knew she was still angry about Roy Holloway showing up that afternoon to take a report on her accident. He also knew she didn't like the man treating it as a true accident and not assault with a deadly weapon. After the sheriff left, Cole had listened to her rant and rave about him for a good half hour. Her insistence that the man didn't deserve to work in animal control was the mildest thing she said about him.

"Calm down, slugger. Let's just enjoy the evening," Cole murmured with another kiss.

She smiled. "You can soften me up all you want, Becker. If you're insisting on spending the night, you're still sleeping on the couch, since Lacey's staying over in the guest room." She sighed. "I think she's adopted us. Fine by me, since I think she's a great girl. Too bad her parents don't realize it. But damn, I think there's way too much going on between her and David."

"He seems levelheaded."

"Everyone's levelheaded until they fall in love." She reached behind him and tucked her hand in the back pocket of his jeans.

"Come on, Cole!" Cody shouted, jumping up and down. "Tilt-A-Whirl!"

"I'll go with him," Sara offered.

Cole gave her a handful of tickets.

She grabbed her brother's hand and headed for the line.

"They're great kids, Bree," he said.

"Yes, they are," she said, pride shining in her face.

"Tonight is what they needed. A chance to forget what's been going on and just plain be kids." A flash of navy caught his eye. He turned his head and noticed Frank Roberts walking through the crowd. The deputy noticed him and nodded.

"One of your co-workers at two o'clock," Cole said softly, using the time to indicate position.

Bree didn't turn her head, but he knew she saw the man just the same.

"In a place like this you need to have that high visibility

factor. It keeps the fights down.'' She smiled and waved back at Cody, who waved wildly at them. ''Do you see David and Lacey anywhere?''

''Nope, but I wouldn't worry about them. David seems to be able to take care of himself.''

''He can, but that doesn't mean I wouldn't worry about anyone else trying something.''

''No worrying,'' Cole chided. ''This is a night for fun, remember? A night for the kids. I'd like for us to find some dark corner and neck.''

''And get caught by one of the deputies?'' she laughed. ''I don't think so. Not to mention I wouldn't care for Sara and Cody as an audience.''

Cole found himself getting dizzy as he shared a variety of rides with Cody, who only shouted with glee. When Bree offered Cole a Coke, he shook his head.

''I'm glad you think it's funny. I used to be able to do this stuff standing on my head,'' he muttered.

''Maybe you should have tried it that way,'' she said all too innocently.

''Wow, Cole, how many rides did you go on?'' David asked, when he and Lacey walked up to them. ''You look seriously green.''

''I'll be fine,'' he said. ''Once I find where I left my stomach. That kid has a cast-iron gut.''

''And to think you wanted to be an astronaut,'' Bree teased.

''Those rides were a lot easier when I was a kid,'' he confessed.

Bree brushed Cody's hair back from his face. ''You had enough?'' she asked.

He nodded as he leaned against her hip.

''How about getting some pizza?'' Cole asked. ''By the time we reach the restaurant, my stomach should be back to normal.''

''Yes!'' Cody yelled at the top of his lungs.

''I won't turn it down,'' David said, after glancing at Lacey, who gave a slight nod.

''And you thought you couldn't relate to kids,'' Bree teased, as they headed for the parking lot.

They walked down the row toward Cole's and David's trucks, since Bree's SUV was out of commission. Cole momentarily paused before continuing. Only Bree noticed his hesitation.

"Three rows to the left," he murmured for her ears only. "The end of the row."

She shifted her gaze in the direction he mentioned and saw what he had. The last vehicle was a large truck. A dually. In the chilly night air, the truck's exhaust showed white. Because of the noise coming from the carnival, they couldn't hear the engine, but they didn't need to. They already knew what it sounded like.

Cole looked at Bree inquiringly, then glanced toward the truck again.

"Want to check it out?" he asked in a low voice.

Before Bree could reply, the vehicle slowly backed up and drove down the dirt road. In moments, it was gone.

"Just wanted us to know he was there," she murmured.

"Yeah. Stay on our tail," Cole said to David, who nodded as he and Lacey headed for his truck.

Cole glanced around as he pulled out of the parking lot, with David close behind him. He kept an eye out for the truck as they drove toward the pizza parlor, but saw nothing. Once inside, he forced himself to relax and joke with the kids as they ate pizza. He even participated when David and Cody challenged him to the arcade games in the back.

By the time they left the parlor, they were satiated with pizza, and a sleepy Cody was leaning against Bree.

David pulled into the driveway first and activated the garage door opener. As she watched it roll upward, Bree felt the tingling sense of something wrong.

"Cody, stay with Cole," she ordered, hopping out of the truck. She opened her fanny pack and took out her weapon. "David! Keep Sara and Lacey with you!" She ran to the keypad by the back door and disarmed the alarm.

"Mom?" Cody's voice shook with terror.

"It's all right, sweetie," she told him as she moved through the brightly lit garage. "Jinx!" she called out. A chill ran down her spine when the dog didn't respond.

When they left the house, Bree had ordered Jinx to guard. She knew he should have come to her the moment she called his name. Something was very wrong.

She went out into the backyard and found the dog lying motionless in the middle of the grass, with one of the new floodlights shining on him as if he was on exhibit.

"No." Her throat closed up as she ran to the dog. The moment she touched him, she felt relief that he was still alive. As she examined him in the light, she found a dart buried in his side. "Cole!"

Hearing her shout, he was at her side in seconds.

"Damn," he muttered.

"Tranquilizer dart," she said crisply. "We need to get him to a vet."

"Here, let me get him." He carefully picked up the unconscious dog in his arms.

"Jinx!" Cody cried out from the front seat of Cole's truck. He scrambled down to the driveway. "Is he dead?"

"No, honey, he's not. Jinx is just asleep," Bree assured him, watching as David hastily found a blanket and laid it in the bed of Cole's truck.

"Is Eartha Katt all right?" the boy demanded.

Bree shared looks with Cole and David. "I'm going to check the house out," she told them. "I need you two to stay here."

"And miss out on the fun?" Cole said, tongue in cheek.

"Let's go then."

She kept her weapon ready as she moved through the house with Cole as her shadow. He touched her arm and nodded toward the alarm keypad. They could see it hadn't been tripped. The kitten was sleeping peacefully in her box. David Boa was curled up in his terrarium. Nothing was out of place and nothing jangled Bree's sixth sense. After making sure nothing was out of place, they returned to the garage.

"You stay here. I'll take Jinx to the vet," Cole told her. His expression was tense as he looked around. "Do you think he'll show up around here?"

There was no question who he was talking about.

She shook her head. "This was meant to frighten the kids,"

she said tautly. "Scaring them makes me angrier, because this person trespassed on my property to do this." She rested her hand on the dog's neck, digging her fingers into the thick fur. "Assault on a police officer," she murmured.

"I'll call you as soon as I know something," he promised, kissing her on the lips.

Bree stood in the driveway watching Cole drive away.

"Nobody better have done anything to my tree house," Cody announced, running toward the backyard.

"Cody Fitzpatrick! You don't go anywhere without me," she shouted, taking off after her son.

She'd barely reached the edge of the yard when her son's screams turned her blood to ice. She sped up, reaching Cody as, still screaming, he scrambled back down the ladder, dropping to the grass. The gagging smell of death reached her at the same time.

"Let me." David ran past her and climbed the ladder. When he came back down, his face was white. "Somebody left a couple dead squirrels up there," he muttered.

"Do me a favor and bag them," she said under her breath.

He nodded. "Gee, Mom, and here everyone thought moving to a small town would be safer," he said sardonically as he walked toward the garage.

Bree looked around. She could see the indentation in the grass where Jinx must have dropped when he was shot with the tranquilizer dart. The horrible smell from the tree house was another unwelcome reminder.

"I guess I had to be wrong sometime."

Bree's worries were alleviated when Cole called to tell her Jinx was all right. The dog had been merely rendered unconscious and would be fine in a few more hours, but the veterinarian wanted to keep Jinx overnight for observation just in case. When Cole returned an hour later, Bree was waiting for him. She set the alarm as soon as he was inside.

"What happened?" Cole asked, seeing the tension etched in her face.

"Cody went out to his tree house and found two dead squirrels in it," she said tightly. "He was afraid to go to sleep. Sara didn't want to be alone and asked Lacey if she'd stay in her room with her." She stepped forward and wrapped her arms around his waist. "I want to find the person who did this and tear him into tiny pieces," she said against the comforting warmth of his chest.

"I'll hold them down for you." He kept his arms around her as they walked into the family room. They sat on the couch with Bree leaning against him.

"I called my sister while you were gone," she said in a low voice. "I asked her to take the kids for a week. She asked if something was wrong. I put her off for now."

"Will she question the kids?" he asked.

Bree shook her head. "She'd want to, but she knows I'll tell her when the time is right."

"I guess our next step is to connect all the dots," he said, also keeping his voice low.

"Exactly." A deep sigh left her body.

She felt the gentle pressure of his lips against her temple. She reluctantly rose to her feet and headed for her lonely bed.

Tomorrow would be soon enough to figure out what step to take next.

"Lacey's coming with us." David stood his ground as he stared down his stepmother. He looked as if he expected an argument and he meant to win.

His truck was already packed with the kids' belongings, and Cody carried Eartha Katt in his arms. Cole had already promised to feed David Boa.

Bree looked beyond the young man to the girl waiting a short distance away. "I doubt Wendy will mind," she said finally. "But she'll have to share a room with Sara." She studied his solemn gaze. "You would have refused to leave if I said no, wouldn't you?"

"We've got each other, Mom. Lacey doesn't have anyone. Her parents are never there for her," he replied.

Bree hugged him. "My David the protector," she murmured. "Make sure Cody takes care of Eartha Katt's litter box."

He nodded. He waved to Cole and loped back to his truck, while Lacey got in the passenger side. Cody looked out the window from the small bench seat behind David and waved.

"Is this what it's like when all the kids have left home?" Cole asked, coming up to Bree and settling his arm around her shoulders.

"I think so," she muttered with a sigh. "Except I'm not happy seeing them go."

He turned his head to press a kiss against her temple. "They'll be back soon." He squeezed her shoulders as they walked back to the house.

Once inside, Bree turned to Cole and gripped his arms.

"I need you so much," she said fiercely.

He easily read the hot request in her eyes.

His name was a bare whisper in the air as he pulled her almost roughly to him. Their mouths fused as they made their way blindly back to her bedroom and fell onto the tumbled sheets.

His touch was fierce as he moved over her body. She gasped, gripping his shoulders as the tremors moved through her body with the force of a major earthquake. Before she could recover, he grasped her hips and lifted her up against him. She wrapped her legs around his hips as he entered her in one swift thrust. His tongue swirled around hers in a demand for a response.

There were no soft loving words between them. No gentle touches because it wasn't what they needed. This time, they acted on pure raw need they both needed so badly.

Bree felt as if she was flying and Cole was right there with her. She dipped her head, nipping his shoulder. He muttered something, she couldn't understand the words, but she knew the emotion because it was the same as hers. His mouth covered hers as she felt herself fly into millions of pieces and a scream rise up in her throat.

Cole's chest rose and fell as he rolled on his back. Bree settled against him as if it was something she did every night. He wrapped his arms around her and rested his chin on the top of her head.

A sigh of regret fell from her lips as she reluctantly moved off the bed and walked into the bathroom. Cole lay in bed listening to the sound of the shower running. It seemed only a few minutes before Bree walked back into the bedroom.

She went into the closet and opened the lock box and took out her weapon and holster, laying them on the bed. Her next step was to pull her clothing out of the closet.

Cole noted the tan pants and navy polo shirt.

"Are we going for the official look?" he asked, sitting on the bed and watching her dress.

"Definitely." She slid her weapon into her holster. She brushed her hair and fluffed the wisp of bangs. Her detective's shield was hooked onto her waistband. "I'm going to stop at the veterinary clinic to check on Jinx, then I'm going in to the station. I'm filling out an official report about last night. I'm filling in everything from the beginning," she said grimly.

"I almost pity the guy once you catch up with him."

"I'm going to find proof once and for all," she said.

"Be careful." Cole stood up and walked over to her. He held on to her arms. "If this bastard has any idea…" He didn't say more.

"Don't worry," she assured him. She laid her hand against his cheek. "I'm very good at what I do," she said without any hint of ego, just a statement of fact. "Whatever it takes, I will get this person. The gloves are off now. My partner was assaulted. My children have been terrorized and, in a sense, my home was invaded. I'm not going to allow that to go unpunished. I will personally arrest whoever is behind all this."

"Boy, this guy doesn't know what he's up against, does he?" He smiled. He picked up his keys and tossed them up in the air. "Let's get this show on the road."

Bree found Jinx a little sluggish from his long nap, but happy to see his human partner. The dog wagged his tail and greeted her with a soft whine and a paw on her arm.

"He's doing fine," the veterinarian told her. "He was given a heavy-duty sedative, but nothing dangerous. I took another blood sample about an hour ago and everything looks good. No reason why he can't leave now."

"Thanks." She scratched behind the German shepherd's ears.

"I'll feel better having him with me." She slipped his harness over his head. His badge settled against his chest. The dog immediately straightened up. He knew it was time to go to work.

When Bree walked into the station with Jinx by her side, she was aware of eyes watching her with open curiosity.

"We thought you'd be staying out for a few days, ma'am," Randy greeted her.

"I only needed a day to get the kinks out," she replied, heading for her desk. Jinx stretched out beside her chair. "Besides, I need to file a report. Someone got onto my property last night and shot Jinx with a tranquilizer dart. Is the sheriff in?"

The deputy looked surprised by her stark announcement, then by her casually voiced question.

"He had to drive out to his sister's," he replied. "He said he'd be back later today. What do you mean, someone broke into your place? Did you call it in?"

"Not broke into my place literally." She switched on her computer. "Just stood on the boundary and shot a tranquilizer dart into Jinx. They also left a couple dead squirrels in my youngest son's tree house. Unfortunately, he was the one to find them."

"What kind of sick son of a bitch would do that?" Frank asked, coming up to her desk. "You don't do that kind of stuff to a kid." His ruddy features turned a dark red color.

"The kind of son of a bitch who didn't mind scaring the wits out of a six-year-old boy." She logged on to her computer. "And I bet it was the same son of a bitch who ran me off the road."

Frank looked intrigued. "You think the two are related?" he asked.

She nodded. "They're related." She looked up, her green eyes glittering like gemstones. "Do you have any ideas?"

"Ideas?" He looked confused, then comprehension hit. "You think me?" He looked as shocked as if she'd just struck him. "Now wait a minute! Okay, I didn't want you here. Hell, the sheriff kept promising me a promotion to detective. I thought I'd get the job. I was mad when I didn't. But I don't hurt dogs and I don't scare kids." His face grew even redder.

Bree held up a hand in hopes of calming him down. "I didn't think you had anything to do with it." She glanced at the computer screen as she brought up the accident report that had to do with her. "Wait a minute, why does this say a small pickup truck ran me off the road?" she muttered, leaning in to read the typed words. "It was a dark-colored dually. Some kind of distinctive sound in the engine."

Frank looked confused. "A dark dually? I was told it was a small pickup."

"Someone got it wrong," she muttered, still scanning the report, then bringing up other reports. One stopped her cold. "Leo was in an accident?"

Randy hovered near her desk. "Yeah, some kid was speeding and sideswiped him. Luckily, he's got that big truck, so the kid had more damage to his car than Leo did. Poor old guy was pretty shook up. Nice truck, too," he added. "But I told him he should see my brother about the problem he had with the engine."

Bree grew very still. "What problem with the engine?" she asked in a deliberately casual voice.

Randy shrugged. "Like a hitch in the engine and a soft whine."

Her senses started singing. "It's amazing that Leo would want to drive something so large. I don't remember seeing it in the parking lot."

"Leo always walks to work. He said he likes being out in the fresh air. The sheriff asked that one of us take the old man home when he was finished working. Said he shouldn't walk late at night even if it's pretty safe around here. Leo said he liked the truck because he could haul stuff around. He uses it a lot when they're needing things for the senior center," Randy replied. "The sheriff offers to do most of the heavy lifting, though. Well, we all take turns over there, but he sure does more than his share."

Bree's mind started spinning like a computer. She could feel the pieces slowly but surely starting to fall together.

"Uh-oh." Randy glanced at the clock. "Time for me to get

out there.'' He offered Bree a shy smile, which she warmly returned.

After making the necessary corrections in the accident report, she shut down her computer and stood up. She motioned to Jinx to follow her, and headed for the front desk.

"Are there any vehicles available for me to use?" she asked Irene.

The receptionist opened her desk drawer, pawed through several key rings and chose one. "The blue Blazer out back," she said, handing her the keys.

Bree nodded.

"You look pretty good for someone who ran into a tree," Irene commented, looking curious and watchful.

Bree smiled, not willing to give away anything. "You should see the tree," she said lightly, as she headed for the door.

"Did someone really leave dead squirrels in your son's tree house and your little boy found them?" The secretary's question stopped her.

Bree turned around. "Yes, someone did just that last night. Probably right after shooting a tranquilizer dart at Jinx."

Irene shook her head. "I've lived here all my life. It was always this small quiet town. There once was a time you didn't even have to worry about locking your doors when you left home. Back then, the worst thing that happened was kids soaping windows on Halloween. Seems no one's safe anymore. It's not right."

"No, it's not," Bree agreed.

She drove over to the newspaper office. Cole was seated at his desk, talking on the telephone, when she and Jinx entered.

He took one look at her face, muttered that he'd call back, and hung up.

She settled in the chair across from him and used a hand cue for Jinx to sit.

"Guess who's been driving a dually?"

Chapter 16

"Leo?" Cole kept shaking his head. "He's not the one."

"No, he's not," Bree agreed. "But the sheriff has used his truck in the past, and I wouldn't be surprised if he has an extra key for it. I need to get out there and see the truck."

"Can I go along?"

"If you behave."

"That's my middle name." He rose from his seat.

Cole directed Bree to the other side of town. All the homes looked postwar housing—small and boxy, with detached garages. Instead of grass, a majority of them boasted gravel front yards or cactus gardens.

"Easier to keep up," Cole explained as he pointed to the second house from the corner.

A dark dually pickup truck sat in the driveway.

They climbed out of the truck and walked up the driveway. Bree stopped to check the front end. She lightly touched the crunched metal.

"We have no idea if this was from his accident or mine," she murmured.

"You're positive it's the same truck?" Cole asked.

"Pretty sure."

"Detective Fitzpatrick?"

They turned and looked toward the now open door. Leo stood on the cement stoop. "Is there a problem?" He looked nervous.

Bree offered him a reassuring smile. "I just heard about your accident, Leo. Are you all right?"

He shifted from one foot to the other. "The kid had it worse than me. But you didn't mean to come out here and ask about me, did you?"

"No, I didn't," she said gently. "Leo, how often does the sheriff borrow your truck?"

He exhaled a deep breath. "I knew you'd be able to do something. Come on in." He turned around and stepped inside, not looking back to see if they followed.

Bree noticed the house was spotless. Leo was in the kitchen pouring iced tea into three glasses. He carefully set them on the table and gestured for Bree and Cole to be seated.

"Does the sheriff borrow your truck, Leo?" Bree asked softly.

The elderly man nodded, wrapping his hands around his glass. "He's called me up sometimes and asked if he could use the truck. That he had things to haul."

"But you didn't think that was the case, did you?" she carefully probed.

Leo looked up. His eyes were damp. "I always felt he was doing something wrong, but I couldn't ever prove it. I wanted to tell you how sorry I was when you had your accident."

"Was your truck gone that night, Leo?" Cole asked.

He nodded slowly. "I think he's done other things, too."

"Such as some of the people who died?" Bree asked.

Leo took a deep breath. "It started a long time ago. Ten years, to be exact. A man named Richard Goodwin discovered he had bone cancer. He wasn't as worried about his death sentence than he was about leaving Marilyn, his wife, with nothing. That's when Roy and Mike had a talk with him. They suggested he take out a life insurance policy."

"No one would insure him with that kind of death sentence hanging over his head," Bree pointed out.

"They would if his cancer wasn't mentioned. All he needed was a good bill of health from a doctor." Leo stared down at the tabletop. "Mike would perform the physical and state that Richard was in excellent health. There was also a double indemnity clause in the policy."

"Roy set up these accidents?" Cole guessed. His skin had a green tinge. "And Mike Warren helped him?"

"Nothing was ever said," Leo explained. "But everyone knew they'd help you. You didn't have to suffer for a long time and you knew your spouse would be taken care of from the insurance. I guess you could say it was one of those untold secrets that gets around quietly. Something no one dares speak of out loud. They have it down to a fine art now. Mike has the opportunity to find out who would require their special services." His lips twisted. "He plays the part of the sincere, caring doctor. He lets them know he can help them with their family's financial future. The insurance policy is written up, and after a decent length of time, when the subject feels ready, the accident or 'death by natural causes' is planned." His eyes glittered with tears. "He used drugs to make some of them look like a heart attack."

"Is that what happened with Anna, Leo?" Cole asked.

Bree reached out and touched the man's hand. "Leo, help us," she pleaded. "What they're doing is very wrong. We have to stop them. Can you help us? Is there anything else you can tell us?"

He nodded. "Joshua thinks they killed Renee."

Bree and Cole exchanged a look.

"Oh, Renee had cancer, but the pain was manageable," Leo continued. "Then the sheriff went to Joshua. He asked if Renee was getting worse. Joshua told them all they were doing was lining their own greedy pockets. He told them to stop. And if they didn't, he'd say something."

"So they thought he was about to say something, and Renee's death was a warning," she guessed.

"How did all this remain unspoken for so long?" Cole asked. "Some of you knew I was suspicious about these deaths. Why wasn't something said to me?"

"Because you would have ended up with the same fate as your uncle Charlie," Leo told him. "Roy once slipped and said something that had me thinking he'd killed Charlie. I knew you had the talent to ferret out this atrocity. I could only hope it wouldn't kill you in the process. But then Bree arrived and you caught her up in your fact-finding. I didn't know they would try to hurt you," he said, turning to her. "I feel like that was my fault."

Cole's features seemed to have turned to stone.

"Leo, are you now willing to make a statement to the district attorney's office?" Bree asked. "We need to close up their shop fast."

He nodded. "I'm ready to do whatever is necessary. I've felt that some of the people who died shouldn't have, but there was never any proof."

"Why do you think Roy never tried to kill you if he thought you knew something?" Cole asked.

Leo smiled sadly. "He knows I keep a journal. I don't think he wanted to take a chance." He sighed heavily. "I guess I didn't want to believe Roy thought money was more important than people's lives. He used to be a good man. I don't know what turned him. He shouldn't have done what he did."

"You're right, he shouldn't have," Cole murmured.

Bree stood up. "Let's get started then," she said briskly. She looked at Cole. "Now it ends."

He stood up and pushed his chair back. "Yes, now it ends."

"This is official business. You cannot go with me," Bree argued, walking out to her borrowed Blazer with Jinx at her side.

"There is no way you're doing this without me," Cole said stubbornly, walking on the other side of her. "I want to see that son of a bitch's face when you arrest him."

She whirled on him. "I spent the last hour arguing and practically promising to give up my pension so I could be the one to arrest Holloway. Officers are already on their way to bring in Dr. Warren. I am not having a civilian screwing up my arrest."

"Civilian? You wouldn't have come this far if it hadn't been for me," he asserted, climbing into the passenger seat.

"Becker, you are a real pain in the ass," she groused, sliding behind the wheel.

He grasped her chin and turned her toward him for a quick hard kiss. "Yeah, but you love me anyway."

She didn't need to say a word. Her fulminating glance said it all. But she didn't throw him out of the vehicle, either.

Bree drove to the sheriff's station. She considered it appropriate that he would meet his downfall in the place where so many revered him.

As if he knew she'd toss him out on a second's notice, Cole remained quiet during the ride.

Bree hated any type of murder. Senseless killings and those for monetary gain she hated the most. She had no idea what she would face when she walked into the station. Just because Joshua didn't think any of the deputies were in on the scam didn't mean it wasn't so. She gave the command for Jinx to guard her. She couldn't have wished for better backup. Cole walked behind them, watchful of their surroundings.

"You will remain silent and in the background," she said quietly.

"Fine, but if he tries to escape, I'm tripping him."

"That I'll let you do."

Roy looked up when Bree walked into his office without waiting for an invitation. Cole remained in the doorway, while Jinx stood by Bree's side.

"I heard you had some trouble last night," he said. "Funny thing, we never had stuff like this happen until you came to town." He grinned, looking as if he didn't have a care in the world. Now she knew just how good his lies were. "You sure you didn't bring along any of your Los Angeles crime with you?" he joked.

"You did that all on your own. Roy Holloway, you are under arrest for multiple counts of murder. You have the right to remain silent…." Bree rambled on, reciting the Miranda. "Do you understand what I have just told you?" she concluded.

Roy sat back in his chair, looking too smug for his own good.

"You can be amused if you want, but you're going to jail for a very long time. That's if you escape the death penalty," she said. "Do you have anything you wish to say?"

He shook his head. "Don't try it on me, Fitzpatrick. I've been in law enforcement a hell of a lot longer than you. I'm going to let my attorney do the talking. He'll have me out on bail in an hour and the case will be dismissed before you can finish the paperwork."

"I don't think so," she said confidently. "Your mistake was you got too greedy, Holloway." She stopped when she heard her cell phone ring. She took it out of her bag. "Fitzpatrick." She listened for several minutes, then hung up. "Looks like there will be one defendant instead of two. Michael Warren just killed himself. Somehow he found out he was about to get arrested. He left a note saying he knew he couldn't survive prison. He apologized to you. He was sorry that he wasn't as strong as you are." Her gaze bored into Holloway's.

"It looks like you'll be alone when you face a judge and jury." She looked down at Jinx. "Jinx, detain." The dog moved over to stand by Roy. There was no doubt the man wouldn't get past the dog.

Roy's face blanched. "No," he whispered, falling back in his chair. "Mike wouldn't kill himself."

"He did," she said bluntly. "He also wrote down the numbers of bank accounts and safety deposit boxes. I guess he figured if he was going to die, you weren't going to be allowed the luxury of trying to get away with it. Now get up slowly and turn around."

He placed his hands on the desktop and slowly stood up. The moment he rose to his feet, Jinx was next to him, watchful of every movement the man made.

The trio in the office were oblivious to the small crowd gathering outside the room, or the low rumble of voices in the background.

Roy left the office with his hands cuffed and his head held high.

"I did nothing wrong," he announced in ringing tones.

"The district attorney might have a different opinion," Bree said. She glanced at the other officers. She hoped there wouldn't be any trouble there.

Everyone stepped back, allowing them to walk out without any interference.

Bree stuck Roy in the back of a patrol car and turned to Cole. "I'm going to be a while," she warned him.

"That's all right. I've got a story to write," he said. "Just remember me when you're finished."

She smiled. "As if I could forget."

"Then we can discuss how to make the two of us a habit," he suggested silkily. "You know what I mean. Lay out terms and all."

"If you only knew what you're in for."

"I do. And I'm in it for the long haul."

Bree kissed him. "You know what? So am I."

Epilogue

Five years later

"What're you crying for now?" Cole teased Bree.

She sniffed and gestured toward the orchestra set off to one side, as the dark-gowned graduates filed to the front of the grassy area. "'Pomp and Circumstance' always makes me cry. It's foretelling a new chapter in a person's life."

"Cole, make her stop," Sara hissed. "I swear, Mom, if you do this at my college graduation I will pretend not to know you." She bounced the toddler in her lap up and down as the little girl looked around with wide-eyed fascination.

"Message for Sara," Cody intoned. "Hollywood is calling."

She glared at her brother.

Cole looked at his family with the same amazement he felt every morning. That Bree had been his wife for almost four years was the first thing he was grateful for. That the three Fitzpatrick children accepted him so readily made him more so. And last, the little girl with her father's stormy-gray eyes and fascination with everything life had to offer completed the circle.

After his story about murdering the elderly for money in Warm Springs hit all the major papers, he had calls asking him to return to the work he'd once thrived on. He'd politely listened to each offer and then turned it down. He'd had more than enough excitement, thank you very much.

Roy Holloway sat on death row for first degree murder, with a count even higher than anyone expected, since Roy hadn't minded traveling to other counties to utilize his talent for homicide. Appeals had been filed, but Cole knew it would only lengthen his stay, since the crimes were too heinous and the evidence much too strong.

His connection to Dr. Michael Warren had begun when they were in high school. Michael's mother was terminally ill, and Roy Holloway had found a way to help Michael ease his mother into death. The secret had bound the two friends together for years, a secret that Roy later brought up as a way to make money.

Joshua was relieved to learn that Renee's death was definitely not a suicide, and many of the senior citizens were relieved to know Roy Holloway wouldn't come knocking on their door one night with an offer to help family members who didn't want to live with terminal illness.

The district attorney's office opted not to prosecute the surviving spouses for their parts in the deaths. It was decided their awareness of what they'd done was punishment enough. It was doubted even time would be able to heal the emotional wounds Roy Holloway's actions left behind.

Bree had been offered Roy's position, and after discussion with Cole and the kids, she'd taken it.

There were days when Cole worried about her and her work. After all, how many sheriffs leave a bad traffic accident scene to travel to the hospital to give birth?

And now his oldest stepson was being courted by every government agency known to man, and a few that remained in the background.

He pulled out his handkerchief and dabbed at Bree's eyes. "Cops don't cry," he murmured.

Her smile tipped his world upside down just as it had that first time he saw her. "This one does."

"Then I'll make you a deal. I won't tell your deputies about the waterworks and you fix my parking tickets."

Bree leaned over, brushing her lips across his ear. "Do us both a favor, Becker. Pay the two dollars." She repeated the time-honored joke, referring to a time when parking tickets had only cost that small amount.

She turned back to watch the graduates file across the stage to receive their diplomas. And thought about the day she'd be sitting here to watch little Jenny accept hers.

She glanced at Cole, who, sensing her regard, turned and looked at her with love shining in his eyes.

Her world was complete.

*   *   *   *   *

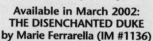

Silhouette

INTIMATE MOMENTS™

presents:

Romancing the Crown

With the help of their powerful allies,
the royal family of Montebello is
determined to find their missing heir.
But the search for the beloved prince
is not without danger—or passion!

Available in March 2002:
THE DISENCHANTED DUKE
by Marie Ferrarella (IM #1136)

Though he was a duke by title, Max Ryker Sebastiani had shrugged off
his regal life for one of risk and adventure. But when he paired up
with beautiful bounty hunter Cara Rivers on a royal mission,
he discovered his heart was in danger....

This exciting series continues throughout
the year with these fabulous titles:

Available only from Silhouette Intimate Moments
at your favorite retail outlet.

Silhouette®

Where love comes alive™

Visit Silhouette at www.eHarlequin.com

SIMRC3

Uncover the truth behind

CODE NAME: DANGER

in **Merline Lovelace's** thrilling duo

DANGEROUS TO HOLD

When tricky situations need a cool head, quick wits and a touch
of ruthlessness, Adam Ridgeway, director of the top secret
OMEGA agency, sends in his team. Lately, though, his agents have
had romantic troubles of their own....

NIGHT OF THE JAGUAR
&
THE COWBOY AND THE COSSACK

And don't miss
HOT AS ICE (IM #1129, 2/02)
which features the newest OMEGA adventure!

DANGEROUS TO HOLD is available this February
at your local retail outlet!

Look for *DANGEROUS TO KNOW,* the second set of
stories in this collection, in July 2002.